Every Night Has A Dawn

THE WINDS OF CHANGE TRILOGY

RACHEL VALENCOURT

PUBLISHED BY MARMONT PUBLISHING

Editors—Dori Harrell, Jenna O'Malley, John Bowers

Format Designer—Dawn Baca

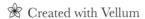 Created with Vellum

Blurb

Embark on a mesmerizing tale of survival within the wild woods of Washington, a compelling coming-of-age journey that celebrates the unbreakable spirit of womanhood.

When Dawn Jensen's family is abruptly uprooted from their idyllic cabin and thrust into a tumultuous existence as nomadic farm workers, this remarkable story unfolds. Experience their extraordinary journey through the luminous eyes of Dawn, a spirited and vibrant girl.

Set against the stormy backdrop of the Great Depression and the looming shadow of World War II, the 1930s becomes the stage where fate weaves an unexpected tale. Dawn's path collides with a charismatic man from Oklahoma, igniting hope for a radiant new beginning. In their connection, her heart blooms, fueled by an unquenchable yearning for survival and love.

Dawn is tested when a chance encounter compels her to safeguard a family secret that threatens to shatter the stability of her adult life. Will she find the strength to withstand the storms that could tear her world apart?

Discover the answers within the captivating pages of this first installment in the epic *"Winds of Change Trilogy"* and prepare to be swept away into the splendor of the natural world. From the rugged lands of the Makah tribe to the sun-kissed shores of California, follow Dawn's remarkable transformation through this breathtaking novel.

Dedicated to the hordes of poor, hopeful people of the Great Depression who toiled from sunup to sunset in the fields of happiness.

Prologue

Dawn Cameron

Ninety years have passed since I first entered this world—a testament to the enduring legacy of my lineage and the indomitable spirit that courses through my veins. As I reflect on a life spanning almost a century, I am reminded of the countless events I've witnessed, the personal battles I've fought, and the triumphs I've celebrated. But let me assure you, dear reader, the fire within me still burns bright, for within this frail vessel resides a mind that refuses to succumb to the passage of time.

In many ways, my mind is more alive now than ever before. Inside, I still feel like the spirited twenty-five-year-old

I once was, even though sometimes I walk into another room and forget why I went in there. But hey, that's been happening since my mid-thirties. I've been blessed by the fact that, while my body has slowed down, my mind has not.

I knew I would live this long; longevity runs in our blood. Mama was born in 1899-a time when women couldn't even vote. She lived to be ninety-four, and somehow, I knew I'd follow in her footsteps. Last year, my family was relieved when I finally stopped driving my cherry red Mustang after a little mishap. But hey, accidents happen, right? Overall, I'm as sharp and stubborn as ever, maybe even wiser.

As the years have unfolded, I've often contemplated whether my life has been truly extraordinary or if that's how I remember it. So many changes, and sometimes I've felt like my life was a reaction to events around me rather than a product of my design. Growing up in a time when women weren't considered equal to men, I was taught to tuck away hardships and hide them in the corners of my mind. But one day, all those boxes came crashing down, and I faced the fallout from years of not confronting my troubles.

Finding my way out of the depths of darkness has been remarkable in and of itself. Now, at ten years shy of a hundred, I've had my share of struggles. Oh, there have been many happy and beautiful moments—in fact, most of them fall into that category. The trick is to keep the challenging moments from derailing your happiness.

When I was a young girl, I didn't realize that I was

growing up in hard times—at that age, we didn't know any better and didn't truly understand what the Great Depression was until many years later.

We shall get to all of that later on in this book. For now, let's focus on the present. On June 5th, 2018, I'm dressed in my favorite sparkly top and sequined shoes, celebrating my 90th birthday. My granddaughter is throwing a huge family party, and I'll be surrounded by my loved ones.

The thing I'm looking forward to most today is having all of the generations together under one roof, from my beloved grandchildren to my precious great-grandchildren and oldest friends. Their laughter and hugs fill my heart with immeasurable joy, a testament to what Ellis and I started to build all those years ago.

As we share stories, embrace memories, and create new ones, I am reminded of the profound love that binds us together, transcending time and space. Today, surrounded by the ones I hold dear, I feel a profound gratitude for the blessings life has bestowed upon me, and I cherish every treasured moment spent in their loving company. The legacy of our family will live on, and in their smiles and laughter, I find the truest measure of a life well-lived. Mama would be so proud.

The funny thing is that the older I get, the more my thoughts drift to the days of my youth. These last few years, I've been lost in the memories of growing up poor in the state of Washington during the Great Depression. I was born at home in 1928, in the early hours of June 5th, the youngest of five children.

As I sit here, waiting for my youngest daughter and her family to arrive, memories of my youth swirl around me, painting vivid pictures of growing up in a time long forgotten. Those early experiences molded me into the strong and resilient woman I am today. As I journey through the annals of time, I realize that my life, though seemingly ordinary in some ways, holds extraordinary moments that have combined to create something beautiful.

My mind drifts to a cherished memory of my sixth birthday—the first birthday I can vividly recall. After relishing a slice of Mama's famous 'Pig 'n' Whistle' cake, Daddy announced a surprise for us children. With eager hearts, he led us on a walk over the hill, promising something special to behold…

PART ONE
Millie Dawn Jensen

How can we live without our lives? How will we know it's us without our past?

—John Steinbeck, *The Grapes of Wrath*

Rising Dawn

SOUTH SEATTLE, WASHINGTON

JUNE 5TH, 1934

Millie Dawn
6th Birthday

My eyes fluttered open to the soft glow of morning light filtering through the cabin's window. Franny, my older sister, laid next to me, fast asleep on her bedroll on the floor.

"Wake up, Franny," I whispered, nudging my older sister.

There were only two proper beds in our home. My parents had one, and my two brothers shared the other. Our eldest sister, Denise, slept on the sofa.

"Shhhh, Millie, you'll wake the whole house." My sister,

with her amber eyes and delicate nose, rolled over and glanced at me.

"I'm sorry. I can't lay still any longer. Not with the sun out and shining like it is. It's my birthday. I'm finally six."

"It's early. Be quiet."

"See for yourself." Despite the rain throughout the week, a single stream of sunlight poured through the window. It had been the first we'd seen in a while. "God's given me a special birthday gift. The rain has stopped, and the sun is out. Let's go pick some wild strawberries for our pancakes."

"Hold your horses. We need to get dressed and cleaned up first."

As usual, Franny rained on my parade with her incessant rule following. As I pulled aside the pretty yellow curtains and gazed out the window into the thick cluster of pine and fir trees, the last whispers of mist shimmered in the dawn light.

Our cabin was made of rough-hewn logs that reached toward the heavens, reminding me of Daddy, tall and strong. It had a sloping roof that looked like it went on forever. Sometimes it leaked, but Daddy always said, "At least we have a roof over our heads."

The fireplace crackled and provided warmth like Mama's loving hugs, wrapping us in a cozy blanket of affection. My mind drifted to the many nights we'd spent gathering around the threadbare sofa to listen to Daddy sing his Irish songs or Mama's thrilling serial dramas on our wireless radio. At that moment, I realized my sister was drifting off to sleep.

"Hurry up," I whispered to Franny, taking care not to wake my parents who were snoring in the other bedroom. Their room had a big bed and an antique vanity table where Mama would comb her flaxen hair before making us the fluffiest, golden, sweet pancakes. Sometimes we didn't have butter or syrup, but we always had flour and eggs from our chicken coop.

My favorite part of our cabin was the creek that ran beyond the wraparound porch. It was a magical place where I could catch tadpoles and splash around in the cool water on warm summer days. Now that I was six years old, I knew I'd be having many more escapades with my older sister and best friend, Franny Jane. I loved exploring the woods around the cabin and playing make-believe with my sister by my side.

"It's a sin to be cooped up inside on a day like this. Come on, sleepyhead." I gave Franny one last nudge.

Realizing the battle was lost, Franny threw her sheets back, climbed out of bed, and started getting dressed. I watched as she meticulously combed her hair. She was perfect, quiet, and graceful. I was the complete opposite—a tiny ball of energy. I bounced around, usually irritating the adults with my incessant questions.

I grabbed Mama's brush and left the room to get myself ready. Hoping to braid my unruly, red hair and impress Mama with how grown up I could look. Usually my hair wandered wild and free, but Mama's eyes would narrow when I returned from my adventures with it a dirt-coated mess.

This morning, of all mornings, my rebellious locks resisted my efforts. They tangled with every stroke. Frustration welled inside me, threatening to burst like a simmering volcano.

Unable to contain my anger, I hurled Mama's brush to the ground. The thud of the brush echoed my frustration. Tears filled my eyes, a mixture of disappointment and irritation. How would I impress Mama if my rebellious hair won't cooperate?

"Let me at that hair of yours." Franny smiled as I wiped my tears.

Franny, sensing my distress, entered the room, and with her gentle touch, she untangled the snarls with patient hands, combing through each knot with practiced ease. As the tension in my body melted away, Franny's soft voice served as a reminder that even in moments of anger and frustration, she could calm me down.

Under Franny's guidance, my hair slowly transformed from chaos to order. I stared at the reflection of my determined eyes and flame-colored braids, trying to see if I looked older now that I was six.

"Mama says my red hair is a warning label, hinting at my fiery temper. How come you never get angry, Franny?"

"Mama says it's because my golden hair is like a halo, and I'm her little angel. That's why I'm so well-behaved."

"Too bad you cry about everything," I teased. I never heard Mama say her hair was like a halo.

"There's nothing wrong with being sensitive." Franny's voice sounded defensive.

Our differences often sparked sisterly clashes, but I had to admit our personalities did complement each other and created a delicate balance within our home. I brought energy and fire, while Franny provided a calm and thoughtful presence. I created mischief and mayhem while Franny helped tone me down. Together, we made quite a pair, I thought, as we headed outside.

We grabbed our worn, muddy shoes from the box on the porch, trying to keep the floors clean and dry. Things were always wet in Washington, but I didn't mind as there was fun to be had outside.

Once outside, Franny thrust a small blue bundle toward me from behind her back.

"Happy birthday, Millie," Franny said with a smile as she handed me a small parcel. Curious, I eagerly took it in my hands, feeling the rough texture of the twine that secured it. As I excitedly unwrapped the package, my eyes widened in astonishment. Inside was none other than my sister's most treasured possession, her beloved Raggedy Ann doll she had cherished for as long as I could remember.

"Are you sure, Franny? Can I keep her?" I hugged the doll to my chest.

"Yes, Millie. I was six when Denise gave her to me. Now that I'm eight, I'm getting too big to play with dolls." Franny scrunched her nose. I didn't believe her for a second. She loved playing with dolls as much as I did.

"Thank you. I promise I'll take care of her."

"Let's go down the creek and brush our teeth." Franny waved her toothbrush at me.

"Last one there is a rotten egg." I raced ahead to my happy place. I was always in a rush, daydreaming with my head in the clouds, but my sister was there to keep me grounded.

I shot Franny a sly grin, prepared to share the plan I'd been devising. I had something important to tell her, and if I could get her on my side, then the rest of the family would follow along.

"Hey ya, Sis! Listen up 'cause I got something really, really big to say, I yelled, my voice all bubbly and excited.

"What's going on, little troublemaker?" Franny turned her head toward me, her eyes shining in the sunlight.

"Guess what I'm gonna ask Mama and Daddy for today?"

"What's that Sis?" Franny responded with curiosity.

"Since they won't let us get a puppy, I'm gonna ask for something super important. I decided I like my middle name better, and I ain't gonna answer to Millie no more. I want everyone to start calling me Dawn, like the sun sneaking up over them hills. I don't like the name Millie. Never did, and never will! It sounds like some old farm horse."

"Oh, my giddy aunt! But Millie's your name... Mama

and Daddy gave it to you. It's a family name ..." Franny exclaimed, her voice laced with an older sister's skepticism.

I squared my shoulders, ready to battle. "I know. Names are like a calling card, and Dawn's the magical word that fits me. It's a beautiful sunrise, and I want to be more like that —the center of the universe."

"You've got gumption, little missy." Franny's face softened, and a laugh escaped from her tight lips. "If Dawn's what your heart's set on, then Dawn it is."

As we skipped to the cabin, I got closer to Franny and nudged her playfully. Our toothbrushes clanked with a happy sound. The babbling creek an eavesdropper to our sisterly banter. We were together every second, and we could do anything we set our minds to. Especially now that I was Dawn, I knew I could blaze my own trail through life's journey.

When Franny and I got to the cabin with our basket full of wild strawberries, the rest of the family was stirring and moving about the cabin. There were five of us Jensen children. Junior was the oldest, born in 1920, followed by Bobby, in 1922. Denise was born in 1924, with Franny Jane and me coming in 1926 and 1928.

The sun cast a golden glow through the yellowed curtains of our kitchen, illuminating the worn, oak dining table. The aromas of freshly-brewed coffee and the sweet smell of Mama's homemade, blackberry syrup filled the air.

Once we were gathered around the table, Franny cleared her throat, trying to sound all grown-up. "Listen up, everybody. We have an announcement to make on Pickle's special day."

Mama's eyes twinkled with curiosity, while Daddy reached for his newspaper. My older brothers, Junior and Bobby, looked puzzled yet eager to know what was going on. With a fancy bow, Franny pointed at me, and her eyes sparkled with delight.

"From now on," she continued playfully, "Millie shall go by her middle name, Dawn."

A hush fell over the room, you could almost hear a pin drop. Mama's eyes twinkled with amusement as she wiped her hands on her blue apron, "Well, it's Sissy's special day, so I guess we can let her have her way."

"Why not? If it makes our birthday girl happy, then Dawn it is." Daddy chuckled, folding his newspaper and setting it aside. Junior and Bobby exchanged grins, their eyes shimmering with brotherly love.

"Sure thing, Sis." Denise stood up to help Mama with the dishes. "However, remember. We might call you Millie when you're being a little rascal."

We laughed together, and I felt warm inside. Maybe Daddy would change his mind now that he was in such a playful mood. I didn't tell Franny that part of my plan.

"Now Daddy, what about the puppy? I promise I'll take care of her by myself. She can have part of my dinner, and she can sleep in the barn. You won't even notice her."

"I already gave you my answer," Daddy said, patting my hand. "I'd love to get you a puppy, but we already have too many mouths to feed. Maybe when things get better we'll talk about it."

I felt disappointed, but at least I had the courage to claim my true name on my special day. From this day forward, I would forever be known as Dawn, a ray of light shining bright. I looked at Franny, my partner in everything. We'd find a way to get that puppy. I was sure of it.

"I packed some baloney sandwiches. Bobby, take the girls to the swimming hole and keep an eye on them. Make sure to be home by four, we are having an early supper. Junior and Bobby shot a stag yesterday, and we're going to have a birthday feast," Mama said as we headed out the door.

We ran through the trees toward the nearby swimming hole where Daddy had hung a rope swing for us to play on. We took turns being Tarzan, swinging and dropping into the icy water below.

After a few hours, Bobby motioned for us to dry off. On our way home, the most amazing smell filled the air.

"Do you smell that?" I asked, my eyes wide with wonder.

"Oh, Dawn, it smells like Mama is cooking up some magic in the kitchen. Let's go find out."

Our excitement grew between us as we got closer to home, following that delicious scent.

"Hello, Love Bugs," Mama greeted us as we burst through the front door, her blue apron dusty with flour. Denise stood beside her, busy measuring ingredients.

"What's cookin', good lookin'?" I grinned at Mama.

"How about you ask that question again, and make it sound a bit more proper? Remember, people judge you by the way you speak."

"Yes Ma'am, whatever could be causing that amazing smell if you don't mind me asking?" I put on the fanciest accent I could muster.

"OK smarty pants, we're making a Pig 'n Whistle cake for your special day," Mama said with a chuckle.

My heart soared with glee, and I exchanged a look of awe with Franny. How did Mama manage to find the ingredients when things were tough?

"Mama," Franny asked, her curiosity showing, "where did you get all this? We've been struggling to find supplies."

"I had a surprise tucked away. In the back of the cupboard, I found the last can of sweet condensed milk and a bunch of walnuts. I saved them for Dawn's birthday. I wanted to make this day unforgettable." Mama winked, her eyes filled with pride.

"What better way to celebrate than with Mama's famous Pig 'n Whistle cake?" Denise chimed in.

Franny and I beamed at our amazing Mama. She knew how to create magic, even when times were tough.

"You're the best Mama in the world. I'm glad you're mine."

"Thank you, my little Pickle. How about setting the dinner table for me?"

We enjoyed an early supper and cake, our bellies filled

with Mama's delicious cooking. Everyone sang me "Happy Birthday" and gave me a few small gifts. Daddy gave me a shiny, new nickel, while Mama gave me a pair of slippers she'd been knitting.

"I have a surprise for the kids. It's near Boeing Field. Before we go, there's one last gift out on the back porch for you, Dawn." Daddy smiled with a twinkle in his eye. This must be why we had an early dinner today.

I dashed out the back door to the most amazing sight— a fluffy ball of clumsiness with floppy ears and oversized paws. It was a beautiful German Shepherd puppy tied to Daddy's rocking chair. She gazed at me with honey-colored eyes, radiating a spirited energy, and her tongue hung out of her mouth in an adorable expression.

I scooped her up as she whined and licked my face.

"How, Daddy?"

"I've been asking around while makin' my deliveries, and it turns out the Stevensons' dog had some pups in the spring. You'll have to train her well. That dog's part timber wolf." Daddy beamed with pride.

"I love her already. Can she come with us on our hike?" I asked, already attached to the puppy.

"Might as well start teaching her to stay with you. She'll be a great protector one day," Daddy said, showing me how to hold the puppy.

"What are you going to call her?" Bobby ran over to pet the puppy.

"Her name is Honey." I smiled as the puppy continued

to lick my face. From that moment on, Honey and I would be inseparable.

"Come now. Time to get going," Daddy said, catching himself before he could use my old name.

"Franny's too busy playing with that pup," Bobby said, looking like a younger version of our father with his tall and lanky stature, long, straight nose, and amber-colored eyes. While Franny and John took after Mama, I got my red hair from Grandma Sallie.

Lately, we'd been hiking everywhere to save on gas. I often trailed behind. Not only because of my short legs, but also because I was easily distracted. Anything that could capture my attention—an anthill, a salamander, or even a ladybug captured in a juice jar—could provide me with hours of entertainment.

This time it was Honey who caused me to fall behind. Keeping her with me proved to be a task. She wanted to run and play without knowing how to obey.

"Keep up, Dawn. You won't want to miss this," Daddy said, glancing over his shoulder.

Once we reached the top of the hill, we gazed in pure wonder as a man catapulted out of an airplane and floated gracefully to the ground beneath a huge canopy of white cloth.

"The army is testing parachutes today," Daddy remarked, watching as several more men landed in Boeing Field. They glided through the air like the dried petals of a dandelion after being blown by the wind. The world was amazing, and I was ready to embrace every bit of it.

I was Dawn, not Millie, after all.

What a magical way to celebrate my birthday. Everyone spent the afternoon together, and it made my heart overflow with joy. Usually, Daddy worked while my brothers hunted elk and fished for king salmon in the Duwamish River.

But today my whole family surrounded me with love and affection, making my birthday truly unforgettable, and it proved to be the best gift of all. Togetherness.

That night, under my snug blankets, I strained to catch the hushed whispers that traveled through the walls. Mama and Daddy's voices were gentle and secretive, filling the quiet of the night with intrigue. Their words held weight, and I sensed that something important passed between them. Confused by their conversation, I wondered what could be so significant.

"I'm glad you had something exciting to show the kids. Lord knows we must find happiness wherever we can. Times have been tough, John," Mama whispered.

"This downturn hasn't been kind to folks like us. With work being scarce, puttin' food on the table has been harder. We're lucky Junior and Bobby shot that stag. It was good to have some meat to serve with supper," Daddy responded, tender and caring. I could hear the worry in his voice. He tried to hide it, but sometimes it crept in.

"I know, sweetheart. It breaks my heart to watch our family struggle. Together, we'll figure it out. This downturn can't last long." Mama continued, "There's something I wanted to talk about. I can't bear the thought of bringing more babies into this hardship. Five little mouths to feed is more than enough."

"What's on your mind tonight?" Daddy responded.

"My sister had this operation, where doctors did something to stop more babies from coming. Adelaide almost died that one time in labor, and they did it to save her. I'm going to see her doctor about having it done, too." Mama took a deep breath, her voice quivering with concern.

"I trust your instincts, my love. If you believe it's the right path, I'm right beside you."

As I lay there on the edge of slumber, a mix of fear and uncertainty filled my heart while an image of the hospital flashed in my mind. I knew it was a place I never wanted to go.

Mama, the glue holding us all together, the one who kept us strong, wanted an operation. If something happened to her, what would become of our family?

Rivers and Roads

EVERETT, WASHINGTON

MARCH 1935

Dawn Jensen
Almost 7 Years Old

T he time had come for Mama to go in for that operation to stop having babies, and I was frightened for her. As I helped Mama pack, I hid a small tin of her favorite tea in her overnight bag. I didn't want Mama to spend even one day at the hospital without her afternoon tea.

"Mama, are you sure you need this operation?" I buckled her overnight bag and placed it next to her vanity table.

"Come sit with me, Pickle." Mama patted the spot next

to her on the bed. "You know how hard Daddy has been trying to keep food on the table, and sometimes you're still hungry, even after we finish supper?"

"Yes, Mama." I blinked my eyes in curiosity.

"Well, we are in hard times right now. Better times will be coming, but sometimes we must do things that aren't pleasant. So things will be better down the road."

"If times are hard now, then how can you afford this operation?" I asked with concern.

"Your Daddy has an agreement with a nice doctor to plow his fields on the weekends that you kids stay with Aunt Hatt. The doctor is going to fix it so I won't be having any more babies. You five are enough, and I love you dearly, but I'm thirty-six years old now. My Mama had babies clear into her 40s. Ten kids total, and it took its toll. I don't want to be like her, especially in these here times."

"Yes, Ma'am." I understood what Mama was saying, but I was still worried for her.

Mama placed her hand under my chin and made me look at her. "You must take control of your life. It's not easy being a woman, but this is a small thing that I can do for our family to make our lives easier. No one is ever coming to save you," Mama's voice was steady and determined. She continued, "You must take care of yourself."

"I understand, Mama, but why are times tough? Daddy said some bubble burst in New York. I don't understand that part."

"It's hard to explain, Pickle. There are more people than

there are jobs, and it causes a lot of hardship. Many families don't have enough money to buy the things they need. Don't you worry though, President Roosevelt is coming up with plans to help fix our economy, and things will be getting better soon." Mama gave me one of her big bear hugs. "Thank you for helping me pack. Now go get your belongings together and make sure the rest of the kids are ready too."

While I gathered my things, thoughts of how quickly this past year had flown by started to fill my mind. It felt as if I had turned six yesterday, but now I was on the brink of turning seven. The previous year had rushed past in a blur. I began kindergarten while Franny moved on to first grade. With Easter Break coming up next week, it was the ideal time for us to pay a visit to Aunt Hatt. This plan would allow Mama to have ample time to rest and recover following her operation.

Even though I was going to miss Mama, going to stay with her sister would probably be an adventure. I loved Aunt Hatt dearly. She didn't have any children of her own, so she spoiled us. Most of Mama's siblings lived in Arkansas, but she and Aunt Hatt were still at home when our grandparents settled in Washington. Mama's sister lived a few hours away in Everett. I was excited to stay with her and her pet poodles. They were fun playmates, but I worried about how Honey would get along with them.

I was also fretful about Daddy losing his job. At night, I often heard Mama and Daddy discussing layoffs at the yard.

Daddy delivered bark and lumber all over Seattle for a local lumber yard. I didn't know why Daddy thought he could lose his job. The boss was also our landlord, and Daddy did whatever Mr. Thorton asked. Daddy said there was no such thing as job stability anymore. Something called a depression had gobbled up the jobs. I imagined it to be this hungry wolf that devoured everything in sight. I didn't fully understand what it meant, but it couldn't be good.

Uncle Jack arrived to transport us to his and Aunt Hatt's little house on the Snohomish River. Saying goodbye to Mama was bittersweet, and the weight of uncertainty hung heavy in the air. I shook off my worry for her and the fear of the unknown that awaited her at the hospital. I had never been to a doctor before, and the thought scared me to the core.

"John, I know this is right for our family. Don't you worry yourself; I'll be home in a jiffy. You've got to keep your spirits up, especially for the children." Mama kissed him goodbye, as the world transformed into a golden sunset. The sun was low in the sky, casting its warm glow over the fir trees around us. The splendor of the moment seemed to go against the heaviness in my heart.

"Come on, Noisy. You can ride with me." Uncle Jack motioned for me to get into his truck. He called me 'Noisy' because of my loud, husky voice, and I was a little noise maker.

"I'll ride with Daddy," I responded, so I'd be able to lean against his strong shoulder and sleep on the way to Everett.

Because of the old truck's relentless heating issues, we drove at night to prevent the car from overheating.

With each mile we traveled, the mountain loomed larger overhead. Its shadowy peaks whispered secrets of uncertainty. After hours of driving, I noticed Daddy's shoulders hung down, weary with exhaustion. The truck sputtered and smoked as we traveled up the last hill. The more Daddy sighed, the harder the radiator groaned in protest.

"Let's pull over and let the engine cool down," Daddy said, his voice strained with concern as he moved to climb out of the truck. Wisps of steam rose from under the hood.

"We'll take a short break here," Daddy motioned over to a spot on the side of the road.

Under the dark night sky, Daddy spread out an old, frayed tarp on the ground. Behind the truck, my siblings and I nestled against the cold earth. Our bodies huddled together, seeking warmth in each other's closeness during the early morning hours. Mama's absence didn't go unnoticed, but Daddy's presence provided solace and support throughout the night.

Daddy and Uncle Jack took turns standing guard. The darkness outside mirrored the shadows in my heart. I didn't like it when we weren't all together. I cuddled Honey, and I eventually fell asleep to the sounds of crickets chirping. I awoke later, startled by a voice.

"Who goes there?" Daddy's yell pierced the darkness like a booming thunderbolt and shook me out of my slumber. Honey started to growl. A beam lit up our camping spot.

Daddy's voice firmly boomed once more, "Step away, or you'll regret it."

My heart raced as I strained to catch a glimpse of the two men who had arrived by car. Their headlights blinded us as they walked toward our truck. Shadows danced and swayed in the distance. I stared, imagining more menacing figures lurking in the dark woods. Uncle Jack appeared at Daddy's side with his trusty pickax.

They were a powerful team, I knew they would give their lives to protect us.

"We don't want no trouble. Get in your car and head on outta here," Uncle Jack yelled. After a moment of hesitation, the intruders heeded the warning and turned around. Slowly, they got into their car and drove off into the darkness, away from our campsite.

"I reckon we best hit the road again. Everybody, hop in the truck. We're movin' on outta here," Daddy folded the tarp. Franny and I sat up front, clutching each other's hands for security. Honey was in the truck bed, her ears perked up in anticipation as if she could sense something was amiss.

"Dear Lord, thank you for keepin' us safe and sound. Thank you for blessin' our family. Give Mama strength to heal up quick. Keep this old truck runnin' so we can get where we need to be. In Jesus' name," Daddy said a prayer before we left. I felt a bit better after Daddy's beautiful words, but my heart was still thumping.

"We'll get through this. We always do." Daddy sighed.

"We only have a little more way to Everett, and then it's

a downhill ride. Hattie will put on some breakfast for us." Uncle Jack chimed in as he climbed into his own vehicle.

Hardly anyone spoke for several hours until we arrived at Aunt Hatt and Uncle Jack's humble home. As predicted, our doting Aunt greeted us with a warm meal.

The next ten days sped along like a river's flow, carrying us swiftly through the lean summer days of 1935. Within the walls of my aunt and uncle's home, the younger kids found solace in the rhythm of our spring break freedom. Mornings arrived with the aroma of breakfast wafting through the air, coaxing us to the table. Simple, sturdy meals of biscuits and gravy greeted us as we started our days. With our bellies full, we did some household chores, as Mama had told us it was important not to become a burden on her little sister.

In the afternoons, the sun bathed the world in its golden glow, the magic of childhood took over. Like explorers of the wild, we ventured to the meandering Snohomish River with our loyal Honey by our side. The cold waters beckoned us, inviting a playful chorus of splashing and laughter. It was a sanctuary of endless escapades. The secrets of the river called to us, enchanting us with the mysteries hidden below its waters.

On occasion, my brothers joined our merry band while Denise stayed behind and helped Aunt Hatt. At fifteen and sixteen, my brothers were young men. Their adventurous spirits guided them on their own explorations. Yet, in the presence of us younger siblings, their playful nature shone through.

We often embarked on crawdad hunting expeditions with our eyes scanning the murky depths for those elusive creatures. With nimble hands and hearts full of anticipation, we tried to capture those wily beings destined for Aunt Hatt's boiler pan and, eventually, our tiny bellies.

I found myself captivated by their allure as the tiny, clawed figures scuttled across the rocky riverbanks. Their shells glistened in the dappled sunlight. Nature was like a delicate song of wonders that called with a hypnotic melody.

"Dawn, what are you doing over there?" Bobby leaned against a nearby dogwood tree, his lanky frame casting a long shadow across the ground.

"Hey-ya Bobby, I'm watching these crawdads. Aren't they something? I reckon they've got their own little world down there."

Junior approached with a mischievous glint in his eyes. "Is today the day you'll catch one, Dawn?" he teased me with a playful smirk. My brothers caught the crafty little creatures like they were born doing it, but I hadn't been able to catch one yet.

"I reckon I will, Junior," My determination flared. "I've got my trusty net right here." I held up a makeshift net Uncle Jack had helped me craft from the wire and mesh materials Aunt Hatt kept buried in her closet.

"If anyone can do it, you can, little Sis." Bobby ruffled my red hair. "Remember, you've gotta be quiet and quick like a sly fox."

With renewed determination, I waded into the icy waters, the river's gentle current billowing my skirt. I carefully positioned the net, primed to scoop my elusive prey.

"Be careful, that current looks powerful." Franny warned me.

"Watch closely." As I made my first attempt to capture a crawdad, the little critter darted away with lightning speed. Junior and Bobby burst into laughter, their voices echoing through the woods.

"You almost had it, Dawn," Junior exclaimed, his laughter infectious.

"Try again, little Sis," Bobby encouraged me, a playful twinkle in his eyes.

Undeterred, I persisted. Each attempt brought me closer to success, and with each failure, my determination grew. It was a war between the natural world and my youthful spirit. After what felt like an eternity, I scooped up a crawdad in my net, its tiny form wriggling and protesting. Excitement bubbled up within me, my heart pounded with triumph.

Squealing with delight, my voice echoed through the woods, "I did it. Look, Bobby. Look, Junior, I really caught one!"

My brothers rushed over, their eyes widened at the sight of my catch. "Well done, Sis," Junior exclaimed, his pride evident in his voice.

Bobby clapped me on the back, a wide grin spreading across his face. "You're a true crawdad wrangler, Sis. Aunt Hatt's gonna be proud."

"Make way, world, for the crawdad wrangler is here."
My voice was filled with enthusiasm as everyone laughed at
my shenanigans. Standing on the banks of the Snohomish
River, surrounded by the rugged scenery and the echoes of
our laughter, I couldn't help but feel a strong affinity for my
home state. The wilds of Washington were like a part of our
extended family. It bound us together, forming an unbreakable bond against the hardships of the world.

As my siblings and I basked in my victory of the
moment, the distant rumble of thunder rolled across the
horizon. A chill crept up my spine, and I couldn't help but
wonder: was this a passing storm, or did it carry a message
from the river, a forewarning of what lay ahead for our
tight-knit family?

Man of Mystery

EVERETT, WASHINGTON

MAY 1935

Dawn Jensen
Almost 7 Years Old

"Who's that man on the porch?" I asked Bobby.

"I don't know, Sis. Let's find out."

As we hiked to the cabin with our basket full of squirming crawdads, my eyes caught sight of a gaunt man sitting on the front porch. The stranger, perched on a rocking chair, puffed a cigarette and cast his shadow across Aunt Hatt's porch. My curiosity surged, and I quickened my pace to get a closer look. Honey ran ahead, barking suspiciously at the stranger.

Aunt Hatt suddenly appeared with a tight smile on her face. "Clarence," she exclaimed, her voice filled with surprise. "Well, looky who's here."

I stopped in my tracks, observing the interaction between Aunt Hatt and the man. His face had a mischievous grin, his eyes twinkled with adventure. I was captivated by him, eager to unravel the mystery that surrounded him.

"Hey there, Hattie. I wanted to swing by and check on my little brother. I didn't interrupt nothin' important, did I?" He glanced over at us kids approaching with our basket of crawdads.

"Nonsense, Clarence. Kin is always welcome here. You caught us by surprise is all." Aunt Hatt waved off his concern with a warm chuckle.

I inched closer, drawn to the energy that emanated from Clarence. There was an air of danger about him, something that set him apart. I could tell he was a man full of stories.

"Well, well, look who decided to grace us with his presence. About time you showed up, big brother." Uncle Jack emerged from the cabin and greeted Clarence with a slap on the back.

"Couldn't resist the call of the wild. Had to see what trouble you've been getting yourself into."

"Trouble? Me? Nah, you know I've settled down now. I'm a changed man." Uncle Jack gave Aunt Hatt a squeeze.

I silently watched this brotherly reunion as joy filled the air. Their boisterous greetings and the way their eyes lit up with shared memories was mesmerizing. Clarence, with his devilish grin and sparkling eyes, drew my attention like a firefly on a warm summer night. Yet Aunt Hatt seemed perturbed about the arrival of her husband's handsome brother.

"Kids, gather round. I've got some news for you. I've received a letter in the post from your Mama. She's healed up and ready for you to head home. It's been nice having you here... But your Daddy will be coming to collect you in a few days, and you know what? Uncle Clare's good with engines I'm sure he'll be able to stop your Daddy's old truck from overheating." Aunt Hatt announced.

Upon learning that Mama was prepared for our return, a sudden wave of longing washed over me. It had been a memorable ten days with Aunt Hatt, and with Uncle Clare's engine expertise, I felt better about our journey back in Daddy's old truck.

In our last days staying with Aunt Hatt, we got to know Uncle Clare (that's what he liked to be called). My usually friendly Aunt watched us with that tight smile on her face as Uncle Clare taught us to play poker and told us stories about his time as a Merchant Marine. We stayed up late on those remaining nights, and one morning, I awoke to the rumble of a truck in the distance. Running to the front yard, my eyes widened as I saw our old truck, kicking up dust in its wake.

"Daddy's here," My heart leapt with joy. There were hugs and introductions as we all gathered around Daddy.

"This is Uncle Jack's big brother Clarence. He can fix

anything and is gonna' have a look at the truck engine before we leave tomorrow," I excitedly introduced our newly arrived guest.

"Glad to meet you. It'll be nice to have a mechanic in the family. How long are you staying in these parts?" Daddy shook Uncle Clare's hand.

"I got me a job waitin' in Seattle. Thought I'd swing by to give my little bro a howdy. Was hoping to hitch a ride with y'all and find somewhere to stay for a while."

"That's great news. We have an old barn on the property that you can stay in until you find your own place. Us Okies need to stick together." Daddy had been a generous man and offered up our barn after only a few minutes of knowing Uncle Clare.

"I was hopin' you'd say that Johnny boy. That's mighty kind of ya. I won't be any trouble, and I'll pay ya for the use of your barn."

"Well, Uncle Clare, our barn has strict rules straight out of the Prohibition era. No speakeasies, no secret jazz performances, and absolutely no smuggling moonshine. We're law-abiding citizens, you see." I chimed in, and everyone laughed at my joke. Daddy reached down and tickled me.

"Where have you heard about all that?" Daddy chuckled.

"Pastor Williams was preaching about it last Sunday. Said I should keep an eye out for any suspicious characters trying to turn our barn into a secret gin joint." I joked.

Daddy's chuckles filled the air as he tousled my hair, his affectionate touch warmed my heart.

"Well, my little eavesdropper, remember, we prefer to keep our barn as a place for animals, not a hidin' spot for bootleggers," he playfully warned. "Rest assured, we may have our share of barn rules, but we'll make sure you're comfortable during your stay, Clarence. And don't you worry about paying rent. Family takes care of family around here."

Uncle Clare grinned, his eyes sparkled with gratitude, "I appreciate that, Johnny boy. I reckon this barn will be a fine temporary home for me. I'll make sure to lend a hand, I can earn my keep."

We woke up early the following morning and embarked on our journey to our little cabin in the woods. Unlike our previous trip, we had the advantage of daylight, and because Uncle Clare had worked his magic on Daddy's old Ford, we weren't worried about the engine overheating anymore. The atmosphere inside the truck was cheerful as we made the long drive home.

Upon our arrival, I pushed open the creaky screen door and was greeted by the soft glow of a flickering lantern and the soothing scent of Mama's favorite tea.

Mama sat at the worn table, the embodiment of grace amidst our simple surroundings. Her delicate hands cradled a porcelain teapot, its patterns whispering stories of generations past. The fragrant steam curled up, mingling with the warmth of the cozy fireplace. Mama's huge eyes held a flicker of determination.

"Hello, Love Bugs." Mama stood up, and we engulfed her in a huge group hug. "I'm glad to have you home. It's been too quiet without our little clan together. Promise me you'll never leave again."

"We couldn't wait to get home and disrupt your peace and quiet, Mama. How are you feeling?" I asked with inquisitive eyes.

"I'm as good as new, Pickle," Mama reassured, squeezing my hand.

Even after her recent surgery, my mother looked as radiant as ever. Her fair skin, golden hair, and gray eyes gave her the appearance of a movie star. When she was a teen, she even graced the cover of a local fashion magazine, and her magnetic charm made anyone feel like they were the center of her world. She could be quite temperamental if you pushed her buttons, though.

"You're as pretty as the day I met ya," Daddy exclaimed.

"Tell us, Daddy," the children chimed in unison, our eyes wide with anticipation.

Daddy took Mama's hand in his, a nostalgic smile playing on his lips. "Well, kids, way back in 1917, your Mama was sitting in her church pew, looking like a vision. I was up in the choir, trying not to hit any wrong notes."

Giggles erupted from Franny and me.

"I felt a spark when our eyes met," he continued, his

voice warm with memories. "Your Mama thought I was the most handsome man in town."

"I knew I'd marry him the moment I laid eyes on him!" Mama planted a kiss on Daddy's cheek.

Daddy chuckled. "Despite the age gap, we fell head over heels in love. Six months later, we tied the knot. And then, I whisked her away to Seattle where we rented this cozy cabin near the lumber yard."

"Did you live happily ever after, Daddy?" I placed myself between them.

"Well, life had its share of twists and turns, but your Mama and I've faced them together. Our love has stayed true." Daddy lifted me up and swung me around.

I loved when our parents recounted the story of how they met, and it was a warm reminder that our family was strong. No matter what troubles came our way, I knew my parent's love would conquer all.

Over the next few weeks, we embraced Uncle Clare as a new member of our brood and he began working at the mechanic's shop in town. Daddy and Uncle Clare got along like a house on fire since they were both from Oklahoma. As the sun set one evening, and enveloped the woods in its warm embrace, I overheard Mama voicing some concerns with Daddy.

"Lenora, you worry too much." Daddy's voice held a touch of defensiveness. "Clarence is a good man. He carries some demons from the Great War."

"I know he's been through a lot, but I fear his drinking

will only lead to trouble. And you, John, you've been drinking more since he's come into our lives." Mama sighed.

"Things are what they are for now."

Mama had recently been on edge when Daddy and Uncle Clare would end their days sitting on the porch drinking moonshine and sharing their stories of Oklahoma.

"That's a temporary fix. He's trying to put a bandage on a broken bone. It won't last, and it won't heal anything," Mama confided to me one night as I helped with the dishes.

In the daytime, Uncle Clare was fun to be around. But after he had started on his bottle of hooch, his language could get harsh, and Mama didn't care for his rude jokes one bit.

That night, over a supper of salt pork and boiled dandelion greens, we gathered around the table, giving thanks for our meager meal set before us. Mama broached the subject again, her eyes cast down, fixated on her worn-out hands. It was time for Uncle Clare to break free from our household and go out on his own.

"John," Mama started, her voice soft yet resolute, "Clarence has been here almost a year now. Maybe it's time for him to find his own home. To start building his own life here in Seattle. He doesn't want to be tied down to us for too long."

Silence hung heavy in the air as Daddy's eyes met Mama's, a mix of understanding and conflict reflected within. His gaze landed on Uncle Clare, who sat at the table, his troubled eyes darting from face to face.

"Don't you worry, Lenora. I've been asking around for a room to rent with one of the boys from work. He has a roommate now, but he'll be movin' on next month. I'll slide right into his spot. Can y'all put up with me for a few more weeks?"

"Stay as long as you need to, Clarence. Us Okies stick together." Daddy cleared his throat when Mama started to protest.

That night I fell asleep feeling a bit better knowing our visitor would soon be gone, and Mama would be happy again. My tranquility was shattered by a booming yell that tore through the silence and jolted us from our slumber. Startled and disoriented, I climbed out of my bedroll, eyes wide with fear. Urgent cries echoed through the house, alerting us to the imminent danger lurking outside.

As I reached the front porch, the heat from the flames warmed my skin and lit up the sky. Our old barn, a steadfast presence in our lives, was now a fiery inferno. Flames danced, hungrily devouring the wooden structure that had been a symbol of our toil and hope.

"Daddy, what's happened?" I whispered. He took in the devastating sight with resignation.

"Boys, go get the neighbors and tell them to bring their buckets," Daddy bellowed, his voice mingling with the hissing from the fire.

Suddenly a noise erupted from within the burning barn. It was the terrified yelping of my beloved Honey.

"Daddy, Honey's trapped in the barn!" I started running

toward the barn, but Daddy grabbed me with his powerful hands.

"No, Dawn, it's too dangerous to go into the barn now. It could collapse right on top of you. Honey is a smart dog, she will find her way out. Start hollering for her, and she'll follow your voice." Daddy had a grim look on his face as I started calling for Honey.

The terrified barks of my dear companion reverberated through the chaos, my heart pounded fiercely within my chest, each beat echoing my escalating dread. The mere image of Honey trapped in the inferno tore at my soul.

"I want you to stay on the porch while we try to get this fire doused." The neighbors had arrived, and Daddy ran toward the barn with a bucket in hand. Mama and Daddy got everyone to form a line from the creek to the barn, so they could pass buckets of water to each other. It seemed as if our whole neighborhood was there, chipping in to fight the fire. The searing heat and smoke filled the air, but my devotion to Honey eclipsed any flicker of trepidation.

"No, Dawn!" Franny yelled, but it was too late.

I was already climbing through the barn window toward Honey. I pressed on, my determination a steady compass. Tears welled in my eyes, blurring my vision, but I adamantly refused to retreat.

Venturing into the smoldering depths of the barn, Honey's desperate whimpers guided my path amid the flickering shadows. Each labored breath was an arduous task. My slight frame quivered with fear, yet I inched forward on all fours, calling out reassuringly to Honey. As I was able to grab onto Honey, a colossal beam plummeted, blocking my exit and trapping me within the fiery inferno.

The heat was intense, almost like the sun was right there with me, scorching my skin. The air was thick with smoke, and I could hardly see anything. The crackling sound of burning wood made me tremble with fright. I called out for help, but my voice seemed small compared to the roaring fire.

I tried to run for the door, but the flames danced and blocked my way. The smoke made me cough and choke. My tears flowed and I felt helpless, like a tiny bird trapped in a burning cage.

"Daddy. Daddy, help me!" My terrified voice called out.

Like an angel summoned from heaven, my father emerged from the haze, his face etched with deep concern. His voice, a soothing balm amid the smoky abyss, called out my name.

"Dawn, I'm here. Can you see me?'

Somehow, my father defied the scorching heat, his sturdy figure fighting against the suffocating smoke. Fueled by love, Daddy tried to lift the heavy beam that blocked my path. He leaned in with all his might, and the massive piece of wood started to shift, creating a narrow escape route. The fumes stung my eyes and I gathered every ounce of courage I had.

"Grab my hand, sweetheart," Daddy pleaded.

Tears streamed down my soot-covered face as I

extended my trembling hand, feeling the strength and love in my father's grasp. Daddy pulled me toward him as his other hand brushed against the searing flames, eliciting a gut-wrenching cry. But still, Daddy refused to let go.

We burst out of the barn, gasping for air, our bodies crashing onto the ground. The taste of freedom mingled with the smoky air. My father's hand, his hero's hand, was marred with deep burns that looked red and raw.

"Oh, John, your hand. We must tend that immediately," Mama uttered, her voice trembling with the weight of her concern.

"That will have to wait." Daddy returned to helping the neighbors as they tried to extinguish the flames engulfing the barn. He left me in Mama's capable hands as he returned to fight the fire. A short time later, the barn collapsed in a thunderous roar.

"Oh, Dawn!" Mama grabbed me in her arms, joining our tear-stained faces together. Her touch was a gentle reminder I was not alone, I was still alive.

Mama's warm embrace offered solace. She held me as my body shook. Her loving presence washed away the residual fear that clung to me like smoke. Her fingers brushed through my disheveled hair, soothing my trembling body with each stroke.

I glanced over at Honey. She limped toward me, her paws burned from the fire as she whimpered and nuzzled against my leg. Despite her injuries, she remained faithfully by my side throughout the ordeal, her eyes reflecting both fear and unyielding loyalty. I gently scooped her into my arms and vowed to nurse her wounds and provide Honey with the care she deserved.

As I clung to Mamma, my small frame wrapped tightly in her loving embrace, she was racked with deep, sorrowful sobs. Her tears mingled with mine, creating a shared river of emotions that flowed between us, each drop carrying the weight of fear, relief, and an almost overwhelming feeling of despair.

The flames had devoured the barn that once stood proud, leaving behind nothing but a charred skeleton of memories. A poignant reminder of the fragility of life's treasures.

"John, let me tend to that hand now." The house was no longer in danger, and Daddy had returned to our side, looking like the weight of the world was on his shoulders.

Determined and steadfast, my mother pulled out her supplies—a clean cloth, a bottle of hydrogen peroxide, and a jar of petroleum jelly—from the cupboard.

Her hands moved with gentle precision, pouring peroxide onto Daddy's burnt hand. Her touch both tender and purposeful. My father gritted his teeth, bearing the weight of agony with quiet resilience.

But my mother wasn't finished. With meticulous care, she smoothed the salve over his wounded hand, her fingers tracing his angry-looking skin. She wrapped his hand in a clean handkerchief, securing it with unwavering tenderness.

"Thank you, sweetheart. You always know what to do," my father whispered, his voice filled with love.

Abruptly, the crunch of gravel seized our attention. The landlord, Mr. Thornton, arrived with an aura of authority, his eyes etched with the weight of the fire's news. "What in blazes happened here? This is your responsibility, and now the whole barn's gone up in smoke."

Daddy's gaze dropped to the ground, his shoulders slumping under the weight of the accusation. "It was an accident, Mr. Thornton. Clarence must have fallen asleep drunk with a lit cigarette."

Mr. Thornton's face reddened with fury. "I won't tolerate such recklessness, John. You've not only cost yourself a job but also the roof over your head. Consider yourself fired." Daddy's face turned white as a sheet. He had dedicated his last few years to the lumberyard, his muscular hands calloused from moving around the wood and shoveling gravel.

"But, sir."

"No buts, John." Mr. Thornton's voice rang out as he walked to his old truck and pulled out a shotgun, his anger unyielding. "Pack your things and get off my property! I won't have a drunken fool endangering my livelihood." Mr. Thornton barked his orders with an air of superiority. His shotgun glinted menacingly in the morning light as a harsh reminder of the power he held over our lives.

As the morning sun began to peek timidly through the haze of smoke, casting an eerie glow upon the charred remains of the old barn, we stood there, a family shattered by loss.

Mama's grip tightened around my hand and her eyes pleaded silently with Daddy. I could see the turmoil on his face, a battle between pride and survival.

"Sir, we'll gather our things and be off your property as soon as we can." Daddy seemed to choke out these words nobody wanted to hear.

Mr. Thornton sneered, and his contempt seeped through his words. "See that you do, John. You're lucky I don't call the sheriff for this mess. A drunkard like Clarence shouldn't have been under your roof in the first place."

Daddy's shoulders sagged, the weight of his mistakes crushing his spirit, and his wounded hand hung limply at his side. My poor Daddy was hurt and it was my fault. I longed to wrap my arms around him to shield him from Mr. Thornton, but I knew I was only a little girl with no power to change our circumstances.

We retreated to our humble cabin, collecting what we could in the short time we had. Mama's eyes glistened with tears as she carefully gathered her precious photograph box, remnants of a past we couldn't afford to lose. Daddy packed our belongings into weathered gunny sacks, his movements slow and heavy with defeat.

The neighbors looked on with sympathy and approached us one by one, offering words of comfort. They knew the trials we faced, for they had weathered their own storms during these hard times. With their help, we loaded our belongings into our old truck.

The truck had seen better days, just like our home. It used to be a pretty blue color, but it had faded into a tired-looking bruise. "Can't we stay, Mama? This was Uncle Clare's fault, he should be the one to go."

Mama sighed as she kept her hands busy packing. "Oh, Dawn, I wish we could, but we can't stay here anymore. We have to go find a new home."

The blow was swift and brutal, leaving us reeling. Where would we live, and how would Daddy make a living without his job at the lumber yard?

On The Road

JOURNEY TO PUYALLUP, WASHINGTON

JUNE 10TH, 1936

Dawn Jensen
8 Years Old

L eaving behind the familiar, questions swirled in my mind, mirroring the dust kicked up by our old truck. How could Uncle Clare disappear like that after causing so much trouble?

Uncertainty gripped my heart as tightly as Mama's hand held mine. Honey sat in my lap, her singed paws wrapped in bandages, and my lungs ached from the smoke I'd inhaled in the burning barn.

My siblings sat on the worn-out wooden planks of the truck bed, their heads hanging in defeat. The wind tousled their hair, and suddenly the heavens opened. It started pouring down rain. Everyone scrambled around for the tarps Daddy always had in his truck bed. Why couldn't it have rained last night? Then the fire would have been put out, and we wouldn't be in this mess.

"I reckon we oughta head up near Puget Sound, Lenora," Daddy drawled. "It's 'bout time for hop-pickin' season, and I've heard there's work aplenty in them fields."

"You might be onto something, John. But how will you work with that burned hand?" Mama responded.

"It looks worse than it feels. I'll make do."

I sat in between Mama and Daddy and captured every word exchanged between them. I felt a gut-wrenching guilt for being the cause of Daddy's burnt hand. No matter what sort of trouble I got into, I knew my Daddy was there to rescue me. But what would happen if he couldn't work?

"We need to find a place where we can make a decent living and regroup after this ordeal. Do we have enough gas to get to Puyallup?" Mama wiped the tears from her eyes.

"We'll make it. Don't you worry. I packed those extra gas cans I kept for the delivery truck." Daddy clutched the steering wheel. The tension in my parents' voices added to the strained atmosphere.

"John, don't ever get mixed up with drunkards again. Nothing good ever comes from it, and you know it too well. Let's put this disaster behind us and never speak of it again." Mama blazed with anger.

I held my breath, my heart pounding, afraid that Mama

would turn her anger on me next. My happy-go-lucky Daddy almost looked like another man as he responded.

"You're right, Lenora. I promise, I won't let myself be led astray. You deserve better." Daddy's shoulders slumped, his gaze filled with tears of shame and frustration. I could sense the weight of his mistakes pressed down upon him.

"And you, young lady. Don't you ever pull a stunt like that again. You scared me half to death." Mama turned her gaze to me.

"Yes, ma'am, I'm sorry Daddy got hurt, and it's my fault," I answered solemnly.

"Remember, your actions have repercussions. Daddy won't always be there to rescue you." Mama continued to stare at the road ahead, her grip on her box of photos a touch tighter.

The air was heavy with unspoken emotions, an unsteady silence lingering in the air. Tears continued to fall from my eyes as I yearned for the warmth of our cabin in the woods.

Noticing my distress, Mama's eyes softened, and I could see her struggling to gain control of her anger. She took a deep breath, exhaling slowly as if pushing last night's tragic events out of the car's open window and out of her mind. "We can't change what's done," she said softly. Her fingers intertwined with mine. "John, do you think we'll find work down south of here?" Her voice sounded less angry now, and there was a glimmer of forgiveness in her tone.

"I know we will," Daddy reassured her.

I held onto that glimmer of hope, desperately wishing

for a place to call home. The reality of not knowing where we'd be staying once night came scared me right to my core.

We drove on for what seemed like hours, and as dusk settled in, I tried to push the events of the night before out of my mind, as Mama had seemed to do. The relentless rain finally ceased, and the sun's last golden rays pierced through the darkened clouds, igniting the sky with a breathtaking display of colors. The horizon transformed into a canvas of vibrant orange and magenta, a sight that whispered of new beginnings.

It was then that we stumbled upon a clearing to rest for the night. Daddy pulled the truck over, parking it beside a babbling creek, the sounds of the flowing water a soothing song of promises yet to come. The scent of fresh, rain-kissed earth mixed with the smoke from the bonfire Daddy had started to build created familiar aromas that brought back memories of our last camping trip.

"Mama, will things get better?" I asked, feeling vulnerable.

Mama's eyes met mine with tenderness. She gently reached out, her hand caressing my cheek. "Oh, my sweet Pickle, don't you fret none. Put that horrible night into a little box in your head, lock it up, and don't think about it again."

"Yes Ma'am," I responded.

"We'll find our way. If we stick together, nothing can hurt us. Keeping our little clan together is what matters most." Mama rummaged around in the back of the truck and found some baloney sandwiches that she had prepared earlier. "Now help pass out these sandwiches to your siblings."

As we ate our meager supper, I clung to Mama's words with a renewed vigor. Our journey was far from over, but she was right—if we stuck together, we could face whatever lay ahead.

The next morning, we rolled into a small town called Puyallup. Daddy stopped at the general store to ask about which farms were looking for workers. When he returned to the truck, he was smiling.

"This is where we will find work." He started up the old truck, heading east toward the hop farms dotting the surrounding area. A short while later, Daddy parked the truck outside one of the farms. He turned to Mama and us.

"Y'all wait right here. I'm fixin' to find the farm manager and see if there's any work up for grabs. Hand me those old work gloves so I can cover up this burned hand."

"You be careful, John," Mama said, and we watched Daddy stride toward a nearby barn. He blended into the hustle and bustle. Anticipation buzzed in the air and my heart raced with eagerness to know if he would find the work we desperately needed. I could see families like ours working hard, even children were helping. We were surrounded by towering trellises laden with hop vines, their delicate cones swaying in the breeze. A man with a hop pole appeared and shouted, "Hop pile," signaling for a new pile of hops to be gathered. He cut down the vines, while the children scurried and collected them into large piles.

"Stick together, my Love Bugs." Mama pulled Franny and me close, her arms enveloping us in a comforting embrace. "We'll be fine. Your Daddy will figure something out for us."

After what felt like forever, Daddy emerged from the barn, his face bursting with relief, a hitch in his step. We gathered around him, waiting for the news.

Daddy cleared his throat. "I spoke to the farm manager, and there's work here for us. We're going to start picking hops tomorrow. There's a spot over yonder where we can set up camp."

Sighs of relief erupted from our little clan. The weight of uncertainty momentarily lifted. Mama's eyes sparkled with tears of joy, while Bobby and I exchanged cautious glances. This was the chance we'd been hoping for.

After setting up camp, Daddy, Mama, and some of the siblings went to explore the grounds of our new home.

I tugged at my brother's sleeve.

"Junior, what are we going to do here? Will I have to work?" My voice was filled with apprehension.

As Junior explained, his tone was filled with a mix of pride and responsibility, "I reckon we're going to be hop pickers now. See those tall vines over there? Those are hop vines. Our job will be to pick those hop cones. You younger kids can drag them into piles to be weighed, and we'll get paid by how many pounds of hops we can pick."

"Do the hops taste good, John?" I pressed him, my curiosity getting the better of me.

"No silly, we pick them because they are used to make beer," Junior replied, his voice carrying a touch of laughter. "Hops make the beer taste good. And when it's hop-picking season, farms like this need lots of workers to harvest the hops."

"Didn't Mama say we should avoid drunkards? Drinking got us into this problem in the first place." I felt confused.

"We aren't going to be drinking the beer. The hops are sent somewhere else to make it for other people to drink. It's honest work, don't try to dwell on it too much. Mama says beer is different than spirits anyway."

As evening approached, we made our way to our campsite. Daddy led us in prayer, his voice soft and reverent.

"Dear Lord, we ask for forgiveness for our past sins and guidance on this journey. Bless this farm, and its workers, and help us to find strength in your word."

I closed my eyes, joining my family in this moment of reflection and hope. The flickering campfire cast dancing shadows around the campsite, and the voices of fellow hop pickers filled the tents around us. In the quiet of the night, I realized we were not alone in our struggles. We were part of a community, bound by shared dreams of a better future.

A huge yawn escaped my lips as I watched Mama clean and redress Daddy's wound, and a fresh wave of guilt washed over me. Why couldn't I have done what I was told?

I was torn between feeling guilty over Daddy's burned hand and grateful that I had Honey by my side.

The darkness of the nighttime sky deepened, and as the stars twinkled like lanterns in the distance, I struggled to fall asleep. I worried about Daddy's hand, and I wondered when we'd have a home to call our own again. The hop farm would be a place where we could work side by side with others, but it was a poor replacement for our little cabin in the woods.

As I nestled into my makeshift bed and drifted off into a restless nights sleep, my dreams were filled with flickering flames and the echoes of my father's reassuring voice calling out to me as I hid from the raging fire that had set us on this journey of uncertainty.

The next morning, I awoke to the bustling energy of people preparing for a grueling day of work. I gently tugged on Junior's arm, directing his attention to a particular group that stood out like vibrant blossoms in the field. They moved with a grace that seemed to harmonize with the swaying vines. The women, their hands weathered by time and adorned with intricately beaded bracelets, had dark and beautifully braided hair. The men exuded a rugged strength born from years of arduous labor; they were adorned with furs and wore beaded jewelry that shimmered in the morning light. I had never seen a man wear jewelry other than a wedding ring or a pocket watch.

"Who are they?" My eyes widened with wonder.

"They must be from the Puyallup Tribe, this entire area

is named after them. They have been living on these lands for a long time. They work the fields like us."

I nodded, taking in these new people that would be working alongside us, their hands moving with practiced ease, an encouraging reminder that we were all connected, striving together to make a living in these uncertain times.

The next day, Mama heated her iron pan over the campfire and heated up a tin of beans. We also had some dry biscuits that were hard to swallow. After breakfast, as Mama washed up, Junior pulled the rest of us kids aside.

"Hey guys," Junior said, his tone kind and understanding. "Today is a big day for all of us. Mama and Daddy have been working hard to take care of us, and now it's our turn to lend a hand. Remember, we're a team, we gotta stick together. Let's try our best not to whine or complain. It's hard enough for Mama and Daddy, and we don't wanna add to their worries."

Franny nodded, her eyes shining with sincerity. Denise shifted next to me, looking kind of uncomfortable. I reached out and squeezed her hand. Junior's voice was warm and reassuring. "No matter what happens, let's stick by each other. Look out for one another, and help out where we can. We might be young, but we're strong. Strength runs in our family, ya know?"

After Junior's pep talk, we made our way over to the hop fields, holding onto the knowledge that our family's strength ran deeper than the roots of the hop vines that surrounded us. I gripped a burlap sack and trudged through the rows of towering hop vines. The morning sun cast a warm glow over the farm, illuminating the lush green foliage that infused the air with a sweet, woodsy fragrance.

"Look at all the hops," I exclaimed, tugging at her sleeve. She scrunched her nose, her blonde curls bouncing with each step.

"Yeah, Dawn. We get to help Mama and Daddy, but you better keep close to me, and don't be asking all your usual questions," Franny said in a bossy tone.

Together, we were in charge of dragging the freshly picked hops into huge piles. We were determined to prove to ourselves. I imagined the coins we'd earn and the other little treasures that awaited us as a reward for our hard work. We all worked tirelessly, and as I worked, I watched as the grown-ups plucked the hop cones from the vines. The rhythm of their labor served as a backdrop to the chatter of voices that filled the air with conversation, and intermingled with the rustle of leaves.

"Careful with those sacks, girls. We need to fill them up, but don't you overdo it, you hear?" Mama reminded us, wiping sweat from her brow.

"We won't, Mama," I assured her. As the day wore on, my arms grew tired, and my legs felt weary from the effort I was putting forth. By the middle of lunch the sight of the hop sacks piling up gave me a renewed sense of energy. Franny and I exchanged encouraging glances. After what seemed like a lifetime, the sun began its descent, and we gathered by the scales to weigh our harvest. The farm manager, Mr. Higgins, had a weathered face and his eyes were cold as he recorded the weight of our bounty.

"The Jensen family has done a good job. You've earned yourselves a decent sum today. If you keep this up, you'll have fifteen dollars by the week's end." The value of our labor became tangible, and the weight of our toil transformed into a reward.

"Did you hear that, Dawn? We can earn so much, Franny whispered, her eyes widening in disbelief.

I nodded, and my tired eyes mirrored hers. "Yeah, Franny, we can. But was all that work worth it for a few dollars? Is it enough for us to get another cabin soon?"

"I don't know Dawn, but let's think of this as one big adventure. I know how much you like camping in the woods."

I raised an eyebrow at Franny's remark. I was feeling tired and sunburned. "Oh, sure, Franny. Who needs a proper home when we can sleep outside and fight off the bugs all night?" I couldn't help but snap at Franny; I was hungry and grouchy after a long day's work.

"Shhh, you don't want Mama and Daddy to hear you. At least it's not raining." Franny shook her head at my remark. I was trying to remain positive, but I missed our little cabin in the woods.

As we walked to our humble campsite, our steps were weary. Mama and Daddy tried to appear hopeful. At least we had money to get more supplies from the general store.

"Chin up, little ones. We're a team," Daddy said as he

ruffled my red hair, echoing what Junior words from earlier. "And together, we can do anything."

Days turned into weeks as hop season wore on. Aided by our meager earnings, we were able to buy more supplies, and none of us went hungry. On the weekends, we picked huckleberries, salmon berries, and the hugest, sweetest blackberries to supplement our small supply of food. Everything that could be eaten for nourishment was used, and nothing ever went to waste. As poor as we were, we had great spirits and trusted in the Lord for better times to come.

At night, as we fell asleep under the stars, our situation weighed on my heart. I often heard the adults talking about "the poorhouse." I had heard that word a lot lately and could only imagine what it meant. I pictured our old, burned-down barn, but something felt worse about the poorhouse.

The next morning, under the scorching summer sun, Franny and I collected the hops from all over the vast expanse of the farm, our bodies glistening with sweat.

"Hey, Franny, what's the poorhouse?" I asked inquisitively.

Franny leaned back and scrunched up her nose like she does when she's concentrating. She took a moment to gather her thoughts before responding.

"The poorhouse is a place where poor folks go when they're having a tough time. It's like a big ol' scary building where they can stay and get some help."

My brow furrowed in confusion. "So, they live there?"

Franny nodded, her gaze focused on the distant horizon. "Yeah, it's like a temporary home for them. They live there if they don't have anywhere else to go, but it ain't like a warm and cozy house. They sleep in a big room with cots all in a line, and they have to work all day to earn their keep."

"But why do they have to go there, Franny? Can't they stay with relatives or friends?"

Franny sighed, her voice filled with compassion. "Sometimes people fall on hard times. They can't afford enough food or even a roof over their heads, and they don't want to be a burden to their relatives. That's why we haven't gone to stay with Aunt Hatt and Uncle Jack. Everyone is struggling right now, I heard Mama say she didn't want to be a burden to them for the summer. The other day she sent them a letter letting them know what happened with the barn."

My heart was heavy with sadness. "That sounds awful. I hope we don't have to go to the poorhouse."

Franny stopped working and looked me full in the face. "Daddy would never let that happen. He's too proud." Franny motioned over to Mama who suddenly appeared beside me.

"You two look like you're ready to break for lunch." Mama interrupted our conversation with a knowing look in her eyes.

I quickly wiped away the tears that had been threatening to fall. "Yes, Mama. I'm a little hungry. That's all," I answered.

She must have caught wind of our hushed conversation

about the poorhouse because compassion filled her eyes. Her sun-kissed face softened with empathy, and she knew just the words to say to calm our worried hearts.

"I couldn't help but overhear a snippet of your talk. It's true, times have been rough, and it's only natural to fret about what's coming next. But I want you to know our family is like them tough old hop vines around us, so robust we can weather any storm. You girls tuck your worries away in the corner of your minds and let us grown-ups take care of everything. Now, let's go find a spot in the shade over yonder to eat the sandwiches I packed for lunch." She brushed her worn hands on her blue apron and motioned over to some trees that were at the edge of the hops field. The ground beneath her worn shoes crackled with dry grass. We looked at her, eyes wide with longing, craving her comfort.

"Yes Ma'am." My stomach growled in response. Hope trickled down my spine along with the sweat from our hard work.

"We're going to be moving on from Puyallup soon. Daddy decided it's time to head down to Selah for apple picking season, but I'm certain that this lifestyle won't last forever. President Roosevelt just gave a speech, and he's working on creating more jobs to get us out of these hard times. We'll hang on for better days. We may not have much right now, but we've got something inside us, deep down. It's a toughness that comes down from our ancestors. Daddy will move mountains to protect us. You can count on me to keep whipping up tasty meals that'll keep your bellies full, no matter what life throws our way. We'll be back in our own home and I'll be banging around my kitchen while you kids are swimming in the creek."

We chuckled picturing Mama bustling around her kitchen, the smell of baked goods filling the air with mouth-watering aromas. Mama's words provided reassurance, reminding us she showed her love through the comfort of her delicious home-cooked meals. It was a small but significant way in which Mama added a touch of stability to our lives.

The image of apple trees filled my mind, enticing me with the possibilities that laid ahead. Yet uncertainties lingered, whispering doubts and fears.

Would Selah bring the fresh start we longed for, or would it be another stop on our journey through hardship and uncertainty?

Don't Sit Under the Apple Tree

SELAH, WASHINGTON
AUGUST 10TH, 1936

Dawn Jensen
8 Years Old

"Alright, kids," Daddy's voice broke through the morning silence, his tone filled with purpose. "Time to wake up and get your things together. We're heading down to Selah for apple picking. It's going to be hard work, but it'll put food on the table. Let's make sure we're all set to leave in an hour."

As Mama had predicted, it was time to leave the hop farm, and by late morning, we were on the road. As we journeyed along a dusty road, the landscape changed before my eyes. Puyallup's vast, open fields and hop farms yielded to the lush greenery of Yakima Valley. Sweet and earthy aromas filled the air on our trek to our next destination. We commenced our journey at daybreak, and my sleepy eyes, laden with dreams, could barely stay open as the truck lulled me into a broken sleep.

Leaning against the car window, my small hand pressed to the glass, I felt the gentle vibrations of the road beneath us. The engine's familiar hum and the car's rhythmic swaying brought a comforting cadence to our journey. After several hours, I finally caught sight of the apple orchards, their trees brimming with red and green fruit, which set my mouth watering.

"Look, Mama! Can we pick some apples to eat?" Now that I'd seen the first apple orchard, I was wide awake.

Mama glanced at me, her eyes shining with a mix of tiredness and hope. "We made it, Pickle. We're in Selah now where the apple trees go on for days. Daddy's going to find some work, and you'll be stuffing yourself with more apples than you can count."

I nodded, my mind buzzing with possibilities. The car pulled up to a huge farmhouse nestled amid the orchards. Daddy stepped out, his tall figure casting a shadow over the dusty ground. His burned hand was healed, but he wore the scars from the night that had set us on this voyage.

I hopped out of the car next to him and my feet sunk into the soft soil. I ran toward the nearest tree and reached up to touch the velvety skin of a ripe apple.

As our parents talked with the orchard owners, I

wandered through the rows of trees, my imagination running wild. I envisioned myself climbing those branches, reaching for the juiciest apples, and filling a basket with my sweet treasures.

Leaves offered plenty of shade as a respite from the sun's powerful rays. Washington was known for its downpours, but we had been having a fairly dry summer and we were thankful we didn't have to spend our nights sleeping out in the rain with only a few carefully hung tarps to provide some shelter.

This was our new beginning. A chance to turn our fortunes around, and I couldn't help but compare this upcoming work to the backbreaking labor we had endured in the hop fields of Puyallup. Those long summer days strained our bodies, but somehow, among the apple orchards, the task of harvest seemed more inviting.

I turned to Bobby, my thoughts bubbling up. "Hey, Bobby," I began, "those hop leaves were light. These apples will be heavier. Do you think we'll make more money picking apples? I hope we make enough money to get our own cabin soon."

"I don't know about that, but at least now we'll be picking something we can actually eat," he responded as we took in the plump apples hanging low on the branches.

These apple-laden trees could never replace the familiar warmth of our humble home. Oh, I yearned for our cabin in the woods, with its comforting embrace and happy memories. The winds of change had blown us away from our cherished home, shattering our hopes and dreams, but I refused to believe my prayers for a place to call home would go unanswered.

Somewhere within this great state of Washington, I knew there must be a house for us where we could build a new life and forge cherished memories once more.

Fall was around the corner, and I had been looking forward to starting school, but I couldn't help but wonder how I'd go to school if we didn't have a home. Now that we were dependent on the crop seasons for income, I would have to work, too. Nevertheless, I tried to put on a happy face for Mama and Daddy. Seeing their strength and unwavering spirit filled my heart with faith. Selah would be another chance to eke out a living, to find stability amid the swaying branches and delicious apples.

Daddy interrupted my thoughts as he returned from his negotiations with the orchard owners. "We've got work, kids. We'll be picking apples like we imagined." Once again, Daddy had found a way to provide, and suddenly the future felt a bit brighter.

Hand in hand, we ventured into the heart of the apple orchard ready to embrace the challenges and blessings that lay ahead. Selah wasn't just a name on a map anymore. It had transformed into a place representing my family's resilience and dreams. A steppingstone toward our future.

We discovered a cozy spot to camp by the riverbank. Lacking a tent, Daddy fashioned one using a couple of large hop sacks and his old trusty tarps. Despite his efforts, I woke in the night to pouring rain and Mama covering us up with an oilcloth, in hopes of keeping us dry throughout the night. The hopsacks had been soaked through, leaving us exposed to the elements.

The next morning we were all soaking wet. Mama started to prepare our breakfast on her large cook stone over the fire Daddy had built—mostly beans, fruit, and whatever vegetables were left over from our supplies on the hop farm.

"You kids go and try to find something dry to put on while I finish heating up these beans," Mama wiped her hands on her blue apron.

As we ate our breakfast, Daddy's eyes scanned the pages, searching for hope amidst the stories of hardship and despair. "Lenora, it says here that almost twenty-five percent of Americans are out of work. We ain't the only ones facin' hard times. Folks from all over the country, all the different races and ages have been displaced."

"I heard they are calling them Shantytowns' and they're popping up in cities everywhere." Mama responded.

"Don't fret, darling wife. We'll have a roof over our heads again before long." Daddy made it a point to get the newspaper often to search for any glimmer of good news about the economy and job situation. The newspaper was our window to the world beyond our life on the road, keeping us connected and informed.

I believed Daddy when he said we'd have a home again, I hoped we'd find it soon. Meanwhile, the first month of apple picking passed quickly. We tried to make the most of our situation until one morning something happened to change the course of our future.

"Bobby, look at all those apples in that tree!" exclaimed Junior.

"Whoa, that's the biggest apple haul I've seen all summer," Bobby replied with a wide grin on his face. "Think about the juicy pies Mama could whip up."

Franny scrunched up her nose, adding, "Don't forget about the apple sauce. It'd be a tasty treat alongside a Sunday roast dinner. Junior, how long before Daddy finds us a new cabin?"

Junior crossed his arms, pondering. "Hard to say, Franny. Apple season's nearly over, and we don't want to be roughing it come winter. Gotta find a warm place before the cold sets in. Daddy must've saved up a good pile of cash by now."

Franny's grin grew wider. "I hope so, Bobby. And you know what that means? Mama can finally bake up a storm in her own kitchen, and we can go to school. I miss having friends."

Junior nodded, his face lit up with anticipation. "And we'll make loads of friends wherever we end up."

Franny playfully teased, "Who knows, Junior? You might find yourself a sweetheart in the next town."

The younger siblings joined in, teasing Junior. We giggled and sang, "Junior and sweetheart, sitting in a tree, K-I-S-S-I-N-G!"

With each apple carefully plucked from the branches,

our hope for the future grew, trusting that soon we'd have a warm place to call our own.

"You lazy good-for-nothing! We don't have time for your games! Get up and get to work or you'll be out of here!" A booming voice carried over the orchards in a sudden burst of commotion. A scene was unfolded at the edge of the field where Bear, an older Native American worker, found himself on the receiving end of Mr. Billings' harsh words.

The oppressive heat seemed to have taken its toll, and the older man struggled to keep pace with the demanding quota. Mr. Billings, the farm supervisor, stood towering over Bear, barking orders and demanding more.

Franny and I watched, feeling uneasy, as Daddy cast a concerned gaze toward the unfolding situation. Old Bear's exhaustion became evident as he tried to get up and finally collapsed to the ground. In an instant, Daddy sprang to action, leaving his work behind to rush to the old man's aid.

"Franny, what's happening?" I sat down my basket and watched the commotion taking place, my heart pounding with concern.

"Stay with me, Sis. Daddy is going to help Old Bear."

Once at Bear's side, Daddy leaned down and felt the man's brow. The supervisor's harsh words faded into the background as Daddy asked, "Bear, you alright?"

Old Bear's breath came in ragged gasps, his face red, and his brow soaked with perspiration. He mustered a weak nod; the deep lines of pain were evident on his weathered face. "Just… the heat. I need a little water. Maybe a quick rest to catch my breath."

Gently, Daddy helped Old Bear sit up, providing support and shade from the scorching heat. "Can't you see the man needs rest, Mr. Billings? He's given his all, and now he needs a break." Daddy did not back down.

"He's slackin' off, trying to dodge work. If he can't work, he's useless to me." Mr. Billings scoffed.

Daddy's eyes blazed, fury flickering within. I had never seen my Daddy that furious. "This aint about slackin' off, Mr. Billings. Old Bear's been bustin' his back since I got here, and you should treat him with some basic human decency. Can't you consider givin' him the afternoon off to regain his strength?"

As Daddy's words hung in the air, a silence settled over the orchard. The oppressive heat seemed to mirror the tension between the men as if nature itself held its breath, awaiting the outcome.

Finally, Mr. Billings relented, his face contorted with a mix of annoyance and begrudging acknowledgment. "Fine, take him to rest. But don't either of you bother comin' tomorrow. You two are troublemakers. Get outta here and don't come back!"

With careful strength, Daddy helped the older man to his feet. The other workers watched, their expressions a mix of relief and respect.

I stood at the edge of the orchard, my eyes fixed on Daddy, and a swell of pride filled my chest. The way Daddy stood up to Mr. Billings sent a rush of admiration coursing through my veins. Then the realization struck me like a lightning bolt.

Daddy had lost another job and an unsettling pit started to form deep within my stomach.

Uncertainty loomed over our family like a dark cloud, casting a shadow of worry and doubt. The weight of the situation settled upon my young shoulders, threatening to pull me into an abyss of fear. How would we make ends meet without the wages from picking apples?

As I looked at Daddy, his face tight with concern, a single question echoed in my mind: What would happen to us now?

The Long and Winding Road

SELAH, WASHINGTON

NOVEMBER 12TH, 1936

Dawn Jensen

8 Years Old

With heavy hearts, we returned to pack up our belongings. As we approached our camp, we noticed a man waiting near our truck.

"I am Elan. Old Bear is my older brother. You showed him kindness when others looked away."

"That was the right thing to do. No man oughta suffer under such harsh conditions," Daddy said in response.

"You are good people. I want to help you, as you helped

my brother. Come to my campfire. There's something important I want to tell you."

Mama nodded in agreement while we children shared hopeful glances. With cautious optimism, we followed the man into the darkness, their steps guided by the moon's soft glow. Elan gestured to a small clearing in the woods, where a flickering campfire illuminated the night.

"Please sit down. Eat. We've got smoked salmon to share." We sat on a makeshift log bench and shared a simple meal of smoked fish and fry bread. The men talked in hushed tones.

"Thank you kindly for your hospitality. This sure means a lot to us."

"It is I who should be thanking you," Bear responded. "You know there's lots of logging work near my wife's home in Neah Bay. It's good work for a younger man like you."

"Work near Neah Bay? That's a long way out."

Old Bear nodded, a solemn expression on his face. "Yes, but a new road has been built. Go and talk to the Makah chief and tell him Elan and Matoaka sent you and they will let you stay. Family is important to them, as it is to us." Daddy grasped Old Bear's calloused hand, gratitude showing on his face.

"Thank you, Matoaka. You don't know what this means to us. We won't forget it."

The men's conversation was interrupted by a sudden flurry of activity, two women emerged from the shadows, their arms cradling baskets brimming with freshly picked apples. The crisp scent mingled with the smoky fire's aroma.

The women deftly placed a cedar plank at the campfire's edge and carefully proceeded to arrange the apples on the plank to roast. Alongside the warmth of the dancing flames, we found a much-needed break from the heavy burdens that had been weighing on our hearts. The hardships and the uncertainty of our future seemed distant in that moment and were replaced by a shared warmth and understanding that transcended culture and circumstance.

As the evening unfolded, laughter and storytelling filled the air. Eventually, we plucked the roasted apples from their fiery perch. After they cooled, we bit into the soft flesh, and a warm sweetness exploded onto our tongues. The rich flavors filled our mouths, and our worries from the events of the day seemed to vanish.

One of their young ones, with sparkling eyes, stood up while holding the basket in his hands. "I wanna tell ya about my Ma's people. They are good people, always giving. Brave enough to hunt the whales where their home is the mighty ocean, and the women weave baskets, the best in the world. My Ma made this basket. She wants your family to have it now." The boy smiled. Mama stood up and graciously accepted the gift. Daddy dug deep into his pocket and handed the boy the small pocket knife he carried with him.

"We thank you and will think about heading to Neah Bay to find those logging jobs you spoke of." Daddy spoke to the men as he motioned for us to start gathering up to head back.

On the way to our campsite, Bobby chimed in, his eyes filled with curiosity, "Daddy, why did you give that boy your knife?"

"That's their custom, and it was a good thing to do. He offered me a gift we could use. I offered him one he could use in return as thanks." Daddy ruffled Bobby's hair.

As we settled in for the night, I could hear Mama and Daddy discussing the night's events in hushed voices. Eventually, Mama's voice filled the air. "Listen up, kids. Your Daddy and I have made up our minds about something."

"It'll be the start of an adventure for us." Daddy agreed, "Come first light, we're hittin' the road and heading to our new lives in Neah Bay."

"But where's Neah Bay?" I asked, always the curious one.

Daddy grinned, his love shining through his eyes. "Neah Bay's a mighty extraordinary spot nestled by the grand, ol' ocean. Way at the top of Washington, right up next to Canada."

"I've never seen the ocean! Will we get a home up there as Old Bear promised?" I questioned. My voice reflected a mix of wonder and puzzlement.

Mama winked at us, her gentle presence reassuring. "In Neah Bay, we'll have a home again. I'm sure of it."

A whirlwind of questions and emotions filled the air— doubts, longing, and a dash of fear. "I know it's tough, moving once more in such a short time, but sometimes we have to grab the opportunities that come our way, that's how we'll create a better life," Daddy addressed us with tenderness in his voice.

"Can we still fish like we did before, Daddy?" Bobby's eyes sparkled with excitement.

Daddy nodded, his grin spread wide. "You bet, Bobby. Neah Bay's got a turquoise ocean, teemin' with fish. We'll cast our lines and live off its bounty."

Mama's voice rang out above our squeals of emotion. "So, rest easy now, my Love Bugs. Come dawn, we'll start our next journey. Neah Bay's calling, and as long as we're all together, trusting in the Lord above, we'll be alright."

I fell asleep with dreams of Neah Bay in my mind, my heart filled with both worry and hope. I was relieved we weren't going to have to go live at that old poorhouse. Franny said if you went into the poorhouse, the children were often split up. It sounded so terrible. I whispered a quick prayer, asking God to keep our family together and out of that poor house.

"Franny, would they split us up if we had to go into the poorhouse?" I whispered to my sister lying next to me.

"I told you before, don't ever think like that, Sis. Daddy won't let it happen," Franny whispered.

"But what about that girl you went to school with? Didn't her family get split up?"

"That was different. Lucy Donnovan's Daddy ran off. Her Mama tried to provide for them for a while." Franny's eyes glistened with unshed tears as she continued. "But they were forced to leave their home, their belongings, everything they had. Lucy and her sisters were separated and sent to different homes and different lives. It was terrible. But our Daddy is a good man, and he won't ever run off from us."

My mind conjured images of a desolate place where families were torn apart and hopes withered away. I couldn't fathom such a fate for our own family, and fear gnawed at the edges of my mind as I drifted off into a restless night's sleep, worrying and praying the Makahs would let us stay, and Daddy would find work. What would happen if this move didn't go as planned?

People of the Rocks and Seagulls

JOURNEY TO NEAH BAY, WASHINGTON

NOVEMBER 1936

Dawn Jensen

8 Years Old

The morning light bathed the world in a soft, golden glow as we continued along gravelly Highway 101, which wound through the majestic Olympic Peninsula. With each mile, the landscape grew wilder, reflecting the emotions swirling within my heart.

Our journey led us through vast fields of golden wheat, rolling hills, and dense forests whispering secrets in the wind. Approaching the coastal region, we encountered many crude log bridges standing proudly over rushing creeks and rivers, their gnarled logs forming a precarious path to the other side.

Hollering over to Bobby from where we sat opposite one another in the back of the truck, I asked, "How much longer to Neah Bay?"

"It'll be another day or so." Bobby ran his hand through his hair. "Daddy said so last night. We'll have to cross more of those old, log bridges you love." Bobby teased. I had recently developed a fear of heights after I took a fall from a tall apple tree during our time in Yakima and didn't like those old bridges one bit.

Throughout the day we had to cross several of the rickety bridges, taking us deeper into the heart of the wilderness. Each primitive bridge felt like a test of our courage and resilience. Some were mere remnants of decaying logs. Their surfaces were worn by time and the elements while others offered sturdier planks for a more stable path.

The most challenging bridge spanned a large chasm, daring us to cross to the other side.

"Is there another way, Bobby?" I asked in fear.

"No Sis, but it will be okay. Don't worry, close your eyes and count to ten. We'll be across before you know it," Bobby replied.

As we approached the intimidating expanse ahead, my heart began to race, matching the tempo of my quickened breaths.

"It may look rugged, but the bridge is steady and true,"

Daddy commented after getting out to inspect the bridge. He returned to the truck, and we slowly began to cross, my heart pounding as the tires clung to the uneven surface.

I held my breath, peering down at the rushing river below. The old bridge seemed to tremble under the weight of our hopes and dreams as we inched forward. Each sway of the groaning logs reminded me of the power of the water below.

We pressed on, with the promise of a new life spurring us on. I held Junior's hand and closed my eyes tightly.

After what felt like an eternity, I heard cheers mingling with the sound of rushing water. Daddy had conquered the log bridge guarding our path. To me, they were more than old bridges; they represented the roadblocks that kept appearing in our journey, trying to derail the stability of our family.

Now that we were safely across, my mind drifted to the unknown awaiting us beyond the Strait of Juan de Fuca. "Junior, do you think we'll like living in Neah Bay? It seems like a long way away from everything."

"I don't know, Dawn, but what I do know is before this road was carved out, people used horses and canoes to reach these parts of Washington. We're lucky to have a proper road."

"But how much further is it?" My questioning continued.

"We should be close to Neah Bay soon. Tonight, we'll find a spot to camp outside the reservation, so we don't startle anyone when we arrive. Daddy has it all planned out. In the daylight, we'll be able to visit the reservation and meet with the chief."

We traveled for many more hours, the morning stretching into an endless day. The road twisted and turned, snaking through forests and along rivers. We passed small towns and hidden coves, catching occasional glimpses of the vast expanse of the Pacific Ocean. As evening approached, we arrived at our destination for the night in Clallam Bay.

Daddy got the fire going while Mama went about preparing a simple dinner of canned stew.

"Any news?" she asked when she returned from the truck.

Daddy stoked the fire, sending a shower of sparks into the night sky. "Well, I got some good news to share with y'all. I had a good chat with the owner of that last general store, and he gave me some leads on logging camps that need workers." Daddy smiled, his voice steady with conviction.

Mama leaned in, her eyes shining with hope. "Tell us, John. What did he say?"

"He said there's one about ten miles yonder, not too far from here. They're in need of hardworking folks prepared to put in an honest day's work. I think it'll be better money than what we were making picking fruit."

A collective gasp of relief escaped our lips, our faces alight with newfound hope. The promise of a fresh start seemed within reach.

"Remember Old Bear said that family is important to the Makah people. If they let us rent a cabin, well, we'll be double blessed, with a job opportunity and a home. I was worried when the foreman fired you, but I didn't let myself dwell on it. No use worrying on things you can't control." Mama stirred the stew with her wooden spoon.

Daddy nodded. "It was probably for the best. Apple season was comin' to an end anyway, and now I'll be makin' more money, and you all won't have to toil under the hot summer sun."

Bobby's excitement couldn't be contained any longer. "Does that mean we'll have a home again, Daddy? A place to stay and settle down?"

Daddy placed a hand on Bobby's shoulder, his voice warm and reassuring. "Let's not put the cart before the horse, son. I need to meet with the chief, but I'm feelin' real hopeful about it."

Mama squeezed Daddy's other hand, her voice soft but resolute. "John, I want you to know how proud I am of you for standing up for Old Bear, but you can't risk the stability of our family by helping others."

Daddy's eyes glistened with understanding as he met Mama's eyes. "When you're helpin' others and standin' up for what's right, God will bless your efforts. Remember that, kids."

In the flickering firelight, surrounded by the embrace of my family, I dared to dream of a future of shelter and comfort in the land of the Makah people.

The following day, as we approached the reservation, a feeling of awe washed over me. Surrounded by thick forests and the shimmering turquoise waters of the mighty Pacific Ocean, the reservation held an enchanting allure.

Once we rounded the final bend, Neah Bay revealed itself in all its natural glory. I was taken in by the rugged beauty surrounding us—the crashing waves, rocky cliffs, with the scent of saltwater heavy in the air.

I beheld a place of untamed splendor, where lush green forests seemed to whisper of ancient tales untold, and a people thrived in harmony with the natural world. Yet it was a land of harsh realities, with rugged cliffs standing tall, and icy waters raging with fierce determination. I could see that fishing here might be dangerous and could test the bravery of anyone who dared to partake in the bounty from the sea.

We arrived at the outskirts of the reservation and camped in the truck bed, right on the border for several nights, unable to meet with the chief. On the third afternoon, as our spirits were at their lowest, a Makah man came and introduced himself as Kwati. He motioned for Daddy to follow him. "I will now take you to see Chief Captain John."

Daddy carried the basket of apples, a gift for the tribe, and followed the man onto the reservation. They didn't return for over an hour. When Daddy returned, he had a spring in his step and a twinkle in his eye.

We gathered around the truck, Daddy's face full of enthusiasm. I could hardly contain my excitement as he began to recount his visit with the chief. I knew something life-changing was about to be shared.

"The meetin' went well. We can stay. They didn't wanna meet right away because they were afraid, we might bring sickness to their tribe. They lost a lot of people during the Spanish Flu a few years back."

"Will we be roughing it out in the open again?" Bobby adjusted his cap.

"No son, there are some empty cabins on the reservation, and they gave us our pick. I found one close to a stream. We'll have plenty of fresh water. It's not much, but it'll do," Daddy announced, his eyes sparkling with exhilaration. "A cozy cabin will be our home, and tomorrow I'll head over to the logging camp to find employment. Junior, you can come with me. You're big for your age, and they might be able to use both of us for work. It's hard work though, son. Are ya up for it?"

"I think so, Daddy." Junior held his chin high, ready for any challenges that lay ahead.

"Our very own cabin? Can we go now and see where we'll be living?" Mama's face was filled with relief.

Daddy nodded, "Indeed, my love. Let's go see this cabin the Makah people are offering."

I couldn't contain my excitement. "Daddy, what was it like when you met the chief? What did you discuss?"

Daddy recalled. "I spoke with Captain John, that's what he said to call him. I shared our connection to Elan and Old Bear from the apple farm. I told him I was hoping to find employment nearby as a logger. I asked if there was a place available for us to rent. The chief pointed me toward an empty cabin in thanks for helping Old Bear. They have a lot of respect for this land and sea and we must try to blend in... keep to ourselves unless approached first."

Franny clapped her hands in delight. "Oh my giddy aunt, we'll have our own cabin, just for us. Did they like the apples?"

Daddy nodded, his voice strong and steady. "They were very happy with our gift and said this was a good place to regroup and find work. It's a remote place, but it's a beautiful place."

As we started to climb into the old truck, Daddy cleared his throat. "Neah Bay, our new home."

"Did you ask if we can hunt and fish here? Will they mind?" Bobby asked.

"You bet we can. There'll be good huntin' and the best fishin' you've ever seen. We'll learn the ways of the land; we need to be careful not to step on anyone's toes. The chief said there were certain areas where we could hunt and fish. We are visitors here, and the relationship between our peoples hasn't always been good. We need to be extra careful about sticking to the right spots. I'll show you tomorrow after I return from the logging camp."

"Yippee!" Bobby exclaimed.

"Kwati mentioned there was plenty of salmon, halibut, and clams that make good eatin'. He called them Razorbacks. There'll be plenty of bounty from the ocean," Daddy replied.

Mama gazed out at the breathtaking landscape, then turned to Daddy with a curious look. "It's amazing how they've built their community way out here, amid such a vast wilderness. Are there any places to buy supplies this far out in the middle of nowhere?"

"This reservation may be sparsely populated, but they've been living here for thousands of years. Living mostly off the ocean and land, but there is a general store that carries most things you'll need," Daddy replied. "These are a resilient people, a tribe of whale hunters. They stopped huntin' the gray whales years ago because the population was gettin' low."

"How come the whales went away, Daddy? Will they ever come back?" I asked, my curiosity getting the better of me.

"I certainly hope so. I read in the paper that the Makah have been hunting those whales forever. It's part of their way of life. The population got low because of those commercial fishing boats coming through. Eventually, the whales started to dwindle down to almost nothing. Now enough talk of whales. Do you wanna go see our new home?"

We spent the next few hours unpacking and settling into our tiny cabin nestled on the edge of Neah Bay. The structure bore the weathered marks of nature's relentless forces, each scar telling a story of years battling the coastal elements.

Its sturdy frame, constructed with cedar logs, stood as a testament to the resilience of those who had built it. The exterior was weathered and showcased a faded appearance, yet it blended seamlessly with the surrounding landscape.

The floors were dirt, and there was a hearth dug out in the corner for making a small fire. There was no chimney, just a hole in the roof where smoke could escape if we needed to build a fire.

"Look at these windows," Franny exclaimed, her eyes wide with surprise. "There's no glass in them, just wooden shutters. I've never seen anything like it."

"Don't worry, those wooden shutters will keep the rain out. It might not be as cozy as our old cabin in the woods, but it beats sleeping out in the open," Mama tried to sound upbeat, but we all knew we were in for some cold nights.

There wasn't much in the way of furniture, a cedar table with a few mismatched chairs. At one end of the cabin, there were a couple of rope beds rigged up. These beds consisted of a wooden frame with interwoven ropes, providing a supportive surface to sleep on.

Though modest in its offerings, the cabin held an undeniable charm. It would be our sanctuary amid the untamed wilderness, a haven where the echoes of laughter and the warmth of familial love could take root and flourish.

"We won't be building a campfire tonight; it looks as if a big storm's comin' in. It will have to be cold beans for dinner. Boys, close up those wood shutters before the rain starts." Daddy ordered.

Just then there was a loud clap of thunder. I looked out toward the ocean, and in the fading light of dusk, I could see a storm on the horizon. Thunder rumbled ominously, and lightning illuminated the rugged cliffs and turbulent waters of Neah Bay.

We had our dinner of cold beans and biscuits, content to have a roof over our heads on that stormy night. As I lay on the floor, curled up under a threadbare blanket, I could hear thunder rumbling loudly, like a giant growling in the distance, and lightning flashing and lighting up the room. I felt a mixture of fear and exhilaration as the storm grew stronger. The wind blew ferociously against the shutters.

A million thoughts ran through my mind. Neah Bay was breathtaking, but it was remote. If we had stayed in Seattle, I'd have been going into the third grade. I was ready to learn new things and make friends. Would there be a schoolhouse on the reservation? And what about the Makah children? Would they be willing to befriend an outsider like me? I longed to explore their forests and hear their ancient tales. I imagined all of us running freely along the beautiful beaches, our laughter blending with the crashing waves.

I could hear Franny, tossing and turning next to me. "Are you scared of the storm?" I whispered, careful not to wake up the rest of the house.

"A little, Sis. It sounds powerful, as if the whole world is shaking."

"I know what you mean. But isn't it fascinating, too? I hope it doesn't last too long. Neah Bay is interesting. I can't wait to explore it."

"I feel the same. But we better be careful to stay where Daddy says we can play until we learn more about the rules here." Franny yawned.

"Will there be a school for us? Will the other children like us?"

"I don't know about a school way out in the middle of nowhere. But we can practice your reading. I saw that Mama brought a few books with her photo albums."

"I'll learn to be a better reader, Franny. Wait and see," I whispered to my sister as we held hands into the night. The storm raged on until the wee hours, as I cuddled with my loyal dog Honey, finding reassurance in her soft fur. If my family was all together, I would be safe, the storm couldn't hurt me, but I couldn't help but wonder, was this ominous storm a sign of things to come?

Blue Skies

NEAH BAY, WASHINGTON

SEPTEMBER 1936

Dawn Jensen

8 Years Old

T he next morning greeted us with a beautiful late summer sun. The rain had ceased, leaving bits of wood and debris scattered about.

"Hey-ya, Franny. Time to go explore."

"Hold your horses. What's the rush? Why are you always in such a rush?" Franny stretched her arms above her head.

"I was looking out the window and spotted the perfect spot to pick huckleberries. Let's go."

Franny got dressed, and we informed Mama that we'd be off looking for berries to pick.

"Be careful, girls, and stay within hollering distance," Mama called after us.

"Let's head over to the forest across the road and check out these berries. If we don't find any, I'm heading home to get cleaned up." Franny scrunched her nose in skepticism.

As we ventured deep into the woods, our anticipation turned to disappointment. Despite our best efforts, we couldn't spot a single huckleberry bush. Franny's stomach growled in protest, reminding us that breakfast awaited back home.

"Let's go home, Sis. I don't see any huckleberry bushes or any berry bushes at all." Franny was frustrated and ready to throw in the towel.

"All right, Franny, let's go home, but mark my words, I'm coming back later to keep exploring. I'll find those berries." Suddenly, I heard rustling in the distance. "Franny, did you hear that?" I caught wind of laughter in the air.

"Look yonder." Franny pointed to some movement she spied in the distance.

"Is someone there?" I tried to sound tough, but inside, my knees were knocking.

A girl my size jumped out from behind the trees. "Gotcha," she exclaimed, sporting a mischievous grin.

Franny and I both screamed, our hearts racing. I was about to blow my top at this mystery girl.

"You think it's funny, jumping out and scaring us like that?"

She had given us a fright, but she laughed and had such a welcoming, yet crooked smile that my anger dissipated into laughter.

"You won't find any berries there," said the Makah girl, standing a few feet away, observing us with mysterious eyes.

"My name is Natalie, but you can call me Talie. I'll show you where the berries grow." She shouted over her shoulder, "You can come out now, they're friendly."

Another little girl emerged timidly from behind the trees. She looked to be a little younger than me. All of us wore homemade dresses but Talie and the other girl were bare-foot, while Franny and I wore shoes.

"This here's Yarlata. She doesn't say much ever since our Daddy died but she asked to come see you after we heard that a white family had come to stay. She wanted to see what you were like. Can we pet your dog?"

"Yes, that's Honey, she likes kids... I'm Dawn and this is my sister Franny." I wasn't sure what to make of Talie, she seemed carefree and independent. Even though we looked about the same age, she had an air of maturity that I didn't possess.

"We've been having trouble finding berries. Can you show us where to they are?"

"Of course, come on, follow me." Talie motioned for us to head east. "I'm watching my sister Yarlata while our mother weaves baskets. You can help me." Talie ran deeper into the forest, as we tried to keep up with Honey following close behind. Eventually Talie pointed to a spot shielded by large rocks, bathed in sunlight. We found several huckleberry bushes growing near an old tree stump and we filled the basket that the boy on the apple farm had given to Mama.

"That's a nice basket. Did your Mother make it?" Talie popped a berry into her mouth.

"No, it was a gift, but look here, Talie. Our Mama has wrapped some of her biscuits and tucked them here for us to find." We located a grassy spot to share our snacks with each other.

"How long will your people be staying on the res?" Talie leaned forward.

"Mama told us we'd be staying as long as Daddy is working and bringing in money from logging nearby. They're saving money for a house near our real home in Seattle," Franny told the other girls.

"Is that where you're from, the big city? What's it like?" Talie's eyes widened in amazement.

"We lived outside of town, but it's a big old city for sure. Lots of hustle and bustle. Do you girls go to school?" I asked.

"Yes, but we don't go during summer. The day school is how I know English so well. I can read some, too. Yarlata will start this fall, but it's only for the children of the tribe. There aren't any other white kids here, right now. Like your family, they come and go." Talie leaned against an old cedar tree.

"Don't worry Dawn, we don't need to go to school. I'll show you what I know, and I'm sure Mama has a plan for us to do some learning of our own," Franny said defensively.

Sensing Franny's unease, Talie deftly changed the subject. "Do you girls want to go clam digging with us? There's a good spot I know right near your cabin. We can dig some up for lunch later."

"But Mama is expecting us by lunch. She usually makes our food," I responded.

"Isn't it better to fend for ourselves? We don't need our Mamas for everything." Talie retorted.

"Let's do it." I rose to her challenge.

"As long as we stop by and tell Mama where we are getting off to," Franny commented, ever so sensibly.

We found ourselves on the beach, outside our Cabin, Talie walked around, her footsteps leaving tiny imprints on the soft sand. She then pointed towards a depression in the sand, her dark eyes gleaming with excitement.

"You have to look for the holes in the sand."

Franny and I ran over with our sticks, our curiosity piqued by Talie's guidance. The three of us started digging, our sticks plunging into the sand with determination. As we uncovered each clam, Talie's nimble fingers gently cradled them into the basket I held out.

"They taste best cooked up into fritters. Let's take them

back to your Mama." We headed to our cabin, Talie leading the way with an air of confidence that fascinated me.

Upon our arrival, Talie got a fire going in our firepit, the flames dancing to an ancient rhythm. Talie showed us how to crumble some crackers and mash them together with the clams.

"Do you have eggs? That's how to make them stick together."

Mama grabbed a few eggs and her frying pan. We watched as Talie transformed our simple catch into the most delicious clam fritters I had ever tasted. It was more than a meal—it was an experience, a testament to the joy Talie found in sharing her culture with us. That day we became fast friends with Talie and Yarlata.

Honey especially took a liking to Yarlata, and found a kindred spirit in her quiet, contemplative nature. They sat together by the shore, their eyes fixed on the horizon, as if silently conversing in a language only they understood.

Over the following days, Talie regaled us with tales of her tribe's traditions, passed down through generations. She spoke of the importance of the ocean and the forest, and most of all, the gray whales that graced their waters during migration season. Talie's eyes sparkled with reverence as she recounted the ancient stories of how the Makah people believed the whales to be sacred protectors and spirit guides.

"The gray whales are a symbol of our tribe, part of the magic of Neah Bay," she said, her voice carrying the weight of generations. I was enthralled to hear Talie speak about the majestic creatures that called Neah Bay home. Talie became more than a friend, she became a guide to the land and sea. She was a bridge between cultures, and her fierce spirit left an indelible mark on our hearts.

As we explored the wonders of the reservation, I discovered that Talie's knowledge extended beyond the practicalities of survival. She was an avid storyteller, her eyes alight with passion as she recounted the legends of her people. Each tale taught a lesson, and I marveled at how deeply they resonated with me.

Talie's fierce loyalty to her family and tribe was evident in her interactions with her younger sister, Yarlata. She lovingly watched out for her younger sister, and their bond reminded me of the protective instincts that bound me and Franny. I sensed that Talie carried great responsibility even at such a young age, and I admired her strength.

As we spent more time together, I realized that Talie's presence had enriched our lives beyond measure. She had opened a window to a world we had never known, and her friendship illuminated our days with warmth and laughter. The Makah girl's spirit was a force of nature, a radiant light guiding us through our days on the reservation.

One afternoon, after a long day of playing, Mama pulled us aside, her eyes narrowing with thoughtfulness. "Those are some nice girls you met, and the clam fritters were delightful, but I need to talk to you girls about your schooling now."

"But there isn't a school here for us, Mama." Franny replied.

"We'll make our own school. I have a few books we can use, and your brother Bobby can help with your arithmetic. We'll start next month when fall is here. For now, I want you to have a carefree summer, living in nature and making friends. Your schooling can start in October." Mama's face was lit up by the golden glow of the sun setting over the ocean.

"Now let's get ready for dinner. Your Daddy will be home soon."

Daddy and Junior returned from a long day of toile and quickly built a bonfire for us to gather around. The crackling fire beckoned us, and its flickering warmth brought a familiarity to the evening.

Daddy's voice was hopeful as he shared his news, "Looks like our lucks turnin'. We got ourselves jobs as loggers. The foreman said we looked like hard workers. It'll be tough work, but it's honest work, and it'll put food on our table."

Junior's eyes gleamed with determination, eager to prove himself. "I know I'll enjoy it, Daddy. We'll show 'em what we're made of."

Daddy patted Junior's back with pride. "That's my boy. I reckon we'll have early mornings and long days, but we'll earn a decent wage. It won't be easy, but it'll keep us going."

Bobby stepped out into the firelight and held up a huge silver salmon he had caught. "Well, you two weren't the only ones to have a successful day. I found a good river for fishing." Bobby adjusted the cap that was forever resting on his head.

"That's great, Bobby, you're doing a good job lookin' after Mama and the girls so keep bringing home these fish you are good at catchin', and we'll keep loggin' until we save enough to get our own place," Daddy explained.

As Mama cooked our dinner, the sweet aroma of salmon rose into the night sky. We nestled in the tender glow of the bonfire's embrace, our souls alight with aspirations for the unfolding days ahead. This marked a new venture, and we got into the rhythm of life on Neah Bay where each heartbeat resonated with promise for a better tomorrow.

The next morning, we met at our designated spot. Talie had brought her younger sister Yarlata, and each girl carried a small basket. Inside, they had some smoked fish and roasted bulbs that grew wild in the area. The girls later showed us how to dig up the small bulbs and roast them into a mildly sweet snack.

They also introduced us to the other children, and soon we were all playing barefoot together in the sandy expanse. Honey was close by, watching over us and playing in the oceans chilly tides. It was summertime, and with no school to worry about, our classroom became the great outdoors.

In our young eyes, cultural differences and skin tones weren't important; we were all united by our humble circumstances.

Food was abundant thanks to Bobby's hunting and fishing. He brought home large salmon and halibut, while his hunting prowess provided us with rich meat from local elk herds. Mama and Denise skillfully prepared the most delicious meals using the bounty of nature, supplemented by the wild camas bulbs, dandelion greens, mushrooms, berries, and razor clams gathered by us younger girls. We also delighted in the canned applesauce Mama had made during our time in Selah.

Each evening, we gathered around the campfire, and Daddy would offer a prayer of gratitude, reminding us of our blessings—having a roof over our heads and food in our bellies.

As the late summer days transitioned into the cool embrace of fall, time seemed to fly on the reservation. The leaves donned vibrant hues, whispering secrets of change with the rustling breeze, and winter was upon us. The air grew crisper, and the days shortened, marking the arrival of Christmas Eve in our modest cabin.

One afternoon, Franny and I eagerly awaited Bobby's return with a surprise for Mama. Bursting through the door, his face flushed with excitement, Bobby carefully maneuvered an evergreen tree into our home, its branches brushing against the low ceiling.

"Mama," I exclaimed, my excitement bubbling over. "Look what Bobby brought us!"

Mama turned, her eyes widening with surprise and emotion. "Oh, my Love Bugs. A Christmas tree is what we needed," she said. "You've all been busy. I can't believe what you've done."

Our faces beamed with pride, our secret plan unfolding as Bobby placed the tree in its designated spot, filling the room with the scent of fresh pine.

I handed Mama a basket of decorations crafted in secret by Denise, Franny, and me over the last few weeks. Strings of popcorn, shell ornaments, and hand-painted pinecones were lovingly created during moments when Mama thought we were exploring in the forest.

As Mama approached the tree, her hands gently touched the delicate shell ornaments and popcorn garlands. Her breath caught in awe, and tears of happiness glistened in her eyes.

"This is the most beautiful Christmas surprise," she whispered.

Denise's excitement was contagious as she joined in, "We can have a wonderful Christmas. Even though it will be different, it will still be meaningful."

Franny's eyes sparkled with enthusiasm, "Oh, and we mustn't forget the carols. Our voices will fill this cabin with warmth and joy."

We joyously decorated our Christmas tree. The soft glow of flickering candlelight illuminated our faces as we carefully placed our handmade ornaments and garlands onto the branches of our tree, our hands moving with care.

Later that night Mama presented Bobby with a bundle of hand-sewn mittens, her eyes gleaming with pride. "These are for you, my son. They'll keep your hands warm during your hunting trips."

Bobby's face lit up with gratitude. "Thank you, Mama. They're perfect."

Denise stepped forward, holding a beautiful hand-drawn portrait of Franny and me. "And for you, dear sisters, a gift from my heart. A memory captured forever."

Franny's wonder was evident as took in the portrait. "Denise, it's breathtaking. Thank you, I love it."

"We can hang it on the wall of our cabin," I chimed in.

Beaming with pride, Bobby handed Mama a carved wooden necklace adorned with seashells. "Mama, I crafted this for you. Each shell represents each of us kids."

Touched to the core, Mama embraced Bobby tightly. "It's truly remarkable, my son. Thank you for this precious gift."

As we exchanged our handmade gifts and reminisced about the past year, laughter echoed throughout the cabin, filling the room with warmth and joy.

Franny's thoughts drifted, "It's hard to believe another year has passed. Things have changed since last Christmas."

Mama drew Franny close, her voice gentle yet resolute, "Yes, my dear, and soon, I know we'll find a permanent home where you'll grow even more."

Gathering in a circle, we joined hands, expressing gratitude and reflecting on our journey. With closed eyes, Daddy led us in prayer.

"Let us remember the true essence of Christmas—the love that holds us, and the joy we share."

Together, we whispered in unison, "Amen."

The cabin exuded warmth and love as we basked in the simple joy of togetherness. The spirit of Christmas enveloped us—a reminder of the potency of love and the resilience of our bonds. That simple Christmas on the reservation showed us that genuine wealth lay not in material possessions but in the treasured moments shared as a family.

Mama departed the cozy room, returning with a glimmer in her eyes. "I have a couple more special gifts for you two," she announced, approaching Franny and me. "These will serve as your study companions to keep your reading on track."

Franny and I unwrapped something that would come to shape our childhood: Brand new copies of *The Wizard of Oz* and another book named *Little Women*.

"I ordered these books right when got to Neah Bay and they arrived just in time." Mama smiled down at us.

Later that week Franny and I sprawled on the cabin floor, immersed in Mama's Christmas gifts. I quickly realized that within these pages, we could journey through enchanting realms, embracing dreams that filled our hearts and the unwavering resilience in the face of life's challenges.

"You know, Sis," Franny said, her eyes gleaming. "These sisters seem so familiar, they are alot like us."

I nodded, turning the page thoughtfully. "Absolutely. She's captured sisterhood perfectly. Their dreams and resilience... it's like seeing ourselves. Do you think I could write a character as good as Jo?"

"Jo's something else," Franny remarked with animation.

"Her spirit, her independence—it's like she could be you. I think you could write a story as good."

I smirked. "I know I could. You are like Meg, with your perfect manners and perfect posture… it would be easy to write about our escapades on the reservation. Our lives are as interesting as the March sisters."

Franny chuckled. "Seems like these characters have taken a page from our book. Jo's fiery independence is like you, and Meg's a lot like me."

I played with my hair absentmindedly. "Remember when I wanted those tight braids on my birthday? Jo makes me realize it's okay to let my hair flow free and wild like it was meant to."

Franny nodded knowingly. "And you should start writing stories, just like Jo!"

My eyes lit up. "Exactly. Daddy brought home those composition books, and I plan to keep a journal of our time on this reservation."

"I think Denise is like Beth. Her gentle nature, loyalty— this book could have been written about us."

I chuckled. "You're not wrong."

Franny laughed. "What if tomorrow, we acted out scenes from *Little Women*? I'll be Beth, and you can be Jo. We'll rehearse and then put on a show for everyone!"

As we conversed, it felt like the March sisters stood beside us. "Jo and Beth," I reflected, "they're more than characters, Franny. They're like our guardian angels."

Together, we absorbed the wisdom from those pages, the

essence of the March sisters' journey flowing through our own lives—sisters united by love, dreams, and an unbreakable thread of sisterhood. With each page, the magic of storytelling unveiled boundless possibilities for a young girl with dreams in her heart.

In those endless afternoons, we'd lose ourselves in acting out our own plays, recreating scenes from the book. I'd step into Jo March's shoes, embracing her fearless spirit and unwavering determination. Jo became my ultimate role model, a boundless source of motivation as I navigated the ups and downs of growing up during hard times.

Franny played Beth March, finding solace in her quiet strength. We even recruited Talie and Yarlata. Occasionally, Bobby would join in and take on the role of Laurie Laurence. We'd practice all week and perform for the family on Saturday nights in front of the campfire. It became a cherished weekly ritual and a beloved family tradition.

In the weeks that followed, Mama nurtured our literary souls, while Bobby taught us mathematics. He made the calculations feel like a game, possessing a knack for turning numbers into puzzles, his eyes twinkling with excitement. Even when I struggled, he never lost his patience with me.

As winter melted into spring, memories transformed into treasures. Through Mama's sheer determination, we were able to forge a path of learning that ignited our imaginations and sparked a love for knowledge.

We found ourselves experiencing our second summer on the reservation, our friendships growing stronger. Mama had established connections with some of the Makah women, while Junior began to spend time with one of the local girls from the reservation. Amidst these growing bonds, we delicately navigated the fine line between two worlds. Although we stood on the reservation's edges, we also found acceptance within its borders.

We soon distanced ourselves from the life we had once known, we gradually became accustomed to our home in Neah Bay. Though not fully part of the community, we were recognized and lived alongside the Makah's harmoniously and cherished our unique, yet temporary home.

In a familiar rhythm, reminiscent of the previous summer, we younger girls ventured into the wilderness, our curious spirits exploring and foraging, while Daddy and Junior would return home tired from their hard days as loggers. Bobby continued to cast his line in pursuit of a bountiful catch, on his journey to manhood. Mama and Denise's bond grew deeper as my oldest sister blossomed into womanhood. They spent their days tending to the home, knitting, and baking together in the wood stove Daddy had brought from our old cabin.

Time passed by and we discovered a newfound freedom that intertwined us within the depths of the reservation. Through ancient forests, we chased butterflies, their vibrant wings painting the air with dreams of the unspoken. Honey was always close by, our protector and guardian.

Our family became cocooned in the embrace of nature's untouched wilderness somehow shielded from the distant shadows of the Great Depression that seemed a world away. The lands of Neah Bay became our sanctuary, a reassuring refuge from the era's uncertainties.

The summer of our youth flew by, leaving behind a trail of laughter, love, and cherished memories. We discovered the power of words, the strength of family, and the untamed spirit within our wild beating hearts.

As fall drew closer, I often heard Mama and Daddy engaged in hushed discussions. I never could quite hear what they were talking about, but the tension in our small cabin could not be ignored.

A storm seemed to brew, not in the sky but within our household. The carefree laughter that once filled our home was now subdued, and I yearned for the joyful moments we had shared a few months before. The tension cast a shadow over our summer, and I longed for the sun to break through, bringing the happiness we once knew.

What would the approaching season bring for our family, and could it mend the fractures that had appeared in our once carefree days?

Raindrops Keep Fallin'

NEAH BAY, WASHINGTON

SEPTEMBER 27, 1937

Dawn Jensen

9 Years Old

As Mama and Daddy sat down for breakfast, the aroma of freshly brewed coffee filled the air. Daddy cleared his throat, breaking the morning silence. "Ya know, Lenora, I been hearin' a whole lotta talk 'bout President Roosevelt and his fight against this godforsaken depression." His voice tinged with admiration.

Mama, with a concerned expression on her face, nodded in agreement. "I've been hearing about those programs he's cooking up, trying to help out us folks who've been hit hardest."

Daddy took another gulp of his coffee before going on, his voice laced with contagious enthusiasm "I heard something this mornin' that might tickle your fancy. The President's comin' 'round here, right to Neah Bay. Ain't that exciting?"

Mama's eyes lit up with surprise. "That's amazing news. It isn't every day the President pays a visit to this neck of the woods. Dawn, Franny, get out my heating tongs. I'm doing our hair up in curls. We'll put a good foot forward for Mr. Roosevelt."

Using the heating tongs and an iron next to the wood-burning stove, Mama ironed church clothes and did her best to make us look our finest.

After getting all dolled up, I headed outside to find the entire reservation buzzing with exhilaration. Word had spread like wildfire that the President of the United States of America was coming to Neah Bay. President Roosevelt was touring the Olympic Peninsula, to rally support for a national park to protect the dwindling elk population as part of his job formations.

Talie and Yarlota emerged from the edges of the crowd to greet us almost immediately.

"Let's go see the Chief of the United States," Talie exclaimed, her excitement contagious. Without hesitation, we joined the other children from the tribe and made our way to the gathering spot.

As we approached, the air crackled with electricity, and even the drizzling rain couldn't dampen our spirits. We eagerly awaited the arrival of a long, black car carrying the leader of our nation. When it finally stopped, a hush fell over the crowd, and there I was, with my bright, red hair done up in Shirley Temple curls. Franny and my lighter locks stood out in a sea of darker-haired people.

President Roosevelt emerged from the car, a commanding presence and a radiant smile. And then, it happened. His eyes swept across the crowd, and unexpectedly, they locked onto mine. He made his way toward us, his smile warm and inviting. With a gentle pat on my head, he said, "What do we have here, a little redhead on Neah Bay?"

Pride surged within me as I recounted the story around the campfire that night. The hope the president had given to my parents filled my heart with gratitude. This moment would be forever etched in my mind and would become like a family legend to our loved ones.

"That's amazing, Love Bug. The president spoke to you because he saw the spark of curiosity and strength in your eyes," my mother said, her voice full of pride. "You've become a part of history now, a moment that you'll tell your grandkids about."

"Your future is wide open, and that encounter proves that anything is possible." Daddy cleared his throat, gaining everyone's attention. "I've got more news to share with y'all. Come Spring, the logging company is moving on from Neah Bay. They're heading to Hoods Canal for the next job, and we'll be going with them."

A hush fell over the family, and I exchanged worried glances with Franny and Bobby. Leaving Neah Bay meant leaving behind our friends and the memories we'd cherished in exchange for more of the unknown.

Deep down, I knew that it was necessary. Neah Bay didn't have a school for us, and Mama's homeschooling smarts could only take us so far. As much as I loved growing up wild on the bay, I had begun to miss some of the things from our old life, like attending church and school.

"But Daddy," Franny protested, "Will we even have a place to live when we move to Hoods Canal?"

Daddy's face softened, and he knelt to meet us at eye level. "I know it's scary, Darlin', but we'll find a home to call our own. We've done it before, and we'll do it again. We'll keep sticking together and make the best of what comes our way."

Mama put a reassuring hand on Franny's shoulder. "We'll be camping out to start, but we'll make it through. Change can be scary, but it also brings new opportunities."

Junior, ever the optimist, chimed in, "Maybe we could find a place closer to a school for you kids, where you can make friends. Neah Bay is remote. Aren't you ready to be closer to a town? We can find one of those movie theaters and I promise I'll take y'all to the picture show with my first paycheck."

Anticipation danced in our eyes as we absorbed Junior's words. I'd never been to a picture show, and the thought of living closer to a town did sound appealing. The crackling fire seemed to echo our flickering emotions.

We had spent two wonderful years on Neah Bay—some of the happiest of my life—but I knew Daddy had to follow the work if we were going to get a long-term place of our own. It was time to move on.

With solemn resignation, I rose from the bonfire's embrace ready to face the uncertainty that laid ahead. The night sky, adorned with a blanket of stars, served as a reminder that no matter where we roamed, we would always be a family.

That night I tossed and turned as a million different thoughts kept me awake.

"Daddy said we'd leave in six months and should appreciate the time we have left. At least we'd have another Christmas in Neah Bay. Why did Mama say not to think too much about it?"

"Mama doesn't want us to be upset, that's all." Franny replied.

"I'm sure gonna miss Talie and Yarlata. Franny, do we have something nice to give them, as a going-away gift?" I whispered to Franny who was lying next to me.

"My giddy aunt, Dawn, let's figure it out later. Now go to sleep."

The months passed faster than I could have imagined. Mama did her best to decorate the cabin for the holidays, and Daddy continued to save money, hopeful for a steady job that would allow us to put down roots. Spring arrived with a burst of color, the daffodil bulbs Mama planted sprouting up all around, and with the flowers came hope for a new beginning. Yet my young heart was heavy with sadness.

We once again gathered our meager belongings into worn-out hop sacks. Talie, our dearest friend, approached with two delicately beaded shell necklaces and tears in her eyes. "Take these as a reminder of our friendship," she said.

I took the necklace, my fingers tracing the intricate patterns of the beads. "Thank you, Talie," I said, my voice cracking with emotion. "I will always wear it."

In return, Franny gave Talie one of our blue ribbons, a symbol of the tie that bound our souls, we also gave her our treasured copy of *Little Women*. Talie smiled through her tears, understanding the significance of our gifts. "You'll forever be my sisters," she said, her voice filled with love.

As we exchanged these simple yet profound tokens, tears welled in my eyes, threatening to spill over. It was a tearful goodbye, an acknowledgment of the bond we had formed during our time in Neah Bay.

The Makah people had given us sanctuary, taught us invaluable lessons of resilience, survival, and how to live off the land. Though we were different on the outside, we were the same in many ways—families trying to make it through a harsh world. The Makah had shown us kindness when it seemed like many others had turned their backs on us.

Daddy knelt beside me, his eyes filled with warmth. "Don't you worry, kiddo," he reassured me. "We'll be camping out at first, but I promise you a roof over your head by next Christmas. I almost have enough saved up, and God will provide the rest."

Mama joined us, her hand resting softly on my shoulder. "Times have been tough, but we'll make it through," she said, her voice filled with grit. "It's time to build a future closer to our kin. Uncle Jack will join us at Hoods Canal. Daddy got him a job with the logging company."

"What about Aunt Hatt?" I asked, tossing my hopsack into the back of the old Ford.

"Aunt Hatt, she's expecting a little one soon. She's staying in Tacoma now with Aunt Bernice, but we'll all be together after the baby arrives." Mama's eyes lit up as she mentioned her two closest sisters.

This was the silver lining I needed to carry me through yet another move when all I wanted was to stay in Neah Bay. I had developed a deep sense of belonging to this magical place.

I climbed into the back of the truck to join my siblings, emotions stirring inside, like the wind that whispered through the trees. How many more times would we be uprooted, chasing work during this unforgiving depression?

Whatever It Takes

Dawn Jensen

Almost 10 Years Old

Our truck bumped along the dusty road, each jolt a reminder of the uncertainty lying ahead. Daddy shared stories of Hoods Canal's long logging history.

As the truck rolled on, Daddy's stories seemed to momentarily distract us from the uncertainty that lay ahead. "You remember that old logger, David Johnson, from the woodyard? He could chop down a tree like it was a twig." Daddy grinned, trying to lighten the mood.

I nodded, a faint smile beginning to spread across my face. "Yeah, I remember. He had arms like tree trunks."

Mama chimed in, her voice tinged with worry added, "He was quite the character, wasn't he? But we've got to focus on the road ahead, John. What do you think awaits us in this place?"

Daddy's smile faltered for a moment, but he quickly recovered, looking at Mama with a determined glint in his eyes. "Don't you worry, Darlin'. This ain't gonna be no long-term affair. We'll be in a home of our own before you know it, mark my words."

As we continued along the dusty road, I found solace in the towering Fir and Cedar trees. They were like silent sentinels, witnessing our struggles and offering familiarity amidst the ever-changing landscape. "I feel safer with these trees around."

"Me too, sweetheart. They've been here long before us, and they'll be here long after."

Suddenly, a beautiful Dogwood tree caught my eye, its white flowers standing out amid a sea of green. "Look, Mama, the Dogwoods are blooming early this year."

Mama smiled softly, her worry lines easing momentarily. "Yes, they add a touch of uniqueness to the world. Like you, my Pickle."

As the truck trudged forward, the prospect of another move weighed heavily on my young shoulders. Each unfamiliar town blurred into a landscape of transient memories, leaving me longing for a place to call home.

It felt like our family was adrift in an ocean of uncertainty, tossed by the waves of economic hardships that marked these times. The truth was, we had become nomads, forever in search of the next opportunity.

As the road stretched on, my mind buzzed with questions and fears. "Daddy, how long do you think we'll stay near Hoods Canal? Will we finally find a place to call home?"

"I reckon it won't be long. The paper's been saying the unemployment rate's going down across the country. That's gotta be a good sign, right? We've seen the worst of it, and things are lookin' up. Gotta keep holdin' on a little while longer, and we'll have a home of our own soon."

Hours later, we pulled into a small parking lot near a bustling diner, we spotted Uncle Jack leaning against his beat-up truck, engaged in conversation with a stranger. Possibly a hobo he'd picked up on his journey, his worn-out shoes scuffing against the pavement. Uncle Jack's eyes lit up as he caught sight of our truck, and he waved us over. Relief mixed with apprehension as we stepped out of the vehicle. Daddy approached Uncle Jack with a warm smile, and they embraced like long-lost brothers.

Uncle Jack murmured, his voice heavy with regret. "Sorry 'bout all that nonsense with Clarence. I feel terrible 'bout him burnin' down the barn."

Daddy's face softened, his forgiveness evident. "No use holdin' grudges, Jack. Family's family, no matter what mistakes we make."

Uncle Jack nodded, gratitude shining on his face. "You're right, John. We may stumble, but as long as we stick together, we'll find our way."

Mama came round the truck, enveloping Uncle Jack in one of her huge hugs. I watched as they caught up on the events of the last couple of years, my heart swelling with love for my imperfect relatives. We were bound by a love that ran deeper than any mistake could. Despite the tension caused by Uncle Clare's actions, Mama's forgiving nature shone through. She easily forgot the past, in order to move forward. Uncle Jack's shoulders relaxed, guilt shifting to gratitude. Their bond would stay strong.

"We'll find a place to camp outside the city for the night, and head to Hoods Canal in the morning.," Daddy motioned towards the truck. With renewed spirits and a shared sense of purpose, Uncle Jack merged back into our family.

We drove along some old, lonely road, flanked by a gentle creek mirroring the waning sunlight. Daddy pulled over, finding a spot that would serve as our temporary home between Port Townsend and Hoods Canal.

"Here's where we'll make camp for tonight," Daddy declared, his voice carrying both fatigue and anticipation.

"John, I managed to save for this big ol' tent. It's big enough for most of us, if we all cram in." Uncle Jack declared.

The tent unfurled, revealing our temporary home. Mama's eyes gleamed with resilience as she gathered the copper boiler pan and old cooking stone to conjure something delicious from our meager supplies.

"Mama, how do you always manage to make the best meals out of nothing?" I asked, my voice filled with wonder.

"It's all about making the most of what we have, Pickle… I also have a secret ingredient."

"What's that, Mama?"

"Love. I put all my love for you into my cooking. That's why it tastes so good." Mama explained.

Around the crackling fire, Uncle Jack shared a glimpse into the realities faced by those less fortunate. His words reminded us of the importance of family, of finding solace in each other's company.

Uncle Jack leaned forward, his voice filled with concern. "You wouldn't believe how bad it is in them cities, brother. Typhoid keeps breakin' out due to contaminated well water. But it ain't just that, bed bugs are runnin' rampant, too, especially among the poor and underfed."

Daddy, listened intently, his face reflecting the gravity of the situation. "That's a real shame, I didn't know things were so awful in the cities. It's a good thing we were livin' on Neah Bay, away from all that. We had fresh water and clean air on the bay."

I absorbed their words, piecing together the harsh reality of the times we were living in. Mama's voice joined the conversation, her tone gentle yet determined. "Being out here, surrounded by fresh air and clean water, gives us the best chance at staying healthy. We don't want to get sick like many others. Best to avoid the big cities."

Daddy nodded, "You're absolutely right, Darlin'. I'll do my best to keep us away from all the diseases and hardships going on in the cities. Our well-being depends on it. We'll get ourselves settled somewhere soon."

"That's something I need to talk to ya about, John. My brother Clarence has been on the wagon and managed to get a job as a mechanic at the airport. Once he's past his probation, he's going to try to get us both jobs there, workin' in one of these New Deal Programs the president started."

"Let's hope he can make it through his probation and keep himself sober. If it's meant for us to get jobs workin' at the airport, then God will make a way for it. I've got a bit of money saved up, but I want to make sure I have steady work before we go puttin' down a deposit. No use renting a cabin if I don't have steady employment to pay the rent," Daddy said with resignation in his eyes.

As the flames danced, stories flowed freely, and laughter echoed in the air. We momentarily forgot about the hardships ahead. Uncle Jack pulled out his harmonica, and the children all danced around the bonfire as he played 'Pennies from Heaven'.

The night was alive with the sounds of nature when a growl filled the air and interrupted our peaceful evening. It was a deep rumble, unfamiliar and unsettling. I looked at Daddy, seeking comfort in his steady presence. His brow furrowed as he exchanged a concerned glance with Mama.

"What's that sound, Daddy?" I asked, my voice trembling with fear.

We all fell silent, straining our ears to hear the mysterious noise again. There it was again, echoing through the trees, closer this time. My heart raced, and I instinctively moved closer to Mama, clutching onto her arm for reassurance. Another roar vibrated through the ground, sending a chill down my spine.

Uncle Jack, the brave one, reached for his trusty axe. His eyes met Daddy's, and without a word, they stepped into the darkness, determined to uncover the source of our unease.

"Don't worry, Dawn. Uncle Jack and Daddy will find out what it is. Stay close to me, and you'll be safe." Mama's reassuring words failed to calm my nerves.

As we anxiously waited, time seemed to drag on at a snail's pace, our imaginations running wild with possibilities. Shadows danced around the campsite, and the rustle of leaves made me jump.

The unknown weighed heavily on my young mind, and I held my breath, praying for their safe return. Where were Uncle Jack and Daddy? Were they in danger?

I Won't Back Down

PORT TOWNSEND, WASHINGTON
MARCH 1938

Dawn Jensen
Almost 10 Years Old

After what felt like an eternity, Uncle Jack emerged from the darkness with Daddy by his side. He held up a hand, signaling for us to stay put. "It's a bear. We need to scare it off. Stay here, everyone."

Hunting rifle in hand, Uncle Jack led the way, Daddy and Junior followed closely behind. Adrenaline-fueled steps moved them toward the sound of the bear. Mama squeezed my hand and instructed. "Find anything that can make noise, start hollering, and we'll scare this bear right out from here," Mama instructed, as she banged her copper pot and pan, creating a sound that echoed through the woods.

As we tried to make a huge ruckus around our campsite, an ear splitting gunshot rang out followed by a fierce roar from the bear that sent shivers down my spine.

Two bear cubs dashed towards our campsite, closely followed by a larger black bear. Yet Mama stood her ground, undeterred by the ferocity before her. She shouted frantically while clanging her pots and pans. It was the ultimate showdown, a clash between the Mother Bear and our own, resilient Mama.

In that harrowing moment, another hero emerged from our midst. Honey, our loyal German Shepherd, lunged forward with unwavering bravery. Her protective instincts kicked into high gear as she sprinted toward the growling bear, barking in fearless determination. With every stride, Honey embodied the spirit of a true protector, defending our camp with her ferocious bark.

The bear's resolve faltered, and she took a step back with her gaze fixed on our Honey. The men saw their opportunity and advanced, making themselves bigger and bolder, their shouts echoing through the night. Realizing she was outnumbered, the Mother Bear turned and ran back into the woods after her cubs, disappearing into the shadows beyond.

Relief washed over us as the tension lifted. The adrenaline in our veins began to subside, replaced by a feelings of triumph and amazement. My Mama, who insisted on sipping her tea from a pretty teacup and saucer, had gone head-to-head with an angry mother bear.

"John, you'd be best not to mess with that woman and her pots and pans." Uncle Jack chuckled, clapping Daddy on his back. Laughter erupted as we gathered around Mama, her face weary but triumphant. She embraced us tightly, tears of relief glistening in her eyes.

"We better pack up and move along," Daddy declared.

We quickly gathered our belongings, folding our tent and securing our supplies. It was time to find a safer place to camp out. We quickly found another spot, a little closer to town, and settled down for the night.

"We'll leave at first light for Hoods Canal. Try to get a good night's sleep," Daddy announced, his voice tinged with exhaustion. The journey ahead weighed heavily on his shoulders, but he remained determined to make it through.

Mama nodded in agreement, her face showing signs of weariness. "You're right, John. We should rest now so that we can begin our long journey in the morning."

Finding solace in the comfort of each other's presence. The gentle lullaby of a nearby brook whispered us into a peaceful slumber.

The next morning we embarked on the long and arduous journey to Hoods Canal. Despite the challenges, our spirits remained steadfast as we arranged another makeshift home by a creek not too far from the logging camp. Our tent provided us with shelter, and Mama wasted no time in making it feel as comfortable as possible. Daddy,

Uncle Jack, and Junior ventured deep into the woods to earn a living, performing the strenuous work of loggers.

One rainy afternoon, as the sun struggled to peek through the thick clouds, Franny and I raced down the creek. Daddy had set up the old cook stove on the river banks, and Mama diligently boiled our clothes, determined to rid them of the grime and sweat from our nomadic life.

Suddenly, she let out a cry of alarm as she struggled with the broiler pan. "The dam must've let out extra water. I was rinsing our clothes, and now they've washed downriver."

We rushed to salvage what was left of our garments, but the relentless current swept many of them away. Exhausted and defeated, we returned to the campsite, our spirits dampened along with our clothes.

Sitting down heavily, Mama looked at the rushing water, her voice carrying wisdom beyond her years. "Our life is like this dang river," she said, her tone a mix of resignation and fierce love for our family. "Every darn thing we put into that water, it's gonna carry down to our future generations."

Her words struck a chord within me, and I made a silent promise to be mindful of my actions and the choices I made. My journey would leave a mark, a legacy for generations to come.

As the river flowed on, carrying our clothes into the great unknown, we sat there, Mama, Franny, and me, pondering her words, their weight sinking into my young mind.

Weeks dragged by, each one shrouded in relentless rain and looming darkness. The struggle to keep our spirits afloat in the face of the ceaseless downpour became an uphill battle. The mud, once an inconvenience, now seemed like an antagonist in the story of our lives. As I trudged through the soggy ground, determination was my lifeline.

"I can't remember the last time my clothes were dry," I muttered, the words escaping my lips before I could stop them.

Mama let out a weary sigh. "We can't let this break us, Pickle."

"It's like the mud has taken over the world." Franny, her voice tinged with frustration.

"I want to have a hot bath and cuddle up next to a warm fireplace." Denise, shoulders hunched, added softly.

Huddled together at night in our makeshift home, we were starting to find it difficult to keep our complaints bottled up. During the day we continued to gather firewood, forage for sustenance, and learn whatever we could from Bobby's sporadic teaching.

Despite the challenges, the bond between us grew stronger, and Mama's love and strength kept us going. Denise grew quieter, but we knew she, too, was weathering the storm in her own way. It got harder and harder to believe that brighter days would come. Would the sun ever break through the depths of our despair?

When it seemed our family was at our lowest point, Uncle Jack returned home with a letter clutched tightly in his hand. Jubilation danced in his eyes as he entered the campground. We gathered around him, eager to hear the news.

"Clarence has come through for us. He's managed to secure jobs for both your Daddy and me at the airport." Uncle Jack's words hung in the air, carrying with them an air of newfound possibility.

Mama's eyes widened, and a smile illuminated her beautiful yet weary face. Daddy's tired features transformed into an expression of gratitude.

The words on the page painted a vivid picture of opportunity and change. In the letter, Clarence acknowledged his mistakes of the past and expressed his sincere desire to make amends.

"I'm thrilled to tell you I've secured jobs as maintenance men for both of you at the airport," Uncle Jack read aloud. "The pay is good. $27 a week, and they are union jobs. I hope in some small way, these opportunities will make up for the trouble I caused in the past."

Tears welled up in Mama's eyes as she listened to the words of redemption. We celebrated with laughter, hugs, and tears of joy, feeling the weight of the world lift from our shoulders. Uncle Jack pulled out his harmonica and played as we danced around in joy. The next chapter of our journey was about to unfold before us, and we were ready to embrace it.

After we ate our supper around the campfire, we shared stories and dreams, painting a mural of hope and gratitude.

Uncle Jack held the letter in his hands, a tangible reminder of the possibilities that awaited us down south.

It ignited a fire within me, a yearning to explore the world beyond the boundaries of our forest sanctuary. I couldn't help but wonder what it would be like to attend a proper school after years of home learning. The thoughts fluttered in my mind, like the delicate wings of a butterfly.

How would it feel to be sitting at a desk alongside other children, listening to a teacher's voice whisk us away on a journey of knowledge? Would I find friends who shared my thirst for adventure and love of reading? What secrets and wonders would the world outside our campsite reveal to me?

As Mama's voice called me to bed, I lay on my bedroll with the questions in my mind interrupting my rest. How would I fit in at a regular school? Would the teachers be ready to handle my boundless energy? Would the other children be open to a feisty spirit like mine? As sleep beckoned, I pondered the endless possibilities that awaited me in the schoolyard.

I knew that entering this next chapter would bring my spark of individuality and a unique perspective to our new town. Life wasn't always smooth sailing, yet a reassuring wave of relief washed over me as I realized that I would have a stable home to call my own. As these thoughts filled my mind, I couldn't help but wonder, would the people of Kent be ready for the unstoppable force that was Dawn Jensen?

You're Gonna Go Far

KENT, WASHINGTON

SEPTEMBER 1938

Dawn Jensen

10 Years Old

My heart fluttered with anticipation as I entered Kent Elementary School. A grand entrance loomed before me, and the school seemed to bask in a radiant aura, like a canvas painted with the colors of possibility and promise.

The scent of fresh paint mingled with polished wood, enveloping me as I walked through the hallway to my classroom. This was no ordinary day—it was my first day at a new school in the small town of Kent. It was finally happening; we were starting our new life, and after two years of at-home learning, I felt both intimidated and excited to be at a real school.

Mrs. Dewitt, our teacher, stood at the front of the classroom, radiating warmth and genuine affection. Her smile stretched across her face as she greeted her students.

"Good morning, Mrs. Dewitt, I'm Dawn Jensen," I greeted her with cheerful determination, my shoes clicking along the linoleum floors.

"Well, good morning, young lady," Mrs. Dewitt replied, her voice a soothing and kind.

"Welcome to the fifth grade, Dawn. Please, find your seat. They have all been labeled, look for your name."

Taking in my surroundings, my gaze landed upon a desk near the window with my name written on a folded piece of paper, a prime spot where I could catch glimpses of the outside world. The playground beyond the glass seemed to beckon me with it's swings and slides. Kent Elementary was a brand-new school, this was everyone's first day on this campus. Not just in our grade, but in all grades.

I instantly liked Mrs. Dewitt, and I knew this would be a great school year. I hoped Mama's home learning had prepared Franny and me well enough for the school year ahead.

"Class, I have an important first assignment for all of you. We are going to write a letter to President Roosevelt. You can ask for something your family needs or share something about your life. Make sure it is at least one page long. I will mail all of the letters off to the White House on Friday after school. Maybe the president will read your letter and answer back."

Mrs. Dewitt's words stirred a whirlwind of thoughts within me. A spark of inspiration ignited, fueled by the hope that my words could reach the highest office in the land. After a short time attending to our papers, it was time for recess, the perfect moment to share my encounter with the president with my schoolmates.

As I stood on the playground, surrounded by excited voices, I felt a sense of pride and nervousness. I had an extraordinary experience to share, one that set me apart from my classmates.

"Hey, everyone. Guess what? I met President Roosevelt and he is the nicest and most handsome man you can imagine."

A boy named Dan challenged me. "We are supposed to believe you met the President of the United States?"

I looked at Dan firmly, refusing to let his skepticism extinguish the flame of truth within me. "Yes, Dan, I did. When he visited the Makah reservation at Neah Bay, I was there. He patted my head and spoke to me."

"Now I've heard everything. Are you telling us you're a redheaded Indian, too?" Sarcasm filled his voice.

A cloud of disbelief lingered in the air, but I stood tall, determined to stand up for myself and my incredible experience on Neah Bay. "I wouldn't lie about something like that. It happened, and I don't care if you believe me or not."

Without thinking, I retaliated by stomping on Dan's foot.

My small but determined act of defiance was meant to push against his rude questioning.

A yelp of pain escaped him, and he recoiled in surprise. The playground erupted into whispers.

"Don't ever doubt me again," I warned, my voice firm and resolute. "I may be small, but I won't tolerate being called a liar. My family lived on the reservation for two years, and I met the president. Ask my sister, Franny, if you don't believe me."

As Dan nursed his foot, the truth of my encounter with President Roosevelt resonated throughout the playground. The whispers shifted from disbelief to curiosity as my classmates began to realize that extraordinary things were possible. Luckily, the bell rang, signaling us to return to the classroom.

With my head held high, I walked to class to start my project. As I entered, Mrs. Dewitt placed a hand on my arm and whispered in my ear, "I don't want to see you do a thing like that again. There are better ways to stand up for yourself." Mrs. Dewitt winked at me.

"Children, you must know that I won't tolerate any bad behavior from the students this year. You must learn to get along better." Mrs. Dewitt put on a stern face as she addressed the class, but I could see in her eyes that she was a sweet woman, and she wouldn't stay mad for long.

Once we settled into our seats, I eagerly wrote my letter to the President. I was happy to learn that my reading and writing skills surpassed most of the students in the class, proving that Mama had successfully kept us up to speed.

With each carefully chosen word, I poured out my hopes onto the page, imagining the impact of my letter on the President. Mrs. Dewitt's words echoed in my mind, reminding me of the opportunity to share our story and possibly receive a response from the leader of our nation.

Dan apologized, and by the end of the week, we were friends. Eventually, the time came to read our letters aloud in the classroom. A smile spread across my face as I reminisced about that extraordinary encounter, feeling a renewed connection to the President.

Dear Mr. President,

I hope this letter finds you well, and that you are enjoying your important role as President. My name is Dawn Jensen, a ten-year-old girl from the rainy state of Washington. We met once before, when you visited the Makah reservation at Neah Bay. Perhaps you remember meeting a little red-haired girl and giving her a gentle pat on her head?

I write to you today, Mr. President, with a humble request. My Daddy, who has recently found steady employment, needs new work shoes. He hasn't had a new pair in years, and his old ones are worn through from a lot of tough work. Daddy spent all his money buying shoes for my sister and me, and he

didn't have enough to get himself a pair. He has dedicated himself to providing for our family, and I hope
you will grant this humble request.

Also, I would be grateful if you could find it in your
budget to send my sister and me raincoats for winter.
When it rains, it can get pretty chilly, and having
good raincoats would not only keep us dry but also
remind us of the importance of kindness and compassion in these times.

Thank you, Mr. President, for your dedication to
our great country. Your tireless efforts to guide us
through these challenging times have not gone unnoticed. On behalf of my family and all those whose lives
you touch, I extend my gratitude and thanks.

Dawn Jenkins

10 Years Old

AFTER READING MY LETTER, I CAREFULLY FOLDED IT AND PUT
it in the envelope our teacher had provided. My excitement
mingled with anticipation at the prospect of receiving a
response from the White House.

That year, Mrs. Dewitt created an environment of
learning and growth, where our minds flourished like fertile
soil. With each lesson, we delved deeper into history,
unearthing the foundations of our nation and the ideals it
was built upon. The stories of trailblazers and visionaries

echoed through the walls, their courageous actions serving as a powerful reminder of the importance of staying resilient through hardships.

NOW THAT WE HAD A PERMANENT HOME, JUNIOR HAD BEGUN to spend his time with a girl from down the street named Eleanor Gates. Their connection blossomed, and as Junior's heart seemed to have found a home, I couldn't help but feel a mixture of emotions. His attention, once wholly dedicated to our family, now shifted to this girl whose parents owned the 'Totem Pole' grocery store.

One evening over supper, Junior made a sudden announcement of an offer presented by Mr. Gates.

"You won't believe it. Mr. Gates wants to help us purchase a plot of land. He's offering his support for Eleanor and me to get married and build our own cabin, a place where we can start our lives together. I want to marry Eleanor." Junior leaned back and looked at all of us across the dinner table.

"Eleanor is a lovely girl, we are happy to welcome her into our family," Mama rubbed my back. My face must have betrayed my conflicting emotions.

As the reality of Junior's possible departure hit me like a tonne of bricks. I grappled with my conflicting emotions of jealousy and happiness over Junior's relationship. What would happen if our family wasn't all under one roof?

"Cheer up. You know I'll always have time for my little Sis." Junior passed the breadbasket as Mama and Daddy's faces beamed with happiness.

"You are nineteen, and it's a perfect time to start your life with a nice, young woman. By this time next year, you'll be out on your own and a homeowner to boot. I'm very proud of you." Daddy's face was filled with pride.

Everyone seemed happy about Junior growing up and leaving our house. I couldn't understand it, but I tried hard to put on a brave face. However, inside it was a different story, I felt as if the air had been sucked out of me. The realization that our tight-knit clan wouldn't all be under one roof upset me to the core, and I couldn't bear the weight of it any longer. Tears welled up in my eyes, blurring my vision as I abruptly pushed back from the table. The harsh scrap of my chair legs echoed through the room. Without uttering a word, I fled from the dinner table, my trusted Honey following close behind.

Outside, the cool evening embraced me, wrapping around me like an old, familiar friend, reminding me of Talie. I missed her so, but my letters I'd sent had gone unanswered.

What would our home be like without Junior's laughter, his guidance and gentle presence? My thoughts drifted to my big brother, and it felt as if a piece of our shared existence was being ripped away. The weight of it threatened to suffocate me, and in the midst of that overwhelming despair,

I sought refuge among the trees, seeking solace in their steady, unchanging presence.

As I collapsed onto the porch swing, the memories of our childhood flooded my mind. The echoes of laughter and the magic of late-night conversations under the stars washed over me. I couldn't help but reminisce about all those nights we spent sleeping under the open sky without a place to call our own. They were uncertain times, but they brought us closer as a family. We shared history and an unspoken connection that only siblings would understand. How could Junior do this to me?

Lost in my sadness, I failed to notice Junior when he appeared on the porch. His footsteps were soft against the creaking boards.

"Dawn." His voice was a gentle whisper filled with concern. "Wanna talk?"

I didn't have the strength to face him, to meet his eyes. My voice was but a fragile tremor as I muttered, "I don't wanna talk. Just… leave me alone."

"I understand. I know it's hard. Please, let me help you understand." His hand brushed against my shoulder.

I turned toward him, my eyes red and swollen. "How can you leave me alone, without our family all together?"

He took a seat beside me, the weight of his presence comforting yet bittersweet.

"Dawn, it's not about leaving you alone. It's about growing, about embracin' my future. Eleanor is someone who's become an important part of my life, and she'll be a part of yours too. You'll have a new sister, and you'll love her, if you give her a chance."

"I'm scared. Mama said we'd all be okay as long as we stuck together. That's all going to change now. What happens when you move out and I don't get to see you every day?"

"You'll still see me lots, and now Eleanor will be a part of your life too. She's going to need your help as her new sister. Who do you think will be there to babysit and help when the babies start coming? You'll have a big role to play, and we are going to be livin' just down the road."

"Promise?" A feeling of assurance spread through me, thawing my fears of abandonment. Maybe this change wouldn't be as unbearable as I had imagined.

"I promise. We'll face these changes as a family, like we always have. Right now, I need you to trust me." Junior squeezed my hand.

"I trust you." I uttered these words softly, but a lingering doubt remained, interrupting my ability to wholeheartedly embrace this uncertain future ahead. Could our family withstand yet another huge shift? Could I truly embrace Eleanor as a sister and welcome her into our tight-knit family?

In My Life

Dawn Jensen

Almost 13 Years Old

I dried my hands on a faded dish towel as I put away the last plate from Sunday lunch. The monotony of washing dishes had become a familiar part of my life, and I was glad for it. After all those years of washing our dishes in the river, I was happy to have a sink and a kitchen.

Today was Valentine's Day, and thoughts of love and affection filled my mind. I reflected on the love shared by Junior and his wife, Eleanor. My sister-in-law's beauty was matched only by her kind and gentle demeanor. Her traits intertwined with our family's tapestry and at thirteen years old, I was beginning to understand the allure of their bond. I even had my eye on a few of the boys at school.

Any lingering traces of jealousy I had once harbored for Eleanor had transformed into genuine sisterhood. Much to my relief, my family did not break up, and Eleanor became an integral part of our lives. Her presence not only enriched our family, but she also came from a large and loving family of her own. Despite this, she had plenty of room in her heart for all of Junior's younger siblings.

Suddenly, the sound of a knock on the door snapped me back to the present.

"Valentine's Day surprises for you, Dawn." Mama's voice carried through the house, bringing the thrill of anticipation to my heart.

I raced toward the door, my cheeks flushed with a mix of delight. Tommy and Dan, Eleanor's brother, and cousin, stood on the other side, dressed in their finest attire. My heart skipped a beat at the card and box of chocolates they held.

"We couldn't resist expressing our affection for the loveliest girl in town." Tommy shifted nervously from foot to foot, his voice tinged with playful charm.

"I picked out the card. Hope you like it." Dan chimed in, nudging Tommy aside.

My heart fluttered, caught between the warmth of their gestures and the uncertainty of choosing between them. It was a moment both endearing and bewildering as I found myself the object of two young suitors' affections.

"Now, Dawn, you must pick one boy to be your Valentine. It wouldn't do for a girl to have two beaus." Mama's voice cut through the air, a playful admonition in her words.

"I choose Dan." Without hesitation, I made my choice.

And just like that, the friendly rivalry between Tommy and Dan escalated into a full-blown tussle on our front porch. Mama quickly intervened, her tone a mix of sternness and amusement. "Break it up, boys. No fighting here. Head home before I tell your Mamas about this little escapade. You better not do it again."

As they dusted themselves off and retreated, I couldn't help but giggle. Little did I know that this simple encounter would become a snapshot of a carefree time when an innocent young love danced on our front porch.

"Dawn, have you finished up your chores for the day?" Mama interrupted my daydream.

"I need to feed the chickens, Mama." I made my way down the steps toward the chicken coop as Franny started to sweep the front porch.

As I entered the chicken coop, my heart was abuzz with the flattery I felt from the two cousins. Rhythmic clucking created a comforting backdrop, especially when paired with the bee box Daddy kept nearby. Lost in my thoughts, I reflected on the afternoon and couldn't wait to see the boys again on Monday at school.

Suddenly, a rustling sound broke through my daydreaming, jolting me from my reverie. My eyes widened in surprise as I turned to see Dan, his mischievous smile lighting up his face.

"Dawn," he whispered. "I knew you'd pick me." Dan entered the chicken coop as the bucket of feed slipped from my hands, forgotten at that moment. A rush of emotions coursed through me as I met his eyes, my heart beating faster with anticipation. I couldn't help but take a step closer, drawn to him like a magnet.

"I had something else to give you," he murmured, his mischievous grin and twinkling eyes revealing his intentions. My heart quivered with excitement as Dan leaned close and planted a big kiss right on my lips. The air crackled with electric energy as our lips locked. Time seemed to stand still, the world around us melted away. It was a moment suspended in time, and my first taste of young love imprinted an indelible mark on my heart.

As quickly as the kiss had ignited, another rustling noise startled us, breaking the spell. We pulled away, our eyes wide with surprise. In the fading light, we saw the silhouette of a familiar figure.

"Well, well, what do we have here?" Franny teased, her voice dripping with amusement. "I thought I heard something egg-citing happening in the chicken coop. Seems like someone should run along home before our Daddy catches you out here canoodling in the chicken coop." Franny scrunched up her nose as she motioned for Dan to get going.

"Get out of here, you spy." I threw a handful of chicken feed her way.

Dan chuckled, stepping back to give us some space. "I should probably be going," he said with a sheepish grin and, a glimmer of laughter in his eyes. "I'll see you at school on Monday."

"Bye-bye, Romeo." Franny relished the moment with a touch of laughter.

I couldn't help but join them in their laughter, feeling a relief wash over me. Franny may have been teasing us, but I was confident that she'd keep our secret kiss to herself.

"I hope you're not planning on mentioning this to anyone?" We made our way onto our front porch as Mama appeared in the doorway.

"Come here, Pickle. You look flushed. Are you running a fever?" Mama looked at me with concerned eyes.

"Don't worry, Mama," Franny interjected, a mischievous smile spread across her face.

"Dawn and I were racing by the chicken coop. That's why she looks red and out of breath."

I breathed a sigh of relief, grateful for Franny's quick thinking and her unwavering loyalty. This kiss would remain a secret shared between sisters.

As Mama continued to fuss over me, her concern gradually eased. I felt lucky to have a sister like Franny—someone who knew how to keep my secrets safe. And though I blushed at the memory of that stolen kiss, I couldn't help but treasure the sisterly bond we shared, knowing that in this ever-changing world, I had someone who would be by my side.

Eventually, Franny and I both had boyfriends, and our afternoons at the soda fountain became even more exciting. The bright neon sign outside the local pharmacy beckoned us with promises of delicious treats and sweet memories. When we stepped through the door, the familiar aroma of freshly-brewed coffee and the sound of soda glasses clinking filled the air.

"Hey, you two! Mind if I join the fun?" Franny's boyfriend, Johnny's voice flowed like a smooth jazz melody, filling the space between us.

"Of course not, silly!" Franny giggled.

As we sat upon the stools at the soda fountain counter, the soda jerk prepared our drinks. I leaned in closer to Franny, excitement bubbling within me. "Can you believe how lucky we are?" I whispered, my voice filled with youthful enthusiasm. "Having boyfriends and getting to share these moments. It's a far cry from Neah Bay."

"It feels like a dream." Franny took a sip from her fizzy drink. Time seemed to be suspended in our little corner of the drugstore. The world beyond faded into the background, allowing us to revel in the enchantment of our first crushes and the comfort of our sisterly bond.

My boyfriend Dan joined us, bringing with him his cocky swagger. He greeted me with a gentle smile and a playful glint in his eyes. "Dawn, you saved a spot for me, right?" he quipped, his tone adding to the playful atmosphere of the moment."

"Of course. You're not getting away that easily."

It was in these moments, surrounded by the buzz of the soda fountain and the chatter of friends, that I felt a deep contentment. In the small town of Kent, we had found a feeling of community that had eluded our family ever since the night of the horrible barn fire we had experienced several years before. This connection to a more stable life was what we had strived for. The years of living a nomadic life almost felt like a dream that had never really happened.

"Life's been treating us pretty good, huh? We'll have countless stories to tell our grandkids about these soda fountain dates and our times on Neah Bay, too." Franny grinned, her eyes sparkling with memories of the past.

"You know, Sis. We may have our differences, but at the end of the day, I wouldn't trade you for the world."

Franny's eyes sparkled with warmth and affection. "Same here, Sis. You're stuck with me forever, whether you like it or not."

After our soda fountain rendezvous, Franny and I began our leisurely walk home, a light drizzle of rain tickled our faces and the scent of fires burning in the fireplace filled the air. With each step, the anticipation of the evening's culinary escapades grew, knowing that Mama awaited our help in the kitchen.

As we strolled along, Dan joined us, his freckles standing out against his reddened cheeks.

"You two ladies are the prettiest sisters I ever knew," he remarked, a touch of banter in his voice. "I'm glad you stomped on my foot that day in the schoolyard."

I linked my arm with Franny's, and a mischievous grin played on my lips. "That's what you get for being a brute."

With laughter and camaraderie filling the air, we continued our journey home, savoring the simplicity and joy of those carefree moments shared between two sisters on the cusp of womanhood. The promise of an evening spent together, crafting memories, warmed my soul. I absorbed the joy of that afternoon, the anticipation of embracing my teenage years in our small town of Kent, where a roof over my head and food in my belly brought a comforting sense of stability to my heart. It felt as though all our troubles were finally behind us.

"I can't wait to be in high school," I said, my voice laced with a touch of excitement,

Franny looked over at me, her eyes curious. "Oh, really? What's got you all dreamy-eyed about it?"

I grinned, my imagination running wild. "Think about it. Attending the same school again, going to dances and football games."

She chuckled, nudging me playfully. "You and your daydreams. Things are really looking up for us, Sis."

My eyes lit up, my enthusiasm building. "Yeah, and the friendships we'll make, the adventures we'll have . . .

"Exactly!" she exclaimed. "It's like a whole world of

possibilities opening up. Attending High school with you is going to be something else."

Franny's smile mirrored mine, full of anticipation. "These are the years we'll remember forever."

"I can't help but think of Talie and Yarlata. Now that we are settled and have a permanent address, we should try writing to them again."

"Let's try again. I'd love to hear how things are going on Neah Bay." I fingered the shell necklace Talie had given to me on the day we left.

'Life feels pretty amazing right now; it feels like nothing could ever disrupt our happiness,' Franny responded. 'But why do you think our letters to Talie have gone unanswered?'"

The unanswered letters weighed on my mind. The question nagged at me: had something happened to them, or was there another reason behind their silence? I couldn't shake the feeling that our peaceful existence might be on the verge of a profound change. What could be keeping Talie and Yarlata from responding?"

A Day That Will Live On...

KENT, WASHINGTON
DECEMBER 7TH, 1941

Dawn Jensen
13 Years Old

"Yesterday, December 7th, 1941—a date which will live in infamy—the United States of America was suddenly and deliberately attacked by naval and air forces of the Empire of Japan."

From where I sat in the small cafeteria of Kent Junior High School, surrounded by my fellow classmates and teachers, the atmosphere was thick with whispers. The entire student body and faculty crammed into our small cafeteria, listening to the radio. Something big was happening that would change our lives forever.

I didn't want to miss out on hearing what the President had to say about the attack on Pearl Harbor. We listened intently to his voice as it crackled through the loudspeaker with an air of authority and strength.

"We must prepare for a long and hard struggle. No matter how long it may take us to overcome this premeditated invasion, the American people, in their righteous might, will win through to absolute victory."

For two years, the USA had avoided joining the battles occurring in Europe, Asia, and Africa. Wars that threatened to bring the world to the brink of chaos for a second time. Now, with the President's resolute proclamation, the actuality of our involvement became a reality.

As the speech continued, his call for unity and sacrifice resonated deep within me. I glanced around the room, seeing the expressions on my classmates' faces—some filled with resolve, others with worry. Afterward, a silence descended upon the room. The air was charged with electricity. Mr. Anderson, our principal, stepped in front of the radio, a grave yet determined expression on his face.

He began, his voice steady and tinged with seriousness. "Please settle down, students. We have had the privilege of listening to President Roosevelt's address to the nation. It's an integral moment in history that could change the face of the world forever. Remember, students, you have a role to play in this great struggle. Each of you can make a difference. Classes will be dismissed early, and you are to go straight home."

Stepping out of the schoolyard, I felt nervous and shaken to the core. I'd heard the stories of the Great War from Uncle Clarence who'd been stationed in Europe, and they had stuck with me. It seemed as if my secure world had been turned upside down.

As I returned home, bursting through the front door with my school bag slung over my shoulder, a familiar scene greeted me. Mama, Junior, Bobby, and Franny were gathered around the table, their faces reflected a combination of seriousness and concern.

I quickly joined them, my chair scraping the hardwood floors, its echo bouncing through the kitchen as Mama handed me a cup of tea and a slice of berry cobbler. As I took a bite, the soft, familiar taste brought a sense of familiarity amidst the uncertain times. I could hear Daddy's car pulling up onto the gravel outside. The news spread quickly, and I imagined families all over the country stopping their daily routines to discuss the impending war.

Daddy's presence soon filled the kitchen with strength and reassurance. He took a seat at the head of the table, joining us for this impromptu gathering.

"Good to see y'all here. I reckon by now everyone's heard."

"Why do we have to go to war?" I looked up with questioning eyes.

"I know it's hard to understand, especially for you, Dawn. This is the first foreign attack on our soil in over 100 years, and the President must give a forceful responce. It makes us look weak otherwise. We must fight for our beliefs. The world is going through a tough time, and our country needs brave people to stand up and protect the values we hold dear."

"But what about the draft? How does it work? Will we all have to go?" Franny wrinkled her face up in concern.

Junior leaned forward, his brows furrowing to match Franny's mood. "The draft is a way for the government to select young men to serve in the military," he explained. "The military will draw numbers to determine who gets called, and if your number comes up, you'll have a duty to fulfill."

Franny's voice trembled as she looked at Junior. "Does that mean you and Bobby might have to go? What if something happens to you?"

Junior's voice held a quiet resolve as he replied, his gaze steady "We don't know what the future holds. But if the time comes, I'll do what I can to protect our family and our country. We'll face it together."

Mama's hand reached out, finding mine across the table, her touch grounding me in the moment. "Remember, no matter what happens, we are strong. We've been through a lot, and we'll make it through anything that comes our way."

I was heartbroken to hear about the island paradise had been attacked by Japanese planes. Many of our Naval ships in the harbor sank, with thousands of casualties. I had never lived through a war and didn't know if I should be afraid. I

hoped it stayed far away and it wouldn't come to the main-
land, I also wondered how things would change for our
family.

Eventually, Germany declared war on the USA, and an
aura of unease settled within our nation. The war was no
longer a distant tale from faraway lands. It seeped into our
consciousness. I looked for signs of assurance that this
conflict would remain far from our shores.

Life in Kent continued to unfold as we tried to keep to
our normal routines, seemingly unaffected by the weight of
the world outside. The streets teemed with people going
about their daily rituals, their laughter and conversations
intermingling in the air.

It was several weeks later, against this backdrop of
bustling activity that Mama, Franny, and I embarked on our
first venture into the world of food rationing.

As we entered Smith's Market in downtown Kent, the
smell of bread triggered my hunger.

"How does this work, girls?" Mama whispered as she
clutched our freshly issued rationing books. This was
uncharted territory for us. Mama wanted Franny and me to
come along and navigate it with her. Ever since Junior's
number had been called up for the draft, Mama seemed as
if she was carrying the weight of the world on her small
shoulders. It was as if the immensity of the war had settled
upon her heart, pressing down with an intensity that had
aged her beyond her years.

"Well, Mama, each item in the store has a certain

number of ration stamps assigned to it. We have to make sure we have enough stamps to cover our purchases." Franny explained.

"Remember what the man at the registration center said. Red stamps are for meat. Blue stamps are for fruits and vegetables. We need to be mindful of our weekly budget. We can't go over our limit or we'll run out of stamps." I rattled off what I remembered from the Post Office visit not long ago.

Mama nodded, her grip tightening around the rationing books. "I understand. We must make every stamp count, but I'm determined to prepare a nice dinner for Junior before he must report for duty on Monday, even if it takes up most of our stamps."

Franny and I exchanged concerned looks as Mama began the selection process, carefully considering their stamp values and the limited points we had available. We approached the counter to make our payment, and Mama handed over our ration books, her hands slightly trembling. The grocer took them with a friendly smile, his experienced hands flipping through the pages to locate the necessary stamps.

"Here you go, ladies. Thank you for your cooperation," the shopkeeper responded. Stepping out onto the bustling streets of downtown Kent, our shopping bags filled with provisions, I realized this was the beginning of our journey through the intricacies of wartime. I wondered what other changes would be in store. . .

More time slowly passed, and as the wars raged on, the realities of wartime existence continued to shape our lives, challenging us in ways we had never imagined.

With Junior fighting alongside the Allies in Europe and the rationing system becoming a part of our daily lives, I wondered: how long would these wars last?

What other sacrifices would we have to make before we experienced peace again?

Wake Me Up

PORT ORCHARD, WASHINGTON

JUNE 7TH, 1944

Dawn Jensen

16 Years Old

"Look at you," I exclaimed. Denise returned from nursing school, and I couldn't believe my eyes. Her short hair looked completely different from the girl who left for work that morning. Women were changing roles during the years of wartime, and Denise embraced that change with flair.

"Mama, look at Denise's hair. It's so different," I said, wide-eyed. Mama turned to Denise, her face lighting up.

"Denise, you look marvelous. I love the new look," Mama said.

"Thanks, Mama. It's practical for nursing duties, too."

Franny nodded approvingly. "Oh, My Giddy Aunt, you're really swingin' that style, Sis. I might bob my hair, too."

The family had recently relocated to Port Orchard and living closer to the water felt more like our time on Neah Bay. When a job opportunity opened up for Daddy, he took it and was finally able to fulfill his lifelong dream of owning his own house. Though we missed Junior and Bobby after they were both drafted for the war, we managed to make our mark in our community.

Suddenly, there was a knock at the door, and Mama's expression changed. Franny answered, finding a man in uniform holding a flag with a somber expression. My heart pounded, and a knot formed in my stomach.

"Mrs. Jensen, I regret to inform you that your son, Robert, was killed in action."

Mama's face turned pale, and tears welled up in my eyes. Denise rushed to console her, and Franny and I joined them, wrapping our arms around Mama as she collapsed into our embrace, sobbing uncontrollably.

My dear brother Bobby was killed by a Japanese sniper in Okinawa at twenty-three. The reality of his loss settled in, and memories of our times together—laughter and sibling love—flooded my mind. It felt like a bad dream from which I couldn't escape.

In the following days, our home felt empty, the laughter silenced. We sought solace in each other's shared pain.

Denise, donning her nurse's uniform, continued to care for others, but sadness lingered in her eyes. Junior, released from duty, was on his way home from Europe.

Two brothers went to war, but only one returned. As the youngest in the family, I clung to memories of Bobby—the hunting trips, his love for the outdoors, and how he patiently taught us algebra all those years ago. The war had taken him from us, but his memory would forever live on in our hearts.

This blow hit us hard, and each of us handled it differently. Junior's return from Europe brought both relief and sorrow. The horrors of war were evident in the weariness written on his face, as if a piece of his innocence had been left behind on foreign soil. Mama clung to him tightly, tears of joy streaming down her cheeks as she held her oldest son in her arms once more.

Franny, ever strong and stoic, tried to hide her emotions behind a brave facade. But I could see the sadness lurking in her eyes from the pain of losing Bobby and seeing the toll of war on her beloved brother, Junior. She spent long hours by the river, sketching the changing landscape, seeking solace in the familiar scenes that had once brought her joy.

Denise continued her nursing duties, caring for the wounded as if they were her dear brother Bobby.

As for me, I found comfort in pouring my heart out onto paper. I often joined Franny by the river and wrote for hours while she sketched. We rarely spoke during those long hours of solitude. The river's gentle flow seemed to carry our thoughts and unspoken words away, allowing us to grieve in our own ways. Sometimes, I would read aloud the letters I wrote to Bobby, my voice choked with emotion, while Franny listened attentively, her eyes filled with understanding.

Amidst the quiet of the riverbank, we found solace in each other's company. We had been close, but the war and its aftermath brought us even closer. Franny's sketches and my heartfelt words became our sanctuary, a place where we could escape from the world's troubles, if only for a while.

Mama, too, had her way of coping. She spent her free time tending to her beloved garden, nurturing the plants as if they were her children. The flowers she grew were not only a splash of color in our yard became a symbol of hope and a reminder that life could flourish even during times of loss and sorrow.

Daddy didn't talk much about Bobby, but I could often hear him weeping when he thought no one was awake to hear. I often found him in the corner, sitting in his favorite armchair, reading the last letter we had received from Bobby.

Dec 31, 1943
Dear Mama,
 I was expecting a letter from home today but didn't get one. Tomorrow is New Year's Day and it will be spent in camp. It rained all day and night... I'm

hoping tomorrow is better. It's hard to believe five years ago we were all together, celebrating the holidays in Neah Bay. I managed to bring home that pheasant for Thanksgiving Day supper. How I miss those simpler times when we were all together. I hope by next Thanksgiving this war will be over and we can all be together. I often find myself reflecting on the things I miss most from home. The simple joys of a hot cup of coffee, the laughter of friends and family, and all your good home cooking. While these memories keep me grounded, they also make me homesick at times.

The camaraderie among the soldiers in our unit is remarkable. We've become a tight-knit bunch, relying on each other on and off the battlefield. The stories we share help to lighten the burden that war places on us. We find comfort in each other's company, sharing jokes, memories of home, and the occasional longing for a hot meal that isn't from a ration pack.

Our interactions with the local people have been interesting. They display a resilience that's remarkable, going about their daily lives despite this war that surrounds them. It helps motivate us all.

Take care, Mama. I hold onto the hope that these words find you well and send my love to Daddy and the girls. I can't help but be reminded of all the cherished moments we've shared as a family during this time of

year... and it'll feel as though a piece of home is right
here with me.
    Love always,
    Bobby

WE EACH COPED IN OUR OWN WAY, LEANING ON ONE another for support in our grief. Losing Bobby was still painful, but we knew we had to keep moving forward. Time carried on, with weeks melting into months. The war had taken much from us, yet it also taught us to cherish what remained. As the seasons changed, we found healing in the rhythm of life. The river kept flowing, the garden bloomed with vibrant colors, and the woods stood tall and unyielding. We found a sense of purpose that allowed us to carry on, though Bobby's absence remained a constant ache in our hearts.

Six months after the blow that had driven us into a deep state of grief, Franny woke up early one morning and prepared breakfast for everyone. As we gathered around the kitchen table, she made her true motives clear over a steaming plate of biscuits and sausage gravy.

"I know we've all been lost in our grief these past months, but I feel Bobby wouldn't want it to be this way. It's time we lock all this grief away and start living again," Franny said, holding back tears.

"Daddy, you need to take Junior and start fishing again.

Mama, I've arranged for you to go stay with Aunt Hatt. A change of scenery will do you some good. Denise is busy throwing herself into her nursing duties over on the military base. Dawn, you and I are going to meet her for one of those USO dances later tonight. The ones the soldiers love so much. We need to dance like nobody's watching and live in the moment, like Bobby would have wanted."

"Oh, Franny, I can't leave you kids alone." Mama's eyes welled up with tears, touched by Franny's determined spirit.

"Mama, Dawn and I are nearly grown now, and we can take care of each other. But it's time for us to start living again and not let this grief hold us back." Franny reached across the table to hold Mama's hand.

Daddy nodded in agreement, a glimmer of hope in his eyes. "Franny's right. We've been stuck in this darkness for too long. It's time to find the light again, for Bobby and for each other."

Mama let out a big sigh, dabbing at her eyes with her napkin. "Yes, girls, I know you are right. Life is for living, and we haven't been doing much living since June. Let's try to tuck this grief away and try to get some joy into our lives."

With newfound determination, my sisters and I spent that Saturday preparing for the evening ahead. We all laughed as we tried on different dresses, selecting the perfect outfits for the USO dance.

Mama packed her bag for the visit to Aunt Hatt's, and Denise came home with a radiant smile, excited to join us for a night of dancing. Junior and Daddy left for a week-long fishing trip on Neah Bay to visit some old friends on the reservation. They were looking forward to fishing in the same rivers that Bobby had found pleasure in all those years ago.

As the sun began to set, Franny, Denise, and I gathered in the living room, ready to head out to the dance. Mama looked at each of us with a mixture of pride and sadness in her eyes. "You girls have grown up so fast. I know your brother would be proud of the beautiful and resilient young women you've all become."

Franny put her arm around Mama, reassuring her, "We'll be alright, Mama. Tonight, we're going to have a good time and honor Bobby's memory by living life to the fullest."

We arrived at the USO dance in an exciting buzz. Soldiers in uniform mingled with local girls, and the atmosphere was alive with energy. Franny and I felt a little jittery at first, but as we took to the dance floor, our worries of the past faded away.

We swayed to the music, feeling the rhythm course through our veins. The night felt like a sweet escape from the somber reality we had been living. We laughed, we danced, and for a few blissful hours, we let go of the weight of our grief, immersing ourselves in the joy of the moment.

As the night wore on, we let our hair down, both figuratively and literally. The camaraderie we shared with the soldiers made us feel alive again. The laughter was contagious, and amidst it all, we knew that Bobby's spirit was with us, guiding our steps and watching over us.

The music from the live band flowed through the dance hall with melodies of Glenn Miller and Benny Goodman filling the air, transporting us away from our sorrow and grief. The smooth tunes of "Moonlight Serenade" and "Boogie Woogie Bugle Boy" had us tapping our feet and swinging to the rhythm. The band's jazzy melodies added an extra layer of charm to the evening, making the atmosphere even more electrifying.

As I observed Franny, her reserved nature and subtle beauty combined to create an aura that captivated yet intimidated the fellas we danced with. On the other hand, at almost 17, I had grown curvier, my body no longer bony like during the depression. My hair remained a unique shade of red, and my fair skin was accentuated by my piercing gray-blue eyes. Standing barely 5'2", I may not have been considered the more beautiful sister by most, but my plucky attitude and confidence drew plenty of attention.

Tonight, I felt ready to take on the world, basking in the excitement of being young and on the brink of womanhood during a time when we longed to forget we were at war and live for the moment.

"Remember that time we snuck some of Uncle Jack's moonshine, and Bobby ended up playing the harmonica while we danced around the bonfire?" Franny's eyes sparkled with fond memories.

I giggled. "Yeah, and Mama found out the next morning when we were nursing the worst hangovers ever."

Denise joined in with her own laughter, her eyes shimmering with joy. "Oh, how Bobby teased us about that for weeks. He knew how to make us laugh."

"Thank you, Franny, this is exactly what we all needed. It's been a rough time for all of us, but I'm betting Bobby's up there rooting for us to get to living and enjoying life." I pointed up toward the heavens above, and with renewed spirits, we danced the night away. We felt Bobby's presence, a guiding light leading us through the darkness, reminding us to cherish each moment and to live each day to the fullest.

When it seemed like the night couldn't get any better, a familiar voice echoed through the air. "Look who's joined the party."

We turned around to see a dashing soldier approaching us with a playful grin on his face. I knew those lips quirking into a smirk. I hadn't seen them since my days in Kent, but I knew them. "Dan. Is that you?"

"Do you ladies mind if I cut in?" he asked, offering me his hand with a charming smile.

I blushed and glanced at Franny and Denise who were already giggling with delight. "Of course not, Dan. How are you a soldier already? You're only a few months older than me."

As we danced, Dan explained how he had fudged his age on his enlistment papers. The world around us spun. We moved, swaying to the rhythm of the music, lost in the enchantment of being reunited with a first love.

As Dan and I got reacquainted, it felt like time stood still. The memories of our childhood were like a warm embrace, and I couldn't help but smile at how fate had brought us together on this magical night.

As we danced to the music, Dan whispered in my ear, his voice filled with warmth and nostalgia.

"You always were a spitfire, Dawn. I kind of hoped I'd run into you again."

"I'm glad you did, Dan. This night has been like a dream, and you being here makes it even more special."

"I heard about your brother. I'm so sorry, but I'm glad I could make you smile."

Dan twirled me around, and I felt like I was floating on air. We laughed and danced, lost in the joy of being reunited. The sorrows of the past months seemed to melt away, replaced by hope for the future.

The night wore on and our jovial group formed a lively circle on the dance floor. The music filled the air, and the atmosphere was alive with laughter and merriment.

In the midst of the dancing and laughter, I caught sight of Franny and Denise, their faces glowing with happiness. They had found their dance partners too, and it seemed like the night had brought a touch of magic to all of us.

"I want to see you again before I ship out to Europe," Dan whispered in my ear as we snuggled close during a slow dance.

"I want that too, Dan," I replied, my voice soft and sincere. "I don't know what the future holds, but I know that tonight has been something special."

Dan smiled warmly, his eyes locking with mine. "It has, Dawn. You're something special."

As the music continued to play, Dan pulled me close, his hand gently cradling my cheek. His lips brushed against mine in a tender, fleeting kiss. It was soft and sweet, filled with promise.

When we finally pulled apart, our eyes met once again, and I could see the same mixture of emotions reflected in his gaze—the longing to stay, the uncertainty of the future, and the deep affection he held for me.

The following week, Dan arrived at our home to pick me up for our first date. I was eager to reintroduce him to my parents and share the joy of our reunion with them.

"What do we have here?" Daddy questioned, a grin spreading across his face.

"I seem to recall a Valentine's Day tussle on our front porch when you were a little scamp. You and Tommy were up to some kind of mischief," Mama said, her eyes twinkling with nostalgia.

"Those were the days, Mrs. Jensen. Tommy and I were quite the pair back then." Dan chuckled.

My dad joined in with a hearty laugh. "You got that right, young man. I remember having to intervene a few times when you two were in cahoots."

As we shared stories of our childhood escapades, the

room filled with laughter and a hint of nostalgia. It was heartwarming to see Dan connecting with my parents. I felt an overwhelming gratitude for my past and present to be reunited.

Dan took a breath, meeting my eyes intently "I'll be finishing my training in a few weeks. After that, I'll be shipping out soon."

My parents sat in rapt attention, understanding the significance of his forthcoming assignment.

"We're proud of what you've done. Serving our country takes courage and determination, and we know you've got both," Daddy said with a solemn voice.

"Thank you, sir. I'll try to do my best," Dan replied, a touch of humility in his eyes.

Mama reached over to squeeze Dan's hand; her voice filled with motherly warmth. "We know you will, dear. Take care of yourself out there."

The next few weeks passed much too quickly. Although he was deep into his basic training, we wrote to each other often. As the day of his departure drew closer, a mix of emotions filled my heart. I knew the time had come for Dan to follow his calling, but it was never easy to say goodbye. I felt myself falling for Dan, and the thought of being apart again was daunting.

A few days before his departure, we found ourselves at another USO dance. The twinkling lights above seemed to whisper promises of hope and love.

"I'll miss you so much, Dan," I said, tears welling up in

my eyes.

Dan pulled me into his arms, holding me close. "And I'll miss you. You'll be in my thoughts every day."

"I'll be waiting for you. Come back to me safely," I whispered, my voice filled husky with longing.

"I promise I will. Before I leave, I want to express how much I love you… And maybe we can talk about getting married when I return. Would you continue to write to me when I'm away?"

My heart fluttered at his words, and a surge of hope filled me. "Of course, Dan. I'll write to you."

We snuck away to a car parked outside. I longed to give myself to Dan, to express the depth of my love before he left. Denise had shared stories of soldiers wanting to make love before shipping out, and I couldn't deny the intensity of my own desire.

As we held each other, the world outside seemed to fade away, and we found passion and comfort in each other's embrace. That night, under the stars and in the warmth of our love, I gave myself to Dan, fully and wholeheartedly. I didn't know what the future had in store, but as we held each other close, the weight of Dan's impending departure didn't seem to matter as much. We had found solace in our love making and my body felt electrified with feelings I'd never experienced before.

My heart was full, yet uncertainty still lingered. What would the future hold for us? How would our love endure the trials of distance and war?

My Heart Will Go On

PORT ORCHARD, WASHINGTON
DECEMBER 31ST, 1944

Dawn Jensen
16 Years Old

"Franny, look what I found," I said, mustering some excitement for the New Year's Eve party. "Carole, my friend from *Best's Apparel* on Fifth Avenue saved a pair for me from their warehouse." I held up a pair of nylons.

Franny smiled warmly, trying to boost my spirits. "You'll look fabulous in them, Sis. And don't worry about the jitterbug contest. You'll have plenty of admirers at the party."

Despite her encouragement, my heart still ached from

recent heartbreak. "It's hard to believe Dan was playing me all along. I thought we had something special. Life can change quickly."

"He doesn't know what he's missing. You're lucky Mama mentioned your reunion to Eleanor. To think that Dan had a fiancée at home all along. The nerve of him. Imagine if you hadn't found out about his deceit. You'd be writing him and pining away for a taken man. Some of these soldiers are scandalous. They want several women writing them to keep them company while they are away. You deserve someone who appreciates the amazing woman you're becoming," Franny said firmly, handing me my hairbrush.

"I know, but it still hurts. I trusted him, and he betrayed me." I sighed.

Franny consoled me, "I understand, Dawn. Tonight is about starting fresh and leaving the past behind. It's a new year, and a time for new beginnings. Maybe you'll meet someone worthy of you at the dance."

"Maybe."

Playfully, she added, "Besides, you should thank Dan for the experience. You'll know how to handle a real man when he comes along. Don't let yourself get hoodwinked again by a handsome face." Franny's anger was evident, but her words soothed the pain I felt from my recent betrayal.

"Franny is right, Dawn. You're a catch," Franny's boyfriend, Will Taylor, chimed in from across the room. He was a war hero, one of the famous Doolittle Raiders who had recently returned from Japan to boost morale on the home front. He and Franny had been dating on and off for years, and now that he was back from war, marriage seemed to be on the horizon. The best part? He treated all of us like his own siblings, but he hadn't asked Daddy's permission yet.

"Thanks, you two. I appreciate it. Let's make this New Year's Eve a night to remember." I mustered a smile and felt a bit reassured by their support.

With renewed determination, I finished getting ready. My hair was perfectly curled, and the nylons added an elegant touch to my outfit.

"Now, get to drawing my line up the back. Not all of us were lucky enough to score a fresh pair of nylons," Franny playfully demanded, handing me a black marker pen.

Chuckling at her request, I took the marker pen from her hand.

"You're right," I replied with a wink. "Now let's get you looking your best for New Year's Eve."

With a steady hand, I carefully drew a straight line up the back of Franny's leg, imitating the look of a seam on a pair of nylons. Franny had a talent for making the best of any situation, and I admired her positive spirit even during the nylon and food shortages of the war.

"There you go, Sissy. You look stunning. No one will ever know you're not wearing actual nylons."

Franny grinned, striking a playful pose. "Perfect. Who needs fancy nylons when I've got a talented sister like you?"

As we finished getting ready, I felt a powerful connection to my sister.

Despite the challenges of these times, we had each other, and that was a great source of solace. Tonight, the USO-sponsored dance took place on the deck of a dry-docked aircraft carrier, promising a memorable New Year's Eve, even without a date.

I wore my favorite Penny Foil dress, a navy fabric with a white collar and cuffs at the elbows. It was one of my first store-bought dresses, purchased with my hard-earned savings. The dress beautifully highlighted my small waist and curvy figure, while my kitten heels and red lipstick completed the look. I emulated the glamorous styles of Rita Hayworth and Ava Gardner by pulling my shoulder-length red hair into victory rolls.

Entering the USO party, the air was vibrant with laughter, music, and the lively chatter of young adults ushering out the old year and welcoming in the new. The dance floor brimmed with couples swaying effortlessly to the music.

Francis and Will grabbed my hands, pulling me toward the dance floor.

"Come on, Dawney. Let's show them how it's done," Francis said with a mischievous grin.

As the music enveloped us, I let go of my worries and allowed myself to get lost in the jitterbug. The joyful atmosphere surrounded me, and for a moment, I felt free from the heartache that had plagued me. Dancing with my sister and brother-in-law brought me joy by reminding me of the love and support I had in my life.

As the night wore on and I watched other couples laughing and dancing, a flicker of sadness crept into my heart. I longed for a connection, for someone to hold me close and dance with me like there was no one else in the room.

I pulled out my compact to powder my nose and looked at myself in the mirror. To hell with Dan. I'm going to dance with every eligible bachelor at the dance tonight, and maybe a few who are ineligible. My gray eyes turned a deeper shade of blue, which usually happened when I ignited my determination.

"Uh-oh, Franny. Your sister has got that look in her eyes. I hope these men are prepared for the tornado rolling into town tonight," Will laughed.

Suddenly, I spotted a tall, dark-haired man gliding across the dance floor, executing the most incredible Lindy Hop moves with grace and ease despite his lanky frame. I felt drawn to him, and my heart raced as I eagerly showed off my own dancing skills, hoping to catch his eye.

That's the one for me," I whispered to my sister, pointing in the direction of the tall, handsome man. It wasn't just his looks that drew my attention; it was also the way he danced, with a passion and gusto that few of the couples on the dance floor possessed.

"Ladies and Gentlemen, we are going to start the dance contest soon. If you need to be paired up with a partner, please head over and see us at the desk near the stage," the band leader announced before asking, "Would anyone not participating in the contest please also clear the dance floor. Thank you."

I looked over at the handsome man I'd set my sights on as he headed away from the dance floor. When he walked by, I acted as if I'd twisted my ankle and stumbled toward him.

"Whoa there, darling. Are you okay?" He grabbed my arm to stabilize me.

"I think the heel on my shoe has come loose. Will you help me over to my table?" I blinked up at my new friend.

"Sure thing, miss," he drawled in a husky voice.

"I'm Dawn," I said.

"I'm Ellis, now let me take a look at that shoe." He picked up my ankle as I sat at the nearest table. "Everything seems to be fine with the heel." Ellis winked.

"Great," I exclaimed. "Because you and I are about to win that dance contest."

Ellis threw his head back and laughed the sexiest laugh I'd ever heard.

"I admire a woman who knows her own mind."

I took his hand in mine and walked over to the sign-up table to enter the dance. As we waited in line, he revealed he was from a small town in Oklahoma, like Daddy. His striking blue eyes sparkled with a mischievous glint, and I couldn't help but feel drawn to him.

Ellis was truly a sight to behold. Tall and lanky, his

frame towered over most people in the room, but he moved with an easy grace that belied his size. His uniform hugged his body in the right places, accentuating his broad shoulders and slim waist, and he looked every bit the dashing hero from a romance novel.

As we chatted, his charm enveloped me, as if I'd become the center of his universe.

With his piercing eyes fixed on me, he shared his dreams of owning a horse ranch someday. "I'm pretty good at breaking in horses."

I couldn't help but imagine him riding a magnificent stallion through the rolling hills of his own ranch. I found myself staring at his muscular and capable hands, with calluses on the fingers that spoke to years of hard work. As we danced the night away, I imagined those hands running over the sleek coat of a powerful stallion, gentle yet firm as he guided the horse through its paces, and I couldn't help but wonder how they'd feel caressing my body in the same way.

Ellis possessed an irresistible charm that captivated everyone around him, and I was undeniably smitten by his magnetic presence. He laughed and joked a lot, with his contagious laughter bubbling up from deep within, and whenever he cracked a joke, his whole body shook with laughter. His eyes would crinkle at the corners and I found myself looking for any opportunity to make him laugh.

We danced until the wee hours of the morning, jitterbugging until our feet were blistered and our skin glistened with sweat. It was an unusually warm January night in Washington State. As the clock struck midnight, Ellis leaned in, and our lips met, sending a jolt of electricity between us. It was akin to the sensation of catching a shock from a metal doorknob on a windy day. The air seemed charged with an undeniable attraction, and for a moment, time seemed to hold still. It felt as though the universe itself held its breath, acknowledging the profound connection that had just ignited between us.

"I've never felt anything like that before!" Ellis exclaimed, before leaning in for a second kiss.

We didn't win the dance contest that night—we came in second—but I felt I'd won something even better. Ellis made my heart flutter in ways that I'd never felt before.

"How about a date tomorrow evening?" Ellis asked after we accepted our prize, a large tin of chocolate-covered toffee.

"I'd like that. We already know that we are wonderful dance partners, I'm curious to know what else we have in common. Can you come to my house tomorrow around lunchtime?"

"Like I said before, I do love a woman that knows her own mind." Ellis gently squeezed my hand. "Tomorrow sounds perfect. I'll pick you up at noon. And who knows, maybe we'll have the chance to dance again soon."

As I watched him walk away, I wondered, could this really be the start of something special, or was it just too good to be true?

Love Walked In

PORT ORCHARD, WASHINGTON

JANUARY 1945

Dawn Jensen

16 Years Old

O n the following day, a rare burst of sunshine pierced through Washington's usual grayness, and a robust knock reverberated on the door. On the porch stood Ellis, dressed to the nines, his charm more radiant than the sun itself. But what truly left me breathless was the transformation in his hair. No longer the midnight black I remembered from the ballroom, it now had shades of auburn, like the hues of autumn leaves. My heart raced, and before I could restrain myself, the words tumbled from my lips, "Ellis, your hair."

He chuckled, running a hand through his auburn locks.

"Did you think it was black?"

"It's dark, but it's still somehow red. It's nice," I responded.

"Thanks, Dawn. I guess you aren't going to be the only redhead in this relationship. This is for you." He handed me a beautiful poinsettia plant. "There weren't too many flowers this time of year."

"It's beautiful, Ellis." I kissed him on the cheek. "Let me place it by the fireplace, and I'll be right out." I was hoping to get away before my parents and Franny could come out and meet Ellis. I wanted him all to myself on this first date, and I knew that once Daddy and he got to talking, we'd never be able to leave for our date.

As I stepped onto the porch and into the sunlight, I noticed how Ellis' rosy complexion seemed to glow, and I found myself mesmerized by the way his freckles sparkled like stars in the sky. I knew I was in trouble. My heart was doing somersaults, and I couldn't help but feel drawn to this unexpected change.

"I couldn't have imagined that you're a freckled redhead," I admitted, feeling a blush creeping onto my cheeks.

Ellis grinned playfully, teasingly. "Well, we all can't have perfect creamy skin, can we?"

I playfully rolled my eyes, trying to hide my growing infatuation. "I guess not."

"Shall we, Miss Dawn? I've got a fun date planned for us." He offered his arm.

Curiosity piqued, I linked my arm with his, a mixture of excitement and nerves coursing through me. "Oh, do tell."

He led me to the *Virginia Inn* in the Pike District of Seattle, and as we chatted over a delightful lunch of fish 'n' chips, I found myself hanging on his every word. He told stories of his time spent breaking horses in Oklahoma, and I couldn't help but be captivated by his natural storytelling abilities. He also talked about his home in the same nostalgic way that Daddy did.

"So, you grew up on a reservation in Neah Bay?" he asked, leaning in with genuine interest.

"Yes. It was a beautiful place, surrounded by the ocean. I've always had a love for seafood, and the memories of the razor clams and cooking salmon on a cedar plank over an open fire are some of my favorites. I still miss my childhood best friend, Talie. I never did find out what happened to her... we moved around a lot in those days... we lost touch."

"That experience sounds idyllic. I can't imagine growing up with such a powerful connection to the sea. I never saw the ocean until recently."

"It was special," I said. "Now tell me how did you end up with a name like Ellis? It's unusual."

He paused for a moment, a thoughtful expression on his face. "Well," he began, "my Mama felt like she was treated less than by the whites in town. She wanted a name that stood for something, one that sounded important to the white man. She came across a story about Ellis Island when she was pregnant and knew that it represented hope and a new life. That's what she wanted for me... Although, I did get teased for having a girls name, the kids at school thought it sounded too much like Alice. Ellis in Wonderland, they used to chant." I noticed how Ellis had a way of not taking things too seriously and how he tried to find humor in every situation.

"That's beautiful, Ellis. Your Mama sounds like a thoughtful person."

As we continued to share our stories, Ellis moved onto his own origins. "My mother, Ruth, she was half Cherokee. Don't let my red hair fool you at all, I'm one quarter Cherokee and my Pa is a Scotsman, you'll love him, he tried to protect us all from discrimination. It wasn't easy for my mother, but they found stability in each other."

My curiosity piqued, and I asked gently, "How did she handle the tough times?"

Ellis sighed, his gaze drifting to the distance. "It wasn't easy, Dawn. She often felt caught between two worlds, not fully belonging to either. And then there was the boarding school."

"The boarding school?" I leaned in, urging him to continue. He nodded; his eyes clouded with emotion. "She was taken away from her family at a young age and forced to live in a boarding school. They tried to erase her culture and forbid her from speaking her language. It was a difficult time for her, and it breaks my heart to think about what she went through at such a young age. It made her resilient."

"I can't even begin to imagine how hard that must have been for her." A lump formed in my throat as I imagined the pain his mother must have endured.

"It was, but she was resilient. She never forgot her roots, her Cherokee heritage. She instilled that pride in me, too, and I'll be grateful for that. You must understand what that's like, growing up amongst the tribe of Neah Bay."

I reached out and placed a hand on his, silently showing my support. "I don't fully understand, but I do know one thing Talie taught me. Our skin does not remove our ability to love each other. As kids, we never thought of each other as different, we were all poor. I think our parents related more to the people of the reservation than the rich white folk we'd come across. They were looking down on us because we were poor. I only had two dresses growing up."

A glint appeared in his blue eyes. "Sounds like we were cut from the same cloth. Times were tough in Oklahoma too."

"Did your Mama ever share her other experiences with you?"

He nodded, a hint of sadness in his eyes. "Sometimes. She didn't talk about it often, but when she did, you could hear the pain in her voice. It's something that stays with you."

"How did it impact her life?" I leaned in closer, wanting to understand him better.

"It made her determined. She tried to break free, to prove that she could be more than what others expected, but she died young. She never fully got the chance."

"That's awful," I said, truly moved by his mother's strength and resilience.

"It is, but it's also a reminder of the injustices done to our people. It's why I feel strongly about treating others with respect."

"You're doing a great job of that. You know my classmates in Kent teased me about being a redheaded Indian whenever I talked about my time on the reservation. It made me mad," I said, feeling a surge of admiration for him.

"I wouldn't want to see you mad. Something tells me you're a force to be reckoned with." Ellis smiled gratefully, his hand squeezing mine.

At that moment, I knew this shared understanding was strengthening the bond between us, and I was grateful for the opportunity to know him on a deeper level.

After finishing our meal, he asked, "Where should we go next? Do you have to get home?"

"No, my parents let me stay out to all hours. Ever since my brother Bobby died... We should go get a drink. *The 5 Point* opened as the prohibition days were coming to an end. It was one of the first legal places to serve alcohol in Washington State. My brother Junior took me there once, they weren't very strict about liqueur laws, and I easily got served."

186

We made our way to *The 5 Point* Café, and as predicted, we had no problem getting served alcohol. As we sipped our drinks, Ellis shared more stories of growing up in Oklahoma, and I was fascinated by his life in Oklahoma.

We had a wonderful night and never ran out of things to talk about. Since both Ellis and Daddy were from Oklahoma, I had an instant connection with him. As we arrived at my house, I realized I was falling for this red-haired cowboy. He was nothing like the men I had dated before, but that only made me want him more.

After that first date, we were inseparable. If Ellis wasn't training, he was running all over Seattle with me. Ellis was lively and had the best sense of humor of any person I'd ever met. He had a gentle confidence, and I imagined it came in handy when breaking horses. I didn't know a lot about horses, but I knew they could spook easily. Because he grew up in rough circumstances, after the Dust Bowl years in Oklahoma, he wanted to make the best of his life. I admired that about him and felt the same way.

I didn't want to say I believed in love at first sight, but our meeting did feel like destiny. To think, I'd almost stayed home that night to nurse my broken heart. Now that I knew how it felt to really fall for someone, I realized my time with Dan was nothing more than an infatuation with the familiar.

I already felt closer to Ellis than anyone I'd ever met. Ellis almost seemed like one of my own family members, apart from the physical attraction I felt for him. We almost seemed to be able to read each other's minds and often finished each other's sentences.

Our connection deepened as the relationship progressed, and I cherished our attachment. As time passed, I didn't get to see much of Ellis once he continued his training. Ellis was able to attend the USO events and I treasured every stolen moment we had together. The world outside seemed to darken, and the thought of Ellis going off to fight weighed heavily on my heart. He never spoke much about his own fears, putting on a brave front, but I could see the uncertainty in his eyes whenever the topic of his deployment arose.

One evening, as the sun's glow gradually faded and the stars began to twinkle in the night sky, Ellis shared some upsetting news.

"Europe? That sounds dangerous, Ellis. Are you sure you're going to be in the thick of it, but you won't face enemy fire?"

Ellis nodded. "That's right. I'll be flying at higher altitudes in a specialized aircraft, I'll be away from the areas where enemy anti-aircraft guns are the most active. The chances of direct confrontation are much lower."

"But you're still fighting?"

"No, no, it's not like that. My job as an aerial photographer will mostly involve capturing images of enemy territory from the air. I won't be directly involved in combat but rather providing information to the front line decision makers. It's considered a relatively safe position. I wish I didn't have to go, but I enlisted before I knew you, and now I don't want to leave you," Ellis whispered, his voice filled with emotion.

"I know, Ellis. It's not fair."

Tears welled up in my eyes, and I struggled to hold back my emotions. "I don't want you to go either, but I know you have to follow your duty."

"I'll return to you," he vowed, his grip on my hand tightening.

Deep down, unease grew inside of me. The war was unpredictable, and the thought of Ellis being far away and surrounded by danger filled me with dread. I didn't want to lose him like I'd lost Bobby.

As we sat there, wrapped in each other's arms, the stars seemed to be dimming, as if mourning the impending separation. I tried to cherish the moments we had left and hold onto him tightly, but the uncertainty of the future hung over us like a dark cloud.

With a heavy heart I whispered, "Promise me you'll come back, Ellis. Promise me you'll be safe."

He pulled me even closer, pressing a tender kiss to my forehead. "I promise, Dawn. I'll do everything in my power to come back to you."

But as I looked into his eyes, I couldn't help but wonder if our love would be strong enough to withstand the trials of war.

Only time would reveal the answer. Would fate be kind to us, or would this distance tear us apart?

One Day

PORT ORCHARD, WASHINGTON

SEPTEMBER 2, 1945

Dawn Jensen

17 Years Old

"Dawn, you won't believe it. The war is over." Franny burst through the front door, her voice brimming with joy and lifting the weight that had burdened us for years. The news of the war's end washed over me like a long-awaited embrace.

"Turn the radio on. Let's see what the news has to say. Do you think Ellis will be coming home?" Franny, who had found a job as a painter's apprentice on the base and seemed to get news before anyone else.

Rushing to the radio, excitement bubbled inside of me

like never before. And there it was, the official announcement that World War II had come to an end. Germany had surrendered, and Japan following soon after. The world celebrated, and so did we. Tears of joy streamed down my cheeks as I clung to my sister, overwhelmed with emotions I could hardly put into words.

"Ellis will be coming home, won't he?" I asked, my voice trembling with hope.

Franny reassured me with a squeeze of my hand. "I'm sure he will, Dawn. Now that the war is over, the soldiers will be returning home, including our brave Ellis."

My heart soared at the thought of seeing Ellis again safe and sound. These past months had been a rollercoaster of emotions, not ever knowing if he was okay. Now I could finally look forward to our reunion. As the days passed, the news of the war's end spread, celebrations erupted all over the world. Our small town came alive with joyous gatherings, and elation filled the air.

Finally, the day arrived when Ellis was due to come home. Franny, Will—who was now Franny's doting husband —and I waited at the port with bated breath, scanning the faces of the returning soldiers, hoping to catch a glimpse of my Ellis. And then, there he was, stepping off the ship with that same charming smile that had stolen my heart.

"Ellis," I called out, running towards him.

He turned towards my voice, and our eyes met, sparking an unspoken connection between us. Without hesitation, I bolted for him, and his arms opened. The world seemed to fade away as we held each other tightly, my feet leaving the ground a little.

"I missed you, Dawn," he whispered into my ear as he lifted me up into a huge bear hug and swung me around.

"I missed you, too," I replied, my heart overflowing with love. I was beyond ecstatic to see Ellis, I tried to ignore the haunted look he had in his eyes.

As we walked home, hand in hand, Ellis shared stories of his time overseas—of the camaraderie among the soldiers and of the longing to return to the life he had left behind. We laughed and cried, cherishing our moments together. Amidst the laughter, I couldn't help but notice the heaviness in his voice when he spoke of some of the horrors he had witnessed during the war. His eyes would drift into a distant stare, and a shadow of pain would flicker across his face.

"You know, Dawn," he said, trying to mask the weight of his emotions as we talked, "I could use a drink right now." With a moment's hesitation, I pushed the image of Uncle Clarence getting drunk on the porch aside and hugged Ellis harder.

"Sure, Ellis," I replied with a smile, trying to be support-ive. "Let's get you that drink."

I couldn't shake the feeling that there was something deeper beneath Ellis's need for a drink. For now, I focused on the joy of having him back and the hope of building a bright future. Settling into civilian life would be the solution he needed, I hoped.

In the weeks that followed, we found our rhythm. One evening as we sat on the porch watching the sunset, Ellis turned to me with a glint in his eye. "Dawn, I've been thinking about our future. I want to build a life with you, to make each day count. Will you marry me?"

My heart leapt as tears of happiness welled up in my eyes. "Yes, Ellis, a thousand times, yes."

As we embraced, I knew the wars end had brought us together, and we had a chance to begin our lives together. We made plans for our future, imagining a home, a family, and the dreams we kept alive in our letters.

"Ellis, did you ask Daddy for my hand?" I looked up into his clear blue eyes.

"We can do it tomorrow night. I wanted to ask you first. Your opinion is the only one that matters to me. You waited for me all those months while I was away at war. I also want your help in picking out the ring."

Excitement and apprehension washed over me. Ellis's admiration touched my heart. He saw me as his equal, and I knew that this was the man I hoped to spend the rest of my life with. However, the thought of leaving my home, the place that held cherished memories stirred a feeling of uncertainty within my soul.

Amidst the joy of our engagement, I couldn't help but wonder how my parents would react when Ellis formally asked for my hand. My mind drifted to my father, a sweet and caring man who could also be intimidating. He had protected and guided me. As his youngest, we had a special bond. I wondered how he'd react to me wanting to get married. I was six months shy of 18, about the same age Mama was when she got married, while Ellis was 21.

Would Daddy approve of our plans, of the life Ellis and I wanted to build together?

PART TWO
Dawn Cameron

I am not afraid of storms, for I am learning how to sail my ship.

—**Louisa May Alcott,** *Little Women*

On The Beach with You

OLYMPIA, WASHINGTON
JUNE 5TH, 1946

Dawn Jensen
18th Birthday

T he courthouse doors swung open, and soft sunlight spilled onto the steps. My heart danced with excitement as Ellis and I stood side-by-side, ready to embark on this new chapter of our lives. In my simple white dress, I felt prepared for anything fate could bring our way.

"Are you nervous, Sis?" Franny asked, adjusting her floral dress with a playful grin.

I chuckled nervously, glancing at Ellis. "Maybe a little, but I'm mostly excited."

"Excited is good. You two are going to have a lifetime of happiness," she said, affection shining in her eyes.

Daddy stood tall, a mix of pride on his distinguished face. "I'm proud of you, Dawn. You've grown into such a fine, young woman."

His words warmed my heart. I reached for his hand and squeezed it gently. "Thank you, Daddy. I'm grateful for your support."

"Alright, it's time," Daddy announced and led the way inside.

The courthouse's interior was bathed in warm light, and I took a deep breath to calm my fluttering nerves. Ellis looked handsome in his military uniform, and our eyes met with an unspoken assurance that everything would be beautiful. The judge's voice resonated through the room, and I focused on his words. This was the moment we had been waiting for, the moment we would become husband and wife.

"Do you, Ellis, take Dawn to be your lawfully wedded wife?"

"I do," Ellis replied, his voice steady and full of love.

"And do you, Dawn, take Ellis to be your lawfully wedded husband?"

"I do," I said, my voice catching with emotion. The exchange of vows was a sacred dance of promises and commitments, and I felt the love between us grow with each word spoken.

"I now pronounce you husband and wife." the judge declared.

Ellis pulled me close, and as our lips met, a surge of joy filled my heart. We were married, bound in a union of love and devotion.

As we emerged from the courthouse, I looked at my husband, Ellis, and admired his easy grace, his uniform mirroring his vibrant personality. The hum of conversation buzzed around him, a testament to the happiness that surrounded this celebration. His presence was a magnet, drawing smiles and friendly nods from everyone.

Stepping forward into the spotlight, a playful glint in his eyes, Ellis' very presence commanded the attention of our assembled guests. "I have somethin' I want to say. Today is a day of love and happiness. And while I may not be the one wearing the fancy white dress," he winked playfully at me, earning a round of chuckles, "I'm honored to now be a part of this incredible family. I have not known you for long, but I do know Dawn. Any family that can produce such an amazing woman is one I want to be part of. And to my wife," he continued, his tone soft but resolute, "as I stand here today, I want you to know that I vow to be the one who shields you from life's storms, who holds your hand when the path gets rough."

As Ellis spoke from the heart, a comforting warmth enveloped me. His playful charm and the sparkle in his eyes stirred a tender affection within me. His expressed desire to join our close-knit family awakened a feeling of comfort I hadn't known I yearned for. When he spoke those solemn promises, my eyes met his, a silent exchange of love and gratitude passing between us.

"You've got a keeper there, Sis!" Franny enveloped me in a warm hug, her eyes shimmering with joy. "Congratulations. I'm happy for you. Where will you be spending your honeymoon?"

"Copalis Beach. It's like a hidden paradise," I replied, taking Ellis's hand in mine.

"Oh, that's going to be amazing, Sis!" Franny exclaimed.

WE ARRIVED AT COPALIS BEACH, LOCATED ONE HUNDRED miles south of Neah Bay.

"I'm glad we chose this spot for our honeymoon." It meant a lot to me to share this small slice of my childhood experiences with Ellis.

"It's gorgeous here." He took my hand in his and brought it to his lips in a tender kiss.

Over the next few days, we strolled hand in hand along the sandy shoreline, collecting seashells and making memories. Ellis had a natural knack for finding the most intricate shells, and he presented them to me like precious treasures.

"Look at this one," he said, holding up a delicate seashell with a soft, bluish hue. "It reminds me of the sunsets we've been watching."

"I'll cherish it forever," I replied, tucking the shell safely into my pocket.

In return, I introduced Ellis to the art of digging for razor clams and making clam fritters the way Talie had taught us. We took long walks along the beach with buckets and shovels in hand.

"Remember, you gotta be quick when you spot one," I instructed, crouching down to show him the technique. "They can burrow deep and disappear in seconds."

Ellis followed my lead, and soon enough, he was digging in the sand like a pro, his face lighting up with pride each time he unearthed a clam. We filled our bucket with the bountiful harvest, knowing we'd be savoring a delicious meal later that evening.

That last night at Copalis Beach, Ellis showed me how to build a campfire from scratch in a way I'd never seen before. After he got the fire going, he leaned in close to wrap his arm around my shoulders, and we gazed at the stars above. It had rained earlier in the day and the sky was crystal clear. Thousands of twinkling stars appeared, a blanket of diamonds dotted across the heavens.

"See that constellation up there?" Ellis said, pointing to a cluster of stars.

"Yeah, what is it?" I asked, trying to make out the shape.

"It's one of the few things I remember from my time with my mother. I was only three when she passed on. The Cherokee call it the Deer Constellation."

I felt a rush of gratitude for this glimpse into his past, for the way he trusted me with his memories and his heart. We shared more stories of our childhoods, our hopes, and our dreams for the future—the intimacy of the moment strengthening our bond even further.

I felt a profound love for my new husband as he leaned in for a passionate kiss and we ended up making love that night on the deserted beach, hidden by the darkness of the summer sky. We cuddled close under our warm blanket, Ellis stroked my back gently as he shared his dreams of one day owning property and having his own horses again.

"I have news to share with you, Dawn, and I want you to consider it. I wrote to my brother, Buck, to let him know we were getting married, and how I'd been honorably discharged from the Air Force. Well, I got his response on the day of our wedding. He was able to get me a job on a horse ranch. It would include accommodations, and we would only be a few miles from my family." Ellis was excited at the prospect of returning home. He promised me that things had started to pick up in Oklahoma, and that we would be happy there.

As I listened to Ellis's news, a wave of emotions washed over me. Part of me was excited at the idea of starting a new life on a horse ranch, surrounded by nature and being close to Ellis's relatives. It sounded like a beautiful opportunity, and I knew how much it meant to him to return to his roots.

Another part of me was hesitant. We would start our life together, true, but I couldn't ignore the sadness of leaving home. Washington had become a special place for us, filled with cherished memories. Daddy would love for me to see Oklahoma but leaving them would be difficult.

"If you don't want to go, I understand. I hate to spring this on you like this. I know your Daddy got me that job on the docks, and I'm willing to stay if that's what you want," Ellis looked deeply into my eyes.

His words tugged at my heartstrings. Ellis was willing to give up the opportunity at the horse ranch and stay with me if that's what I truly wanted. I felt torn between the adventure before me and the thought of leaving my relatives and the state of Washington behind.

"This could be an incredible chance for us. We'll have a home, a job, and my family close by. It's everything I've ever wanted. I hoped you would want it, too," Ellis continued.

His earnest eyes were brimming with love and sincerity. Ellis had sacrificed during the war, and I knew being back in Oklahoma meant the world to him. I tried to be a supportive wife, even if it meant leaving behind my own family and comfort zone.

"I trust you. If this is what you truly want, then I'm with you all the way. I'd love to see where you come from and get to know your relatives better, too," I said, placing my hand over my heart, my gaze meeting his with affection.

A smile graced his lips, and he pulled me close, wrapping his arms around me protectively. "Thank you. You have no idea how much this means to me."

Strawberry Wine

Dawn Cameron

18 Years Old

In the spring, our lives took a transformative turn as we embarked on our trip to Oklahoma. Daddy had generously helped us buy an old Ford truck, and Ellis, who had learned to drive during his deployment in England, finally owned his very first vehicle.

"Are you sure you remember which side of the road to drive on?" I playfully nudged him.

He shot me a mischievous grin, his eyes sparkling with amusement. "Heck, I might have started on the wrong side, but now, I reckon I can drive circles around you on any side."

"You think you're smooth, don't you?" I teased.

The road stretched out before us like an open book, filled with countless adventures waiting to unfold. Our destination was Hugo, Oklahoma, a place deeply intertwined with Ellis's origins.

Upon arriving at the homestead, Ellis's relatives welcomed us with open arms, making me feel instantly at home. Ellis proudly introduced me to his relatives. Buck, the oldest brother was tall and dark-haired like Ellis, he had a witty sense of humor that kept us entertained. Biggin was the gentle giant and Ellis' middle brother. He didn't speak much, but when he did it was usually something endearing.

We spent the first night with his older brother, Buck, and his wife, Daisy May. Their warmth and hospitality reminded me of my own family back home. We shared stories, laughter, and grew even closer as the evening progressed.

As night fell upon us, the men stayed up late, exchanging jokes and singing old country songs they grew up on. I couldn't help but smile, feeling grateful for being a part of this fun-loving family.

The next day, despite the imbibing of the previous night, Ellis was up early and brimming with enthusiasm. We hopped into the old Ford and drove about ten miles to the Diamond L. Horse Ranch. The vast landscape of southern Oklahoma spread before us, and I marveled at the lush greenery that contradicted the tales I'd been told of the Great Dust Bowl.

The state had truly recovered from those hard years when Daddy decided to come out west.

We parked outside, Ellis said, "Old Man Lockhart knows my Pa, and he's a fair but burly man. Don't let him intimidate you. The Diamond L. has been raising and training American quarter horses for thirty years. They are the fastest at quarter-mile races—that's why they call them quarter horses. I'll be breaking in any new horses brought to the ranch and eventually I'll be running the whole shebang."

Ellis and I stepped out, taking in the picturesque surroundings. The late afternoon sun cast a warm golden glow over the sprawling ranch, and the scent of hay and horses permeated the air.

A handsome man greeted us, but he didn't look like the man Ellis had been describing. "Welcome to the Diamond L. I'm Charles Lockhart, the ranch manager. You must be Ellis and Dawn."

"Nice to meet you." Ellis replied, shaking the man's hand firmly. "This is my wife, Dawn. We're excited to be here. Where's Old Man Lockhart?""

"He'll be out to meet you shortly. I'll be the one training you, for now. I'm his oldest son.

"Fair enough, either way, I'm ready to get to get started."

"Well, you two are in for an adventure here. And

speaking of adventures, I have someone I want you to meet." He motioned toward a husky young boy standing nearby, who had been busy tending to a group of horses.

"This is my little brother, James Lockhart. He's thirteen years old and has been raised around these parts. He'll be helping you both settle in and get acquainted with the ranch. If you two need anything, he'll be your errand boy."

James, a husky and energetic boy, approached us with a huge wide grin. His glasses hid his gaze, but they could not hide his huge green eyes. "Hey there. Welcome back to Oklahoma."

"I'm pleased to meet you. We're glad to have you as our guide," I responded with a warm smile, and Ellis shook the boy's hand.

As James helped us unload our belongings from the truck, he regaled me with tales of the ranch's history, the horses, and the many escapades he had experienced here. He answered all my questions with ease. His passions for the land and the animals were infectious, and he had me captivated by his storytelling.

"I'm sure gonna miss this place," James said wistfully, "My Daddy decided to move us to California, and I really don't want to say goodbye to all this."

Placing a reassuring hand on James's shoulder, I said, "Change can be tough, but remember, you'll carry these memories with you wherever you go. And hey, who knows, maybe one day, I'll come to visit you in California."

"Yeah, have you ever been there?"

"No, but I grew up in Washington State my whole life, and I even lived right beside the Pacific Ocean when I was a young girl. Have you ever seen the ocean?" I asked.

"I haven't, what's it like?"

"It's magnificent," I replied, my voice filled with memories, "The sound of the waves crashing against the shore, the vastness of the ocean stretching as far as the eye can see. It's both calming and invigorating. The salty breeze on your face, the feeling of sand between your toes. It's like being connected to something much bigger than yourself while also knowing it can swallow you whole with love, never to return."

James mused, "I've always wanted to see it. Maybe California won't be so bad after all." James straightened his glasses. "I've been reading about it. Do you like to read?"

"I do, and I love to write. There's something magical about getting lost in the pages of a book and letting your imagination take flight. And as for writing, it's like painting with words by expressing thoughts and feelings in a way that can touch someone's heart."

"I wish I could write like that," James admitted, a hint of self-doubt in his voice. "I need to get going, but I can come back tomorrow around three if you think you'll be ready to learn how to ride these horses."

"I look forward to it," I chuckled to myself.

"I'll see ya tomorrow." He called over his shoulder as he rode off.

What a nice young man, I thought to myself as I started

to unpack my belongings. I wondered when Ellis would be done with his first day as I unpacked. Things were quiet and I quickly realized I'd need to get a radio to keep me company in the day. I never lived on my own, and the house's quietness conjured shivers down my spine.

Later that night, on the front porch of our ranch home, Ellis and I savored the cool, evening breeze. Twinkling stars adorned the night sky, accompanied by the distant serenade of crickets and owls. Ellis poured us sweet strawberry wine, and we clinked glasses, feeling content.

"To new beginnings," Ellis toasted with a smile.

"Cheers," I replied, taking a sip of the delightful wine. It tasted like honey and sunshine, a perfect match for the enchanting evening. With a soft sigh of happiness, I leaned my head on Ellis's shoulder, and we both gazed up at the stars.

"There's something magical about this place, especially with you by my side."

"I'll take you shopping for supplies tomorrow, maybe buy you a sewing machine.

"That sounds nice, Ellis, but I think what I need is a radio. It will be nice to fill this home with music and listen to the familiar tunes that bring comfort to my heart."

"A radio it is, and I'll start my training after lunch tomorrow."

"Make sure to have me back by three. I have a riding lesson with James," I added eagerly.

"Don't worry, I promise to bring you back in time. I saw the way he was making eyes at you." Ellis teased.

"Oh, please. James is a young boy. I'd rather spend my time with you, listening to music and dancing around this cozy house." I playfully rolled my eyes.

Ellis embraced me warmly and continued to make our plans to explore the town together, shop for groceries and have lunch at a charming spot on the main strip.

Our love story had begun, filled with possibility and hope.

The next day, James joined me on the porch to introduce me to a beautiful horse for my riding lesson. After a fantastic morning exploring Hugo, I was thrilled to embark on this adventure. My morning activities in downtown Hugo with Ellis had left me excited to explore more of this charming town, but now I was transfixed by the beautiful horse I was about to ride.

"How was your first morning in Hugo?" James climbed off his horse and joined me on the porch.

"It was wonderful. Ellis and I had a great time exploring the town, and we even found a radio for the house. I'm looking forward hopefully I can get a sewing machine next."

"That's great to hear. I'm glad you're settling in well. Let's get you acquainted with this sweet girl. Her name is Buckles." He patted the mare gently, and she nuzzled against him affectionately.

James patiently guided me through mounting and holding the reins. As we rode around the ranch, my nerves vanished, replaced by a sense of freedom and connection with the horse blended. James praised my natural affinity with her, and we returned to the ranch exhausted and elated.

"Thank you, James. I had an incredible time," I replied, feeling a surge of gratitude. "I see why you love this place and the horses as much as you do."

As we entered my cozy ranch house for a glass of sweet tea, a feeling of accomplishment mixed with an ache for my sister, Franny, my closest friend. She wouldn't believe how well I rode.

"You did amazing out there," James complimented, admiration in his eyes."

"She's stunning," I said, my voice tinged with sadness as my thoughts had drifted to Franny, I felt an immense longing for my dear sister.

"Are you okay? You seem a little sad," James asked, concern showing in his gaze.

"I'm fine, just a headache. I might lay down for a bit," I assured him.

"Should I come back tomorrow at the same time?" James inquired.

"I should be ready for more riding tomorrow. Thank you, James." I dismounted and went inside to freshen up before preparing dinner.

A few hours later, as I sat at the dinner table, our dinner growing cold, a sense of panic gripped my heart. The minutes turned into hours and Ellis hadn't returned from work. Worry consumed my heart. He was rarely late without notice. I tried to dismiss thoughts of accidents, hoping it was only a small delay.

As the evening wore on, that fear intensified. I paced the kitchen, glancing out the window, hoping to see his truck. The once welcoming space now felt suffocated. Where was Ellis? Why hadn't he come home? What tragedies loomed on the horizon?

Don't Come Home A-Drinkin'

HUGO, OKLAHOMA
SUMMER, 1946

Dawn Cameron
18 Years Old

T he clock had long struck past midnight when the front door creaked open, and Ellis stumbled into the house. His footsteps were heavy and unsteady. I stood at the living room entrance, arms crossed in a tumultuous blend of relief and anger washing over me.

"Where have you been? Do you have any idea what time it is?"

"I was with the guys from the ranch. They insisted we grab a drink after the long day," he muttered.

"That's no excuse, Ellis. We moved across the country for a fresh start, to build a life together, and this is not what I expected." My anger flared, and tears welled in my eyes.

"I'm sorry. I didn't mean to stay out late. Time, it got away from me." His words were slurred and his glaze blurry.

My anger boiled over. "I thought something bad happened to you, Ellis. I won't live like this, wondering where you are at night as I sit home with no one to talk to."

"I promise I'll do better. It won't happen again." He staggered closer, attempting to reach out and touch me, but I stepped back, avoiding his touch.

"No, Ellis. This is not what I was expecting of our new beginning in Oklahoma. I left my home behind to build a life with you and follow your dreams!" I exclaimed, throwing my hands up in frustration. "I thought moving here would bring us closer, but I didn't sign up for this."

"I didn't think one night out with the ranch hands would be such a big deal, there's nothing to be mad about," Ellis slurred.

I shook my head, the weight of the situation heavy on my shoulders. "I left everything behind, my family, my friends, and my old life… But I can't help but think you're battling something. You know, when I was a child, we lost our home to a relative who drank too much. You remember the cabin I lived in before the one in Neah Bay? The one I loved? All of it was ripped out from under me and I won't stand by and let it happen again. I'm lonely all day and I look forward to having dinner together each night. You don't know what it's like for me. I need you."

The room fell silent, with the weight of my words hanging in the air. Ellis's drunken state had torn down the walls of a happy home we had built, leaving us standing on shaky ground.

"I'm sorry I scared you, Dawn," he finally whispered, his voice tinged with sadness.

"You are starting to remind me of my Uncle Clare. I can't watch you become him. I don't want to lose us," I replied, my voice softening. "But things need to change, Ellis. I've seen how drinking leads to worse in a single night. I've also seen someone become a better man after. Can we skip the burning part to get to the point where you become a better man?"

"I think you might be overacting a bit, but I understand why you'd be upset. I'm not your Uncle Clare." Ellis responded with tears in his eyes, we embraced, and I started to feel safe again.

Tears streamed down my cheeks. "I hope so, Ellis. Because I can't bear the thought of this beautiful dream slipping away because of you coming home drinking too much."

The next morning, we had a calmer discussion over breakfast. Ellis explained that this is what some of the men do here to blow off a little steam, but he wouldn't make it a common occurrence.

The tension from the previous night lingered, but there

was also a glimmer of hope. Ellis took a deep breath, his eyes filled with remorse.

"I'm sorry, Dawn. I know my actions hurt you, and I'll make sure to send word if I'm going to be late. I promise."

"And what exactly is that promise?" I clarified, sliding my hand over his.

"I'll be sure to send word if I'm going to be more than an hour late. Otherwise, you can come looking for me if you want."

I nodded, the weight in my heart beginning to lift as I saw the sincerity in his eyes. "Thank you, Ellis. I want us to be honest with each other and build a life together. One we can both count on. I want you to keep an eye on your drinking. Don't let it take over our happiness."

He reached across the table and took my hand in his. "I want to be the husband you deserve and the man who supports your dreams as much as you support mine. I'll try to cut down."

Later that day, during my riding lesson, I shared my concerns with James. I know I probably shouldn't have, but I was lonely and frustrated.

"You know, Ellis came home drunker than a skunk last night," I confided.

James listened attentively as I spoke, but he clarified, "Some of the men like to tie one on at the Saloon after work. It's something they do. sometimes they stay out 'til all hours. I'm not saying it's right, Dawn, but he said he's sorry.

Men make mistakes. What matters is how they move forward from them."

"You're right, James. We all have our flaws, I'm trying to be patient with him. Don't mention that I said anything to anyone about this. You know you're pretty smart for a thirteen year old?"

James looked up and blushed, a shy smile tugging at the corners of his lips. "Thanks, Dawn. I guess I've learned a thing or two from living here and spending time with my uncle and the other ranch hands. Now let's get back to this lesson."

I hoped James was right and went feeling hopeful, yet cautious about my future in Oklahoma.

March 21, 1947

My Dearest Dawn,
*   I was overjoyed to receive your letter! It feels like an eternity since you left Washington, and reading about your escapades on the ranch brought a big smile to my face. I can't help but feel a sense of excitement and a tinge of jealousy as I picture you riding horses and embracing the Oklahoma country-side. It sounds as if you're truly living the ranch life to the fullest! Have you visited where Daddy was born? I'm curious to know what it is like...*

Your account of the ranch and learning to ride horses sounds like those westerns Daddy watches. I can hardly believe Mama watches them with him. Mama and Daddy are doing well, but unfortunately our dear sweet Honey passed away shortly after you left. She made it to a nice old age of 12, we had a small ceremony for her and put her to rest by the river where you and I spent all those hours in solitude after we lost Bobby. Don't you worry about things here, Mama is already on a mission to get a new puppy and I think it will bring youthful energy to their house.

I was concerned to hear about Ellis's drinking getting out-of-hand. After what happened with Clarence when we were kids, I could see why it would bother you. Unfortunately, it's not uncommon. Many of the soldiers returning from war struggle with the bottle. We both know life isn't perfect and how tough it can be when the person you love faces their demons. Be understanding and patient with Ellis, he'll come around but most important, take care of yourself first. too! Focus on your marriage and getting to know your husband's people. Your sweet moments under the stars with Ellis, reminded me of the magical evenings we spent as kids, chasing fireflies and dreaming of our future. Well, sis, our future is here and it's not always going to be roses.

Your feisty spirit and determination have been an

inspiration to me. Remember, our beloved Jo and Meg from "Little Women" found their happily ever after and so will we! We deserve it, dear sister, and if you ever need someone to talk to, I'm forever here for you. Distance may separate us, but our bond is as true as ever!

I miss you dearly, and I can't wait for the day we can reunite, whether it's on the ranch or back in Washington.

In the meantime, keep embracing life with your fire within. Cherish those beautiful sunsets, ride those horses like there's no tomorrow, and know that you have a loving sister cheering you on from afar.

I'm sending you all my love and hugs, my adventurous sister. The children keep asking about their daring auntie and we eagerly await the day they can see you again. Until then, stay strong, and remember you have the strength to face whatever comes your way.

With love and sisterly affection,
Franny

PS. I'm painting up a storm, and Will is getting invited to speaking engagements all over the US. Everyone wants to meet the big war hero, the famous Doolittle Raider. Maybe we'll even make it to Oklahoma on one of his engagements.

. . .

MY SISTER'S TOUCHING WORDS STIRRED MIXED EMOTIONS within me, evoking longing for my family and the woods of Washington state. I started to doubt my decision to move that far from everything I'd ever known.

As spring gave way to summer, my worries gradually subsided. Ellis stayed true to his word, coming home promptly after work, or communicating otherwise. Often, we spent evenings strolling through the ranch, hand-in in-hand, admiring the sunsets over vast fields. Our connection felt stronger than ever, and I allowed myself to believe that we had overcome our rough patch. The blissful memories we built on the ranch brought immense joy, and the memory of our late-night argument seemed like a distant echo, fading with time.

However, the idyllic moments weren't destined to last, as another late-night escapade at the saloon unfolded. Ellis returned home, engulfed in an alcohol-induced haze, and his promises of change were forgotten. Soon, the communication stopped, too. It happened more frequently, and with each occurrence, my heart sank deeper. I tried to be patient and understanding, reminding myself of Franny's wise words about the challenges men faced after returning from the war. But his drinking became a bone of contention between us, threatening the happiness we found on the ranch.

Suddenly, the harsh reality hit me like a punch in the gut —This life wasn't for me. Each passing day brought a deeper acceptance of that realization. As Ellis drifted further away, his presence in our home was inconsistent. I found myself spending countless hours isolated, and the loneliness crept into my soul. The vastness of the Oklahoma's landscape was both beautiful and overwhelming, they amplified my isolation.

I yearned for companionship beyond that of a thirteen-year-old ranch hand, who was friendly but not quite the friend I needed. Ellis seemed more interested in his own pursuits than building our life together.

My evenings became the loneliest moments, with Ellis absent, drawn to the allure of the local saloon. I longed for the joy of genuine connections, meaningful conversations, and laughter with friends. With no one to turn to, I became like a stranded woman alone and often angry in this unfamiliar place. The walls of our home closed in on me, and the silence only magnified my time alone. I yearned for more and deep down inside, I knew I couldn't endure these endless nights of solitude any longer. The question lingered in my mind—what was Ellis thinking? This wasn't the life I had imagined, and I knew

I deserved more than this desolate existence in a place where I had no relatives of my own.

"I'm not happy here, Ellis. I hardly see you, and I'm lonely at night. I won't sit around and knit baby booties while you run around until all hours of the night," I raised my voice in frustration.

"You'll start to meet people at church, and you'll be busy soon enough when the little ones start coming." Ellis was referring to that conversation we had on our first night on the ranch.

I went to bed that night angry and had a restless slumber. The following morning, I began to devise my escape plan. I told Ellis one rare evening when he came home in time for dinner. "I'm riding into town tomorrow and doing some shopping. I want to get a few things to make the house homier."

"That will be good for you. Get the house set up how you want it, and you'll settle in. I'll leave some cash for you on the counter," Ellis said nonchalantly.

While in town, I called Daddy from the pay phone. I had to get out of this situation before I became pregnant and was tethered to this life forever. I knew if Ellis and I had babies in Oklahoma, it would be harder to leave.

"Dawn? What's wrong?"

"Daddy, I've made a mistake. The men on the ranch wake up in the morning and head off to the ranch. Then after work, they go to a saloon. Ellis doesn't come home until all hours. It's not what I thought, Daddy, Ellis isn't who I thought he was," I explained over the phone, barely holding back the tears that threatened to fall.

"Did he hit you?"

"No, nothing like that. I'm not the quiet woman that's going to sit at home while her husband runs around all night. There isn't much for me here, it's nothing like Washington, and I miss you all. I even miss the rain!"

"Come on home. If he loves you, he'll follow. The woman decides the type of treatment she'll accept. You're Mama never put up with no shenanigans, and neither should you. Remember, Ellis is a young man and bound to make mistakes. Don't be too harsh on him, but don't put up with any carousing either. No good can come from a man hanging in bars without his wife. Come on home if it gets too bad."

"Are you sure, Daddy?" I whispered into the phone.

"Yes dear, I'll wire you money for a bus ticket, and you come on home. We'll figure this out together," Daddy cleared his throat.

Once I had the money to escape, I wasted no time packing my suitcase and left for the bus stop the following week. A note on the kitchen table waited for Ellis whenever he returned home. I poured my heart out, explaining my reasons for leaving and where he could find the old Ford, parked at the bus stop with the key under the floor mat.

I loved the Ellis I knew in Washington. This other man felt like a stranger, and I would never find happiness in Hugo, not with him. Building a life like this with someone who wouldn't be around much wasn't what I signed up for. At nineteen years old, I had my whole life ahead of me. I couldn't bear to spend it feeling lonely while my husband hung at the saloon, getting drunk and neglecting me. This wasn't the happily ever after I had envisioned; it was a letdown of colossal proportions.

On that bus ride home, I had a lot to think about. I'd never known anyone who got divorced. I hoped Ellis would realize his mistakes and love me enough to give up everything to be with me on my terms.

Daddy and Mama were there to meet me at the bus stop, never mentioning my disastrous marriage. I moved back into my old room and got a job at the local drugstore. Women working outside the home had become more accepted, and I needed the distraction (and the money).

As days turned to weeks a lingering unease filled my soul, a feeling I couldn't quite shake off. My energy felt drained, and I wondered if I might be coming down with the flu. I often came home and took naps after work and could barely keep my eyes open during dinner. Mama, ever observant, noticed my exhaustion and approached me with concern in her eyes.

"When was the last time you had a cycle? You've had a glow about you, do you think you might be with child?"

Her words struck me like a thunder bolt. I hadn't experienced my monthly cycle since before we left for Oklahoma. In the midst of trying to convince myself it was merely stress-related, Mama's intuition tore through my doubts. The possibility of being pregnant filled me with conflicting emotions—excitement for the prospect of new life, yet the fear of the unknown and how it would alter my path.

As the days passed, I couldn't shake the feeling that something significant was happening inside me. My thoughts drifted between visions of a future with a child, one who might bring joy and healing to my fractured heart, and the harsh reality of facing motherhood alone.

More Than Words

PORT ORCHARD, WASHINGTON

DECEMBER 1947

Dawn Cameron

19 Years Old

E arly one rainy morning, a knock on the door made my heart race with hope. Not in the exhilarating way of my youth, but with a cautious anticipation that it might be Ellis. Nervousness amplified my anticipation as I approached the door, my pulse quickening with every step. When I opened the door, there stood Ellis, his eyes reflecting a mix of nerves and determination. He looked thinner, as if he had shed the weight of his past mistakes.

"Hey, Dawn," he said, his voice a blend of regret and hope.

"Hey, Ellis," I replied, keeping my emotions in check.

Ellis took a step closer, uncertainty etched on his face. "I've missed you. I came all this way because... because I can't imagine my life without you."

"I don't know Ellis. You hurt me deeply. I needed you, and you shut me out."

His hands clenched into fists as he looked down. "I know, and I'm so sorry. I was wrong, Dawn. I was stubborn and foolish, and I realized I can't lose you. I love you too much." Ellis looked down and fiddled with his wedding ring.

"Love is more than words, Ellis. It's actions too. We need more than promises." Tears welled in my eyes. "I haven't been to a doctor yet, but I might be pregnant."

"Pregnant? You could be carrying my child?" His eyes widened, and he took a step back in surprise.

"I think so, but if you want to be with me, it will have to be here. I won't go back to Oklahoma, knowing what tempts you there."

His eyes searched mine, desperation was evident in his gaze.

"I'll do whatever it takes to make things right. We can start over, here, in Washington. I'll find a job, support you, and be the husband you deserve."

Taking a deep breath, I tried to steady my racing heart. "Ellis, it's not about finding a job or starting over. It's about trusting and rebuilding what we had. I need to know that I can count on you again. You've got to cut down on the drinking."

He nodded, determination in his expression. "I promise, Dawn. I'll do whatever it takes to earn back your trust, to be the man you need me to be."

Tears spilled from my eyes, and I couldn't hold back any longer. Pulling him into a tight embrace, I whispered, "I want to believe you, Ellis. I want us to be a family, to raise our child together."

He held me close, his arms wrapping around me protectively. "I understand. We'll take it one step at a time, and I'll show you that I'm committed to making things right again."

A tap came from the door. "Is it safe ta come on in?"

"Oh, I forgot to mention, my brother, Biggin, is coming to stay. You don't mind, do you?" Ellis said, looking at me with hopeful eyes.

I placed my hands on my hips, pondering the idea. "For how long?"

I want this to succeed, you're my wife," he replied earnestly. "Having Biggin around won't change that. I'm committed to making it work, and I promise you, nothing will come between us again.

"Don't you worry, you won't even know I'm here, unless I need to keep Ellis in line, then everyone will know!" Biggin drawled.

Their words filled me with a sense of hope, and I knew that with his brother Biggin by his side, the pull of Oklahoma would no longer haunt him as much. I had admired Biggin. He was such a gentle giant, and he would be a protective uncle.

I enveloped Biggin in a warm hug, "Come here, big guy. But let's keep the drinking to a minimum, alright?"

"Strictly weekends only. We'll keep it under control, don't you worry."

The days that followed proved Ellis was true to his word. He found a job in Washington, working hard to support our little family. He was by my side during every doctor's appointment, holding my hand tightly as we heard our baby's heartbeat for the first time. My heart began to heal, and I allowed myself to embrace the possibility of love and happiness once more.

We found a three-bedroom house in Tacoma, and I was thankful it sat close to Franny and Will's place. Ellis found a job as a butcher, while Biggin took up a job as a mailman. During a visit to the Post Office to register our address, I was surprised to encounter a familiar face.

"Talie, is that you?" I exclaimed, unable to believe my eyes.

"Dawn Jensen, as I live and breathe?" Talie replied, equally surprised. Our eyes lit up with recognition, and we hugged each other like long-lost friends.

"It's Cameron now," I said, showing her my wedding ring. "I'm married to a wonderful man, and we're expecting our first child."

Talie's face beamed with joy as she came around the counter to envelop me in another huge hug. "Congratulations! I knew you'd find your happiness and I'd often wondered if our paths would ever cross again."

I ran my finger along the delicate shell necklace I wore around my neck. "I always wear it and wonder how your life has been. I'm sorry we lost touch."

Talie reached from behind the counter and pulled out a worn copy of *Little Women*.

"And I've kept this book close," she said, her voice tinged with nostalgia. "Remember how we used to imagine our lives unfolding like the March sisters'? It's been quite a journey, hasn't it?"

I smiled, touched by the shared memory. "It truly has, but finding you again feels like a page right out of our own story. I did write to you, but our address changed so much in those days, I never got a letter back."

"I married and left the reservation a few years after you left and never got them. But now that we've found each other, let's never lose track again." Talie clasped my hand in hers.

As we stood there, catching up on the years we'd missed, a notion of familiarity settled in as if no time had passed at all.

We talked of our childhood in Neah Bay, and we laughed about the mischief we got up to there. Talie was the same spirited, witty friend I remembered, and we picked up right where we left off.

"What are you doing these days?"

"I work part-time at the post office now," Talie said with a chuckle. "It's not as glamorous as being a writer, but it's a steady job. I enjoy it."

"I can see that. I miss those days on the reservation. Running around on the beach, digging for clams and dancing by the bonfire during the summer nights. Things seemed simpler then."

Talie sighed wistfully. "Life was slower, and we had all the time in the world to chase our dreams. You know, I couldn't wait to get off the reservation and see some other parts of this big ol' world after meeting you."

We shared stories of our families and the challenges we faced as young women finding our path in the world. Talie's love for her own family was evident, and she spoke fondly of her husband, Chuck, and their little one Frankie.

"You look happy, Talie."

"Thank you. I can't wait to meet this cowboy of yours. Can you come for dinner this weekend?"

As time marched on, our bond deepened, and I felt truly blessed to have Talie back in my life. She reminded me of our simple beginnings, the joy of cherished friendships. Once again, Talie's wit and strength became a constant source of light in my life. She was an inspiration to everyone around her, reminding us of the values we held dear.

As Ellis and I continued our journey as parents, Talie's presence enriched our lives in ways we couldn't have imagined. She offered unwavering support and was a connection to simpler times in Neah Bay that brought an inkling of peace and grounding to our busy lives that I hadn't realized I'd missed so much. Talie was the final puzzle piece, infusing a special spark into the life of contentment I'd been searching for.

The babies continued to come, and we found ourselves the parents of multiple children. Talie had three girls, and I had three boys named Buck, Bobby and Randall. We also had a daughter named Susan.

Chuck and Ellis grew close, and our families got together often. Those gatherings were full of laughter and stories. It felt as if we were once again those carefree girls running wild on the beach with the wind in our hair and the taste of salt on our lips.

Five years quickly slipped through our fingers, transforming our once-young babies into older children. Each day brought its own blend of joy and challenges as we built our life together in Tacoma. Yet, amid the routines that became our anchor, unexpected twists of fate brought surprises that tested our strength. Our journey was far from predictable, and every corner we turned held the promise of both joyous moments and heart-wrenching sorrows.

Dream a Little Dream

PORT ORCHARD, WASHINGTON
JULY 1951

Dawn Cameron

23 Years Old

"My Pa has died. I need to take the train to Oklahoma and go to the funeral," Ellis confided in me one morning. His voice trembled, and his eyes glistened with unshed tears.

I rushed to his side, wrapping my arms around him in a tight embrace. "Oh honey, I'm so sorry. But the train is expensive. How can we afford it?"

"My Pa had some acreage in Hugo. His will says we are to split it up between the three brothers. I'm going to get five acres. I plan to sell my portion to Buck. We'll have enough money to give us a fresh start and maybe even enough to buy a house," Ellis shared, his voice filled with both sadness and determination. I could sense his yearning to create a stable and loving home for us, to fill the void left by his distant relationship with George Cameron.

"Every cloud has a silver lining, I'm truly sorry about your Pa," I said gently, rubbing Ellis' muscular back for comfort. As we discussed our plans, the loss of Ellis' father weighed heavily on us. Ellis would travel to Oklahoma for the funeral and take care of selling his portion of the Cameron homestead. Meanwhile, I would stay behind, preparing for the arrival of our baby.

Unbeknownst to me, Ellis would return from Oklahoma with a proposition that promised to change our future forever.

"When I get back would you consider going on an adventure with me?" Ellis had that special glint in his eye.

"What do you have in mind?" I respond with excitement bubbling up inside.

"The Lockharts have built up a pretty good-sized construction company in a place called Pomona, California. Do you remember the ranch manager, Charles? We've kept in touch over the years, and he says there's lots of opportunity down there."

"Oh, Ellis, I don't know. Why do you want to leave Washington?" I asked, torn between the familiarity of my home state and the allure of possibilities.

"I'm tired of the rain and gloom. I didn't grow up this way, it gets me down sometimes. If you give California a try, I know you'll love it. The weather is perfect, and Charles says lots of Okies moved there during the dustbowl. We can come back to Washington if it doesn't pan out. Try it for three months, if you don't like it, we'll come right back to Tacoma," he pleaded, his eyes shining with hope and excitement.

Ellis' enthusiasm was contagious, and despite my reservations, I couldn't help but feel the enticement from a promise of journey and the idea of a fresh start held its own allure.

"You drive a hard bargain, Ellis Cameron." I chuckled with a glimmer in my eye. The prospect of change both thrilled and terrified me, but I knew deep down that I would follow him anywhere.

"I wanna build a life together, and I hear California calling," Ellis exclaimed, standing up from the couch and pulling me into a huge bear hug. His warmth and conviction enveloped me, and I couldn't help but believe in the vision he painted.

In the following weeks, excitement buzzed in the air as we planned our move to California. Ellis' words about the land of opportunity had piqued the interest of our dear friends, Chuck and Talie Fisher. They also caught the California bug, eager to embrace a new beginning, like many before us.

As the days passed, we savored the time we had left in

Tacoma, cherishing the memories we had created in this city. Our anticipation grew with the thought that soon, we would embark on a journey to establish ourselves in California.

With the arrival of spring, we prepared to bid farewell to the familiar streets and faces we knew, and since the Sunday before we left fell on Easter. Mama planned a huge sendoff dinner for us.

Everyone attended, Junior and Eleanor, Franny and Will and my oldest sister, Denise, who was head nurse over at Tacoma General Hospital.

Between Franny and I, there were five grandkids. Our families continued to grow and Mama loved to spoil them with Easter Egg hunts and baskets full of sweet treats.

We all gathered in Mama and Daddy's living room, the atmosphere thick with love. The soft glow of lamps created cozy pockets of light, illuminating our faces in a warm embrace.

Will, always one to get straight to the point, leaned forward, his gaze fixed on Ellis. "Driving all the way to California with kids in tow? That's quite the undertaking. Why not fly?"

Ellis exchanged a knowing look with Junior, who was already nodding vigorously. "Well, we've been considering it, but we figured a road trip would be more of an adventure. Gives us a chance to see the coast together, soak in all those sights along the way, and we can bring more of our belongings with us."

"Plus, Ellis is a master storyteller. Those little ones will be hanging on his every word." I jumped in, laughter dancing in my eyes.

I couldn't help but chuckle at the thought of Ellis regaling the kids with his tales from Oklahoma while we drove along the western coast all the way down to California.

Franny, cradling her youngest, nodded with a smile. "I think it's a wonderful idea. You'll remember this trip forever."

"And you'll be sure to check in regularly, I want to know that you're all safe and sound." Denise chimed in.

As the night wore on, laughter and conversation flowed freely, the anticipation of our impending journey adding to the excitement of our grand family adventure.

Ellis and I could feel the love and support from our loved ones, a reminder of the foundation we were leaving behind. Mama's warm presence and delicious cooking provided a sense of comfort that I knew I would miss dearly.

As the meal drew to a close, Mama brought out her famous Pig N' Whistle Cake, a sweet finale to our gathering. We savored each bite, the taste of home lingering on our lips.

After dessert, Ellis stood, a newfound determination in his eyes. "I want to thank all of you for being here for us, for supporting us in this new chapter. We're leaving with heavy hearts, but also with hope for what's to come. We'll miss you all dearly."

The next day, as we stood around the loaded truck, hugs and well-wishes filled the air. I looked at Ellis and gave him an encouraging smile. We were embarking on a new journey, alongside our dearest friends and a growing gaggle of kids.

Turning away from the porch, I caught Daddy's gaze, his eyes holding both pride and a hint of melancholy. He walked over and placed a hand on my shoulder, his touch steady and reassuring.

"Take care, Pickle," he said, his voice tinged with a quiet wisdom that seemed to cut through the noise of the world. "You're embarking on your next great venture, but remember, you'll always have a home here."

I nodded, blinking away tears, grateful for his steady presence and the love that flowed from him to all of us. "I'll remember, Daddy. We'll come to visit, I promise."

With one final round of farewells, we climbed into the truck, the engine rumbling to life. As we pulled away from the cabin, I stole a glance at Mama and Daddy's porch, wanting to etch the memory in my mind. This was the beginning of something new, and the promise of the open road stretched out before us.

The scenery transitioned from the lush evergreens of Washington to the breathtaking vistas along the west coast of California, where stunning beaches stretched out towards the horizon, their golden sands kissed by the gentle caress of the Pacific Ocean's waves.

"Alright, California, here we come." I gazed over at Ellis and our hands found each other, fingers intertwining, as we set off on a journey filled with hope for the opportunities and adventures that lay ahead.

California Dreamin'

POMONA, CALIFORNIA

MARCH 1957

Dawn Cameron

Almost 29 Years Old

Dearest Dawn,

My heart leapt with joy upon receiving your letter! It brought me great delight to hear that life in California has been treating you well and that you're happy with the decision you made in '51. Your happiness means the world to me, my spirited sister, and I pray that this letter finds you and your precious family in good health and high spirits. Write soon and let me know if Will and I can come visit in the summer. Will has bought one of those Airstreams and we are eager to come see you all.

I must admit, your news about Ellis's hours being cut has troubled me. Times can be challenging, I know, but you've been fiercely determined and full of fire. It doesn't surprise me one bit to learn that you've taken up hosting Tupperware parties to bring in some extra money. You're a force to be reckoned with, my dear, always putting family first and finding creative ways to overcome any obstacle.

Life in Puyallup has its usual routines and small-town charm. The weather has been typical for this time of year—dreary drizzles followed by bursts of sunshine that never last long enough. I must say, though, the thought of visiting you in sunny California has been lingering in my mind...

As for myself, I am still painting. Will is writing a book about his time in the war, and the children are thriving with their activities. We've come a long way from picking hops and running wild on Neah Bay, Sis!

I can't help but reminisce about the days when we were side by side, sharing laughter and secrets. My heart aches with longing to see you in person, to witness your unwavering resolve and the spark that ignites when you set your mind to something. It feels like an eternity since we were last together.

Time might have separated us physically, but our bond remains unbreakable. I yearn for the day when

I can board a train and head south to reunite with you and your fiery determination. I long to see my nieces and nephews, to hear their laughter, and to fill our days with endless chatter once more.

Until that day arrives, please know that you are always in my thoughts and prayers. You are the spirited flame that ignites my own determination, and I am forever grateful for your presence in my life.

With all my love,

Sister Franny

PS. Say hello to Ellis and the children for me. Send dear Talie and her brood my best and give everyone a warm hug from their auntie. Until we meet again, my heart is with you.

As I read my sister's letter aloud to Talie, I couldn't help but reflect on how far we had come since our move to California. All of our families had grown. I now had five children—Buckie, the oldest was born in 1948, Susan born in 1949, Bobby in 1951, followed by Randall and Rory in 1953 and 1958.

Talie also had five little ones of similar ages, and we both craved a much-needed respite from our time spent as dutiful mothers. Although money was tight, I was hopeful that work would pick up for Ellis, and tonight's event was the perfect opportunity to make money and let off some steam. My job required me to host home parties showcasing kitchen products, and tonight was special because, for the first time, I was hosting the party in my own home.

"Chuck, Ellis, you know the drill," I playfully shooed our husbands out the door. "Come back after ten. Tonight's for us ladies."

"You know where to find us? We'll be at 'Lucky Penny' until it's safe to come home," Ellis called over his shoulder as he winked, giving me a reassuring smile. Chuck, who had recently got a job at the local police department, laughed and gave a mock salute before closing the door behind them.

"Think they'll stay out of trouble?" I asked Talie.

"Not a chance," She responded, and we both broke out in laughter.

Even though money was tight, I couldn't help but feel optimistic about our future in California. Our husbands had grown accustomed to our routine—our little escape from the whirlwind of motherhood and household responsibilities. As their footsteps faded down the sidewalk, the air in the house seemed to change, carrying with it a newfound liberation.

Once the men were gone, Talie helped me make Margaritas as our friends and neighbors started to arrive, each carrying Tupperware catalogs and a contagious enthusiasm. Laughter filled the air as we gathered in the living room, savoring the joy of being together without the kids.

I poured the margaritas into glasses and couldn't help but giggle knowing that these Tupperware parties were more about getting tipsy on cocktails and gossiping than the items I sold. It was a fun way to make a little extra money and a good excuse to get away from the house and kids every so often.

"Here's to a night of fun, ladies." I held my glass up to our small gathering in the front room.

Suddenly, there was a knock on the door, and a glamorous blonde entered the room. My neighbor, Stephanie, raced to open the door. "I hope you don't mind, ladies. I invited my cousin, Janice."

Janice Dixon was a vivacious addition to our group, and her infectious laughter quickly blended with ours. Throughout the evening, we shared stories of motherhood, life in Pomona, and dreams for the future. The Tupperware catalogs lay mostly forgotten as we bonded over the camaraderie of sisterhood.

"Would you like another margarita?" Talie motioned toward the blender.

"Oh, Stephanie, you didn't tell me Dawn had a servant," Janice slurred, silencing the room enough to hear a pin drop.

My face turned red as I was about to put this tipsy newcomer in her place, but before I could say anything, Talie made her way over to Janice with a margarita in hand and a smile on her face.

"You seem to be confused, dear. I am Talie Claplanhoo

Fisher, and I come from the Makah tribe of Whale Hunters. Chuck, my husband, is a police officer in this area. I am not a servant to anyone."

Stephanie was horrified when Janice responded, "How sweet. Do they allow your kind onto the police force?"

"Stephanie, I didn't realize your cousin is rude and ignorant," I chimed in. "It's quite evident you're not used to encountering someone as culturally rich and radiant as Talie here. She's more than a friend, she's like a sister. While you're stuck in your narrow-minded bubble, Talie embraces her heritage with pride and grace. While you are in my home you will not disrespect my oldest friend."

"Now let me serve you your margarita, dear." And just like that, Talie poured the contents of her glass right over Janice's head.

"I think we should leave. I'm sorry about this. My cousin has apparently had a little too much to drink." Stephanie jumped up and led her soaking-wet cousin out the front door.

"I'm sorry to ruin your party, but I know her. Her boys are the ones that have been bullying our kids at school. It looks like the racist apple doesn't fall far from the racist apple tree. Her boys have put mine through hell with all their taunting and Mama Bear came out."

"Talie, I'm sorry. I didn't know that was happening. That's terrible. She deserved every drop of that margarita. I hope it turns her hair pink." I turned to the rest of our guests, trying to salvage the night. "Let's not let one wet bigot ruin our good time."

The party continued without a hitch. I felt terrible about Janice's snide remarks and wondered if Talie had to deal with people like that often. I reminded myself to ask her about it the next time we were alone. For now, it would be another unpleasant thing to lock away and think about later.

The people who remained at the party were there to have a good night away from their husbands and children. With every sip, the room buzzed with stories and laughter. Talie and I talked about how happy we were living in California and how we had truly found our own little piece of paradise.

"Despite that snob, Janice, I love your neighborhood," Talie exclaimed.

"It's like a close-knit community where everyone looks out for one another. Everyone else went out of their way to make me feel welcome, despite the few odd people being rude."

"There's always one bad apple in the bunch, and you took care of her." I chuckled.

"Oh, you bet I did! Don't mess with me or my kids, especially when I have a drink in my hand." We both burst out laughing over the incident, feeling our bond growing stronger.

The rest of the night, we gossiped, shared recipes, and celebrated our lives in California. It was more than a party; it was a testament to the newfound happiness we had discovered together. The children were having a sleepover at Talie's house, one town away, giving us a rare night to let our hair down. As the hours passed, the margaritas flowed, and our spirits soared. The night seemed magical, reminding us of the importance of taking time for ourselves amidst the responsibilities of family life.

When the clock struck ten, the men returned, finding us all in high spirits with smiles that lit up the room.

"Looks like we missed quite the party," Ellis chuckled, his eyes dancing with amusement.

"You have no idea," Talie said, winking at me, and we all erupted in laughter.

The party had transcended its original purpose, becoming a cherished tradition of bonding, laughter, and the celebration of friendship. I knew that I had found the stable life I'd been looking for, and the future was filled with hope and promise. But life was a constant ebb and flow, a roller coaster of experiences, and in a small corner of my mind, I knew that the peace and stability might be too good to last forever.

Stormy Weather

Dawn Cameron

30 Years Old

"Careful there, young chef," I affectionately guided our oldest son, Buckie, who was meticulously measuring flour into a mixing bowl. "You've got a great helper in Bobby."

Buckie's face lit up with a proud smile, his eyes sparkling with a mixture of excitement and camaraderie. "He's a natural chef, Mom."

"And he's not afraid to let us know if something doesn't meet his high standards," Susan chimed in. My oldest daughter had a demeanor that was sweet yet assertive, reminiscent of Franny at that age.

"Up Mama, up!" Our youngest, Rory, was trying to climb out of her highchair and doing her best to get my attention as the rest of us were gathered around the countertop. We were immersed in the cherished ritual of making Grandma's famous Pig 'n Whistle cake.

"Did you know that my Mama used to make this same cake for all of our birthdays?" I interjected, as I picked up Rory in my arms. "She believed it brought luck and happiness to anyone who prepared it. Your Grandma had a way of making everything feel magical."

Randall, our youngest son, had been rearranging the ingredients on the counter to his liking. He seized the opportunity to contribute, "Well, I think this cake is destined to be the best one ever. I can practically taste the magic already."

"Of course, there's going to be magic. We're Camerons, after all, descended from the medicine people of the Cherokee nation." Susan continued to mix the batter as she gave her opinion on the matter.

"I see Daddy's been telling you some of his old stories from Oklahoma." Buckie's nurturing instincts came to the forefront as he gently patted Susan's shoulder.

"That's right, and it's not just the stories, but the heart of our ancestry that's passed down to us. Our heritage is like the secret ingredient that makes everything we do special." Susan added.

As the cake began to take shape under our collective efforts, the kitchen filled with lively conversations and love.

Each child brought their distinct personality and skills to our household. Buckie's careful consideration, Susan's decisive direction, Bobby's gentle soul, Randall's unwavering resolve, and Rory's infectious joy all melded into a delightful and happy atmosphere.

"Looks like the Cameron's are crafting a masterpiece." Ellis entered the kitchen, his presence infusing a touch of warmth into the already cozy room.

Susan's eyes danced with a mischievous spark. "Daddy, you're not supposed to be in here yet!"

"The aroma was too inviting to resist. I must be the luckiest man to be surrounded by such room of good-looking cooks."

"Happy Birthday, Daddy!" George seized the moment to proudly hold up a spoon.

Ellis quirked an eyebrow in a manner of mock surprise. "Why, thank you, my son."

As the cake baked, we settled around the kitchen table in anticipation for the upcoming celebration. My heart swelled with gratitude, and the unbreakable bond that held our family together felt more robust than ever. Gazing at our children, each uniquely wonderful in their own ways, I couldn't help but be overcome with profound thankfulness for the life Ellis and I had created.

As the laughter and excitement continued to fill the kitchen, a sudden ringing cut through the air, momentarily silencing our jovial time. Susan picked up the phone from the wall, her expression a mix of surprise and concern.

"Dad, it's Buck, your big brother, calling from Oklahoma," Susan announced.

The once bustling kitchen was still as Ellis got up to take the call.

When Ellis ended the call, his expression bore the weight of the conversation. The atmosphere had shifted, leaving behind a heaviness in the air.

"Dad, is Uncle Buck alright? He didn't sound good." Susan, who normally exuded unwavering confidence, was the first to vocalize our collective concern.

Ellis raked a hand through his hair, weariness, and sadness evident in his gaze. "Buck called to wish me a happy birthday, but he's been battlin' cancer for over a year," he confided, his voice tinged with the heaviness of the news. "His condition has worsened, and hearing him like that… It's incredibly tough."

A hushed silence seemed to stretch on as the weight of the word 'cancer' hung in the air. My hand found its way to Ellis's arm, offering a wordless gesture of solidarity. "We're here for you, Ellis. Whatever you need."

"Thank you, sweetheart. It's just… Buck's been the pillar of strength in my family. Hearing him vulnerable like that is difficult."

"Maybe we can send him our thoughts and prayers, Dad. Perhaps that will help." Bobby glanced up at his father with his innocent blue eyes.

A wistful smile formed on Ellis's lips as he looked at our children. "Thank you, son. That means a lot."

The call from Oklahoma had cast a shadow over our celebratory mood, a stark reminder that life could change on a dime. As I held Ellis's hand across the table, I was reminded that our journey, though marked by happiness, was also rife with challenges.

"Dad," Susan's voice had softened into a soft tone of empathy. "We're here for both you and Uncle Buck. Maybe he'll get better soon."

"I appreciate that, Sweetpea. Unfortunately, I don't think that's the case."

In the ensuing days, I noticed subtle changes in Ellis. He seemed more distant, preoccupied, and I often caught him occasionally staring into space with a far-off look in his eyes. I wanted to ask if there was more than his brother's poor health bothering him, but a part of me feared the answer. Instead, I tried to be a supportive and loving wife, hoping that his troubles would pass with time.

But it didn't.

One evening, I found Ellis sitting in his favorite armchair, smoking a cigarette with a half-empty bottle of whiskey by his side. His shoulders were slumped, and his eyes held a weariness that tore at my heart. "Ellis, what's going on?"

He hesitated, as if battling with himself, before finally speaking.

"I'm about to lose my job. They sold the company, and I'm one of the casualties."

It felt like my stable world had suddenly shifted. The

storm that I had sensed on the horizon was raging in full force, threatening to tear apart the life we had built. I tried my best to hold it together, to be the strong one for both of us, but it was taking a toll.

"Oh Ellis, you'll find something else. I'm sure of it." I proclaimed.

I found myself torn between wanting to help Ellis through his struggles and desperately holding onto the stability I had worked hard to achieve. The fear of losing everything we had built together ate away at me, but I refused to give up without a fight.

I prayed that somehow, we'd find our way to calmer waters. Little did I know that the true test of our love and resilience was about to begin, and the path ahead would be more challenging than anything we had ever faced before.

Cry To Me

POMONA, CALIFORNIA
JANUARY 1959

Dawn Cameron
30 Years Old

T he news of Ellis losing his job was a heavy blow, hitting us at the worst possible time. The company's offer to keep him on with a pay cut and a new manager didn't sit well with his pride. Ellis took the two weeks' pay offered, believing his experience would land him another job quickly, but fate had other plans and with each passing week, hope seemed to fade.

Ellis's once vibrant and joyful demeanor started to change. His visits to the local bar increased again. The news of Buck's declining health and eventual passing shook Ellis to the core. Dealing with the dual loss of his job and his big brother took a toll on Ellis's spirit. He became irritable and distant, snapping at me and the children over trivial matters.

Desperate to help our family stay afloat, I started booking more Tupperware parties and luckily, my oldest daughter was able to watch the young ones while I worked elsewhere in the evenings. The income was meager, but it kept us going while Ellis searched for opportunities. My decision to work more often caused some unexpected tension in our marriage.

Ellis couldn't appreciate me being the sole breadwinner, and it drove a wedge between us. "I'll come and go as I please," he said to me one night after I asked him to stay home with the family.

"This is our home, not some flop house. I don't want you coming home drunk at all hours. I left you in Oklahoma over this, remember? Don't do this to me again. We have children, and it's not good for them to see you like this."

"They don't have to. I'm leaving. You don't need me now that you have your fancy job, gallivanting around town attending your lady parties." His nostrils flared in angry huffs.

"You know that's for a bit of extra money, and so what if I enjoy it! What I really need is for you to get your act together, Ellis. We aren't a couple of kids anymore. Drinking your life away isn't helping anyone," I proclaimed.

"I need some time to cool off." Ellis headed for the door, and my heart pounded in my chest. He had never walked out after a fight before. Silence lingered as he stormed out, the door a newfound escape.

Days quickly passed by, but there was no sign of his return. My heart held a mix of panic and relief, an iron weight in my chest. Not living at Ellis's whims was a relief, yet my mask for the children threatened to crumble under the mounting pressure of being a single mother. I'd held onto the belief that everything would be alright as long as my family was together, and with Ellis gone I felt like a ship lost at sea.

As the end of the first week without Ellis approached, my anxiety grew. A letter from him arrived. He was in Hugo, promising to send money for the rent, but I was left with a lingering doubt about him keeping his word. The weight of our financial burden felt unbearable, and I prayed for a miracle to pull us through. Nightmares of the poorhouses I'd heard about growing up filled my nights as I wondered how I'd make it without a father for my children.

How could Ellis let me down in this way?

In an attempt to distract the kids and myself from the stress, I decided to take them for haircuts at the new barbershop in town. As we entered, a familiar Oklahoma accent greeted me.

"Well, I'll be. Did Dawn Cameron decide to make an appearance in my humble, old barbershop?"

"James Lockhart?

"You do remember me?"

The once husky, thirteen-year-old boy had grown into a

strapping, handsome man. I'd heard he was in town but had no idea he had turned out to be that good looking. After he finished with my children's hair, we settled on a cozy bench to catch up on old times. Like years ago in Oklahoma, I found myself opening up to him about our struggles, and James empathized with our situation.

"You're doing an incredible job. Ellis doesn't deserve you," James said, giving my hand a comforting squeeze. "And you don't have to do it alone. I'm here for you, and so are many others in town. You have people who care about you here."

"That means a lot. Thank you for being my shoulder to cry on. It's been tough, but I'm trying my best to stay strong for them. But enough about me, is there a Mrs. Lockhart in your life?"

He took a deep breath, as if gathering his thoughts.

"Naw, I've just broken up with someone… You know, when I was younger, I had a bit of a crush on you. I was devastated when you left the ranch so suddenly to move home," he admitted with a shy smile. "I never had the courage to say anything, and I know it's not the right time to bring it up, but I wanted you to know you're as pretty as ever."

I was taken aback by his confession, my cheeks flushing.

"Oh, James," I said softly, touched by his honesty. "You were such a kind and caring young man."

He smiled, relieved that I didn't seem upset by his revelation. "I'm here, and I'll be here if you need someone to talk to or lean on." The genuine care in his eyes melted my heart with gratitude.

"I'll remember that."

"Would it be okay if I took you and the kids for a picnic?"

That weekend, James took us to Lake Puddingstone. The sun's reflection on the water stirred memories of my childhood by Neah Bay. James's easy-going nature and genuine kindness endeared him to my children, creating a special kinship between them. I found myself drawn into James's understated charm. We had shared good times before, and I wondered why our paths hadn't crossed until now.

As we relaxed by the lake, I turned to James, curiosity in my eyes, and asked, "How did you come to own the barbershop?"

"After I joined the Air Force, I thought flying would be my passion. I had this vision of soaring through the skies but as it turned out, flyin' wasn't quite what I expected."

"How so?" I questioned.

"It wasn't how I thought it would be. Turns out, I like my two feet here, safely on the ground. When the opportunity arose to train as a barber, I jumped at the chance without hesitation. It felt like a calling or a sign that this was my path. I saved every penny, and when my tour of duty was up, I came to Pomona and opened my own shop."

Listening to James's story, my admiration for him grew.

It took courage to change careers after dedicating himself to the Air Force.

"That's wonderful," I said, gazing into James's striking green eyes, which bore a resemblance to Elvis Presley, albeit with lighter hair and captivating green eyes. His handsome features intrigued me.

Our conversation flowed effortlessly, and stealing glances at him sent a flutter of excitement through me. "Thank you for inviting us out. Since Ellis left, I've been feeling lonely for adult conversation."

"I can imagine it must be tough," James drawled, his voice gentle and understanding. "But you're an incredible mother, and still beautiful. I can see the love you have for your children. They're lucky to have you." James softly gripped my hand, and his genuine compliment warmed my heart.

James started coming over on Fridays, bringing groceries and staying for supper. I felt a closeness to him that transcended age and circumstances. I felt a connection to him, and I had a feeling he felt it too. Could this younger, handsome man be interested in me, a mother of five?

"HELLO?" I ANSWERED THE PHONE LATE ONE EVENING, MY voice filled with both surprise and apprehension. "Ellis, is that you?"

He was distant, and the line was unstable, but it was Ellis on the other end of the line

"I'm still in Oklahoma, I have a job here."

"What about us? When are you coming back?"

"I'll be sending money for the rent when I can," he replied before the call abruptly ended.

Reeling from my call with Ellis, I knew the only solution was to call Daddy. He'd know how to get me out of this mess. I dialed my parents' number, and after a few moments, I heard his familiar voice.

"Daddy, I need to talk."

"The last time you said that it meant coming home. Are you coming home again?" His voice sounded exhausted and weary.

"Not exactly. But Daddy, you don't sound good. Is everything alright?"

"I didn't want to worry you, it's a small bout of walking pneumonia. The doctor said I'll be good as new. I need to rest up a bit. Tell me about your problem."

"Oh, Daddy, are you sure you are all right? How long have you been sick? Maybe I should come home."

"You'll do no such thing. I'm a stubborn old man, and it will take more than a little cough to do me in. What's troubling you?"

"Ellis… has run off to Oklahoma, and he's not himself. He's drinking again. I don't know what to do." There was a brief pause on the line, and I could picture Daddy's furrowed brow as he carefully contemplated his response.

"Listen. You're a grown woman," he began, his tone both loving and firm, "with a family of your own. It's time to stand on your own two feet and take care of yourself and the kids. I know you can make it with or without Ellis."

Tears welled up in my eyes as his words sank in. I knew he was right, but it was hard to accept.

"But what about Ellis? What if he needs me?"

"I understand how you feel, but you can't fix him, Daddy drawled gently. "Sometimes, folks gotta find their own way, even if they gotta do it alone. You'll make it through. I won't always be here for you to come runnin' to. You need to trust your instincts."

His words hit me like a heavy weight, and I swallowed hard, trying to hold in the tears.

"I want our family back together."

"I know you do, and maybe that'll happen." Daddy cleared his throat, his voice filled with compassion. "But right now, you need to focus on takin' care of yourself and the kids. You're a strong one, Dawn. You'll do whatever it takes to survive."

Sweet Surrender

POMONA, CALIFORNIA

SPRING 1959

Dawn Cameron

30 Years Old

S urrounded by the aroma of brewing coffee and a tangible air of tension, I confided in my oldest friend, Talie Fisher, the overwhelming feeling that everything was falling apart.

"It feels like everything's falling apart. Ellis is gone, and with Daddy ailing… I'm just so overwhelmed."

"You'll make it through." Talie held my hand in hers as she gazed into my eyes. "You've been through harder times than this, and we'll survive anything life throws at you, together."

My confession carried the weight of my troubles, and the storm on the horizon felt all too real.

My voice wavered as I shared another secret, both a lifeline and a pitfall.

"James has been stopping by, offering help. It's like his presence fills this void inside me, this loneliness I've been trying to shake."

"Be careful, you're playing with fire. You know, Chuck got a phone call from Ellis yesterday. He asked Chuck to look out for you. Ellis has found employment in Oklahoma, and he's coming back soon as he has enough money to start his own business," Talie replied.

This news hit me hard. I couldn't believe Ellis would share his plans with Chuck and Talie but had failed to share them with me, his wife.

"Well, if he's coming home, he'd better let his wife know his plans," I said with more fire in my voice than I meant to show. "Did he give Chuck any sort of time frame? It could take months before he has enough money for that." I felt like my whole world was crashing in.

"He didn't. I'm sorry to be the bearer of this news, but you know I love you, and I'm here for you. No matter what."

"I know, I'm sorry I snapped at you. You are my best friend and love you, too. I wish Ellis had called and told me this sooner. Before I had gotten close with James. I think I've started to fall for him."

"Take things slow. Maybe Ellis will come back, and you can sort things out. I don't want to see you getting hurt."

I knew Talie was a good friend, but I didn't heed her warning. My visits with James became the highlight of my week. After nearly two months with James coming around every Friday evening, it was no surprise what happened next.

"How are you holding up? Any news from Oklahoma or Washington?" James and I sat on the back porch, sipping strawberry wine on the warm September evening. The children were in bed after a tasty spaghetti dinner, and my oldest daughter had handled putting the younger ones to bed.

"I'm tired," I admitted. "Daddy is doing good. Mama's feeding him enough chicken soup to feed a small village."

"Any word from Ellis?" James leaned forward.

"Not in weeks. He seems to keep in touch with Chuck Fisher, though." I twirled my hair in contemplation.

"You know, you have other options if he doesn't want you. Someone else here does." James held my hand, his desire for me evident.

Feeling lonely and uncertain about raising my five kids alone, I found myself at a crossroads. Resting my head on James's shoulder, I felt desired and safe.

I snuggled in closer as James gently turned his head towards mine, cupping my chin in his hand. I looked deep into James' emerald-colored eyes. I saw not only the desire within, but also a future for myself and my children. This was a dependable man that wanted me.

He leaned in for a passionate kiss, and I felt a spark inside that I hadn't felt in a long time. I was shocked that this younger man was attracted to me in this way. I know my body wasn't what it used to be, after my five pregnancies. Now that I was a single mother, I was feeling worn down by the burdens of facing life without a partner. This kiss reignited something deep within me, making me feel sexy and wanted again.

We lost ourselves in each other's embrace, savoring the taste of forbidden passion. The chemistry between us was undeniable, and I managed to push the guilt away as I gave into the pleasure of my flesh. In James' embrace, I felt wanted again. The recent rejection from my husband amplified my desire. After we spent that first passionate night together, things quickly progressed, and I couldn't find it in me to suppress my need for companionship and intimacy.

The following week, I finally called and confided in Talie about my intimacy with James. "You know, something happened between James and me."

"Oh, Dawn, no. You didn't." Talie's voice reflected both surprise and concern. "I can't believe you crossed that line."

I sighed as I dropped my head into my hands. "I know, I know. It just… happened. I never intended for things to go this far, and I've agreed to meet his parents tonight for dinner."

Talie's voice softened with understanding. "You've been

through so much, it's only natural to seek intimacy where you can find it. But you have to be careful. This could end badly for everyone involved. Especially if Ellis comes back. He'll rip James apart."

"Ellis is the one that ran out, but why do I feel guilty?" I responded.

"Because you're a good person. You love your husband, and he let you down. I'll let you know if Chuck hears from him again. Life is easier when you have the embrace of a man that loves you."

"Thank you for your understanding, Talie."

Later that night, James and I approached his parents' cozy, two-bedroom house, my heart aflutter with nervous anticipation. The Lockharts greeted me with genuine warmth, their Oklahoma hospitality shining through. If they had any reservations about their youngest son dating an older woman with a husband and children, they kept them well-hidden.

After dinner, we ventured to James's little apartment over their garage. A mix of curiosity and anticipation filled me as I stepped inside. The cozy studio apartment, a pull-out sofa, a threadbare armchair, and a record player—the books scattered around, companions during his moments of solitude.

That night was a turning point in our relationship—our emotional connection deepened, and our love grew stronger. Our time spent together became more meaningful, and I cherished each moment. On a rare date night at the

Pomona Valley Mining Company, James and I engaged in heartfelt conversations that made me feel truly seen and understood.

"I can't tell you how much I appreciate our talks," James said, his eyes filled with warmth.

His words made me smile. "Me too, James. It's like time flies whenever we're together."

His chuckle was soft and endearing. "I've been looking for someone like you ever since I met you at age 13, and now I get to be with you."

A surge of warmth flooded my heart, and for a moment, we sat in a comfortable silence, our eyes locked, and the world around us faded away. But I knew there were things I needed to share with him, worries I couldn't keep hidden.

"I have to be honest, though. It's not always going to be smooth sailing," I confessed.

He reached for my hand, his touch grounding and reassuring. "Tell me. I want to know everything, even the tough stuff."

"The children are struggling. The loss of their father has hit them hard. With you in the picture, they're finding it even more challenging, in some ways. The boys have been calling you names behind your back and their behavior is starting to worry me."

"Their Daddy leaving must be difficult for them, and for you, too." James ran a hand through his thick hair.

"I appreciate you taking an active role in their lives— taking them to their music lessons and baseball practices, encouraging them on." I squeezed his hand from across the table.

"They're great kids, and they deserve someone to believe in them," he said, his conviction shining through.

"I'm amazed at how you've become a positive influence in their lives so quickly." His support and encouragement for my children touched me deeply.

"It's easy to be there for people you care about. Don't you worry, the kids will come around." James assured me. His care and dedication made my heart swell with affection.

"Thank you, James. For everything." I tried to believe his words, but the turmoil inside me refused to subside. As much as I appreciated his support, I couldn't shake the nagging feeling that if Ellis returned, it could bring both joy and chaos. Joy for my children, but chaos for me and James.

Not long after that night, I found myself feeling exhausted and needing to take naps in the afternoon. I thought what I might be feeling was depression brought on by my situation, but then I also started to gain weight. Realization struck me like a bolt of lightning from the past. Day after day, the signs grew more apparent, and my suspicion intensified.

I looked at the calendar and realized I was three weeks late.

The revelation hit me like a ton of bricks. Pregnant. With a baby that wasn't my husband's. How could I have been this careless, to let myself get into this situation?

As I sat alone in the kitchen, I couldn't help but wonder

what the future held. What would this mean for my future, my family, and my reputation? Would James step up and take responsibility, or would he disappear from my life once the reality of the situation set in? Apart from his time in the Air Force, he'd never even lived away from his parents' house. Could he truly be the man for me to build a life with?

One thing was certain—everything was about to change forever. I'd made a poor decision, a choice that would have consequences for years to come. But I couldn't deny the feelings I had for James or the hope that we might be able to find a way to make things work. The next morning, I met him on his lunch break. "James, I've missed my period. What are we going to do? I was not anticipating this, and I feel like a rug has been pulled out from under me."

"Are you sure?" James had a shocked look on his face as I nodded my head. He took a moment to take everything in, and with a calm demeanor, he responded, "You'll have to file for a divorce from Ellis and marry me. I'll move in and help you raise all the children together. I will be here for all seven of you. Always."

I nodded my head, relieved that he wasn't going to run from this, but at the same time, I felt a pang of longing for the future I had planned for—a future with Ellis.

"Are you sure about this James? You are a young man with your whole life ahead of you. Isn't there a woman your own age you're interested in?" I had a nagging thought in the corner of my mind that he didn't know what he was getting himself into. He'd never known the demands of marriage and fatherhood, and this would mean facing it all at once.

Then he knelt before me. "I'm sure, and I love you. Always and forever." I wrapped my arms around him, and he held me as I wept tears of relief.

I called home to share my news that evening. "Mama, you've got to come down to California. I need you." I explained the situation and hoped Mama wouldn't be too shocked at my news.

"Are you sure Ellis isn't coming back?"

"Who knows what Ellis is doing? I don't even know if he's still in Oklahoma. I haven't spoken to him in forever. He consistently mails money, but there's never more than a few words on the letters he sends. I'm getting tired of the children asking when their daddy is coming home."

"Book me a flight. I'll start packing." Mama responded.

As I called and booked Mama's flight, I felt a sense of panic. What if Ellis did come home? The possibility of facing him again filled me with trepidation. I knew I had to confront the unresolved emotions that lingered from our past, but the mere thought of it made my head ache.

I prayed I was making the right decision. In the midst of uncertainty, I started to prepare for the children's recital. I needed to set a strong example for them and I had to tuck these emotions away in the corner of my mind, at least for the time being.

Now that I was going to start building a life with James,

this recital was the perfect opportunity to introduce him to the world as my partner.

As we approached the school entrance, my nerves ran rampant on this highly anticipated recital day. I was grateful not to be alone, especially with the town's whispers about Ellis running out on us. As I entered the auditorium, I held my head high – I wasn't the one who'd left my loved ones behind.

"It means a lot that you're here to support me and the children," I admitted, nervously twirling my hair.

James grinned, warmth twinkling in his eyes. "Can't wait to see them perform. Don't worry, everything will turn out. We are going to be a family now." He placed his hand over my tummy.

Bobby took the stage, his steel guitar glinting under the spotlight. Susan stood beside him, adjusting the microphone with a blend of excitement and nervousness.

I gently squeezed James' hand. "There they are," I whispered, a rush of affection for my kids surging within me.

The recital began, and the children's enchanting performances unfolded before us. Bobby's fingers caressed the steel guitar's strings, each note resonating with his dedication and love for music. His eyes sparkled with concentration and passion, his hands moving gracefully to coax out soulful melodies that tugged at my heartstrings. The sound enveloped me and I felt my eyes growing misty as the beauty of his music touched my soul.

Susan's voice soared with grace, filling the space with

her captivating charm. Later, Buck and Randall's magic tricks left the audience enthralled, laughter ringing in response. The Fisher children also performed in various skits and musical acts, showcasing their boundless creativity and infectious enthusiasm. The evening turned into a celebration of talent, a testament to the vibrant spirit of the community that thrived on shared moments of joy and togetherness. As the curtain closed on the night's festivities, it was clear that the bonds woven that evening were not just of family, but of a town that cherished every unique contribution and reveled in the collective brilliance that made each person shine.

Leaving the auditorium, I spotted my friends, Talie and Chuck. "I'd love for you to officially meet James," I said, introducing him.

Talie's eyes lit up as she warmly extended her hand. "Wonderful to finally meet you."

Chuck nodded, a faint smile on his lips.

"Hello, Dawn. James," he greeted with a handshake.

During our conversation, I sensed Chuck's reservations about James. Unresolved tensions lingered in the air.

"Ellis mentioned he's coming home soon." Chuck's gaze fixed pointedly on James.

"Shh, here comes the children." Talie nudged Chuck.

"Did you like it, Mama?" Bobby and the other children joined us.

"It was beautiful, son! Everyone did a fantastic job, but

my lovebugs made the proudest. I love you all." I hugged them tightly.

Driving away from the school later, I sighed contentedly. "I'm glad everything went smoothly."

James gently squeezed my hand. "Your kids are amazing, Dawn. They've inherited your talent and spirit."

Smiling, my heart warmed at his words. The melodies of the recital echoed in our minds, a reminder that today was about the harmonies of togetherness. As we turned onto Elm Street, the neighborhood gossip, Janice Dixon, came into view.

"There's that busy body, Janice. Try not to make contact. She's been a rude neighbor. Always in everyone's business" I whispered to James.

"I've handled worse than her," James said with a chuckle.

I rolled my eyes as Janice Dixon's disapproving glare fixed upon us. She leaned against her white picket fence and called out, "Well, well, Dawn, didn't expect to see you with such a younger man. Guess while the cat's away, the mouse will play."

James shot me a questioning look, and I shrugged, hoping he wouldn't take the comment to heart.

Without missing a beat, James turned a playful grin towards Janice. "They say judgment ages you faster than anything else. You might want to keep your nose out of our business if you're concerned about staying youthful." With a wink, he turned away, leaving Janice momentarily stunned with her mouth hanging open.

"I guess we'll always have the neighborhood peanut gallery," James said, his laughter contagious.

I nodded, laughing softly. "I suppose so, but I'm glad you can handle it with such grace." On the outside, I smiled and laughed it off, but on the inside, a little nervous flutter remained. It was hard not to wonder what everyone in town would say, what kind of tales they'd spin about us once I was walking around with a big pregnant belly.

I let out a sigh and pushed those worrisome thoughts out of my mind and focused on James, with his hand holding mine, and the memory of the recital's melodies still in my mind, his presence was a steady reassurance that we were strong enough to face anything. This version of my family might just work... despite the prying eyes and wagging tongues of the neighborhood.

Hard to Handle

POMONA, CALIFORNIA

FALL 1959

Dawn Cameron

31 Years Old

My Dearest Dawn,

I hope this letter finds you well. I must admit, reading about your new love has me feeling torn between feeling happy for you and concerned for you, at the same time. I know new love can be exhilarating, filling every moment with passion and excitement. I can understand how tempting it must be to find solace in James' arms, especially with Ellis gone.

However, I feel compelled to caution you about the potential repercussions of this affair. While it might feel like a lifeline and a glimmer of hope in the midst of your struggles, you must remember that actions have consequences. I worry that getting involved with someone outside your marriage could complicate matters further and potentially hurt those involved, including your children.

I know you never signed up for being alone on this journey. But, my dear sister, you are strong, resilient, and capable of handling anything that comes your way. I believe in you, and I know you can find the strength to stand on your own two feet.

Before allowing this romance to sweep you away completely, consider the impact it could have on your family and the stability they need during this time. You and your children deserve love and support but remember the importance of making choices that align with your values and the well-being of everyone involved. No matter what you decide, I will forever be here to support you as your loving sister.

Take care, dear sister, and remember I love you, I am here for you... I'll stand by your side through thick and thin. I believe in your strength and your ability to find the best path forward.

With all my love,
Franny

My sister's words echoed in my mind, mingling with the growing doubts and fears that had taken root. The advice was well-meant, but the pull of emotions, the need for connection, and the intoxicating allure of James still had their hold on me. I was feeling run down, I wanted to climb into bed and never get up.

As the days passed and I grew more evidently pregnant, my belly rounded with the life growing within me. The weight of the decision I had to make felt heavier with each passing moment, and I tried to prepare myself for whatever the future held.

One afternoon, I opened my door to see Talie standing there with a distraught look on her face.

"Ellis is on his way back. He knows everything. Chuck spilled the beans about James, the baby, everything."

"Why now? He's going to kill James. Did he think he could run off for all this time with no repercussions?" My heart raced, and I tried to remain calm. I was supposed to pick up my mother from the airport that afternoon. "Do you know when he'll come home?"

"He's already left Oklahoma. It should take him a couple of days before he's in California," Talie answered.

"Thank goodness Mama is coming. I need all the support I can get. Can you stay here with the kids while I go to pick her up at the airport?" I asked.

"Of course. You know I'm here for you, always." Talie squeezed my hand.

On the way home from the airport, Mama weighed in with her thoughts on the situation. "Well, this is certainly a tough one. You're going to have to pick one," Mama said after I informed her of Ellis' impending arrival.

"I don't know what to do, Mama. I need to talk to Ellis. I don't even know if he wants me. Even if he does, how can I ever count on him again? I don't know if I have it in me to forgive his drinking a second time. I'm in love with James, and I've moved on."

"Men will do desperate things when they feel they can't support their family. Many ran out during the Depression. Some did worse… I think you need to search your heart. Talk to both Ellis and James. Pray, baby. You'll need a lot of prayers. I don't believe there's just one man for each woman. You can have many loves in your life, but you can't change the past. Ellis certainly put you in a predicament when he left for so long. No one could blame you for finding someone else."

The next day, Mama met James over lunch, and as expected, they got along great. "He's a fine man, Dawn. You have my blessing, whatever your decision is."

"I almost wished you didn't like James. It would make things much easier." I rubbed my temples.

"I'm sorry baby. They are both good men. Ellis has stumbled, but I believe in him. He's been a good man for most of your marriage. Marriages go through these rough patches, but I know you can fix it that's what you want."

"What about James, Mama?"

"James reminds me a lot of your Daddy, when he was that age... but you need to figure out what's best for YOU and your family. You can't make this decision based on anyone's feelings. Which life do you want?"

"That's the problem, Mama. I can see it working out with either one of them. I have love for them both."

"Don't worry Pickle, everything will work out. You'll see." Mama rubbed my shoulders in solace.

The following evening there was a soft knock on the door. It was Ellis, and in his arms wriggled a little German Shepherd puppy. The sight of him brought a flood of memories, the good and the painful. My heart wavered, torn between the past and the uncertain future. He looked better than he had in a while, apart from the dark circles under his eyes.

"I thought you could use some company. Her names Honey Two" Ellis traced his finger around the dog's collar, his gaze fixed somewhere between regret and determination. "Before you say anything, I've got something I want you to hear... I ain't blind to the fact that I've been a real jackass, not givin' you half of what you deserved, but I still love you. I always will."

"Daddy!" The children all came running out on the porch, hugging Ellis, and interrupting our conversation. They enveloped him in a group hug, everyone chanting, "Daddy's home."

They were elated to see him.

Mama appeared behind them. "Come on children,

bring that pup into the backyard, and Susan, you get a bowl of water. That dog looks thirsty. Let's give your Mama and Daddy some space to talk."

"What happened to you, Ellis? How could you run off for that long?" I asked.

"Sometimes people turn to the bottle to escape their demons. Damned if I ain't one of 'em. I know now that have a drinking problem. I'm not holdin' out hope you'll forgive me or take me back, but if you decide to give me another shot, I swear I'll stick by you. Our life can be better than the one we had before. I'm a better man now I've quit drinking for good. I'll never touch the stuff again."

Doubt filled my heart as I shot back words tinged with skepticism. "You think you can disappear for months, and suddenly you've seen the light?" I was fuming inside, all those months of pining away for Ellis flashed through my mind.

Ellis' voice, husky yet genuine, held a hint of raw honesty. "Dawn, I ain't got no fancy explanation that'll make this all make sense to you. It was like a punch in the gut, realizing how much I messed up. This whole pregnancy bombshell, it's made me see what I'll be missing, what I threw away. The thought of you moving on with someone else, building a life, it's a bitter pill to swallow. I miss you and I won't give you up without a fight."

"Showing up with a cute little puppy doesn't fix everything you've said and done," I responded.

Ellis gently interrupted, his voice sincere. "That's the start. There's something else you should know." He took my hand in his. "I've saved up a down payment for a fixer upper, and that house flipping venture I've been talking about. It's happening. I want you with me. A fresh slate. Let's start over, one more time. Don't throw away all those years of happiness over a drunken' fool… and besides, you know the children will want their Daddy."

In a heartbeat, memories flooded my mind—our first kiss, receiving the keys to our first home, even the births of our children. Good times, tough times, and plenty more ahead. Could we truly start over again?

"I'm not sure, Ellis… what about this baby I'm carry-ing?" He seemed confident and hopeful, nothing like the man who had left me all those months ago. There was a fire in his eyes I hadn't seen for years. This was the Ellis I had fallen in love with and married all those years ago, but why was I hesitating? This is what I had yearned for all spring. But now that it was happening, I couldn't help but think of James, the man who had been there to rescue me from despair.

"Please, give me that chance to put things right. You're still the beat in my heart, even though I've let you down, I'm still your husband. That baby, she's every bit a Cameron, no matter what went on between you and James. I swear, I'll step up to be the best damn daddy and husband you deserve. One more shot," Ellis's words cut through my thoughts like a sharp blade, slicing away the doubts that had been clouding my mind.

"I don't know Ellis. Could you really raise another man's child?"

"The kids, they already know me as their Daddy, and this little one... She'll know me as hers, too. A true Cameron. All those tough months, we can let them go if you're willing. You're my only love. I'm nothing without you and the kids. Let's mend our family." The fervor in his gaze held the weight of his conviction—he truly believed his every word. While my mind saw the logic in Ellis's plan, my doubt lingered.

"Oh, Ellis, why couldn't you come home sooner?" I sat down on the porch swing, my head in my hands, feeling completely overwhelmed.

Ellis gently placed his hand at the nape of my neck and lifted my face toward him. "I love you and I always will." He leaned in and kissed me tenderly on my lips. His mouth felt familiar and inviting that I melted into him. The kiss was like sitting in front of the fire on a cold day. It felt like coming home and my heart began to pound. After we pulled apart, we looked at each other like the teenagers we once were.

"Couldn't resist you. You're my person. You always will be," Ellis whispered, his forehead against mine.

"I need time to think," I responded.

"Call me in the morning, no matter what. I'm staying with Chuck and Talie."

"I will." Tears threatened, but I held them in.

"I hope you'll take me back." Ellis looked down and fiddled with his wedding ring.

"You hurt me deeply. I needed you, and you shut me out."

"I'm going to spend the rest of my life making it up to you," Ellis said as I closed the front door.

Inside the house, I lay on my bed, hugging myself as my heart continued to race. The kids all looked ecstatic when Ellis returned, how would they feel if I didn't take him back? It would crush their little hearts. Would they ever forgive me?

And then there was James. Lovely and dependable, like Daddy. James who had stirred up feelings inside me that had laid dormant for a long time. He was kind, caring and... new.

What on earth was I going to do?

As Ellis was leaving, I could hear another car pull up into the driveway.

'What do you think you're doing here?" James called out.

"You dirty SOB, how could you go after my wife? I thought you were my friend?" I heard Ellis respond. I jumped up and ran out to the front lawn.

"You left her. I was here to pick up the pieces. What did you expect to happen?"

The two men squared off in the yard, and Ellis threw the first punch. It was a terrible fight, seeming to go on forever. James was younger and quicker, but Ellis was a bigger and tougher man. They were evenly matched. The police arrived and broke up the fight. They said they wouldn't arrest anyone if both men agreed to leave and cool off.

That night, I worried for both men. I knew how stubborn each of them could be, and I needed to make this decision quickly. If I didn't, someone could end up seriously injured or worse.

This was the most confusing and painful time of my life. I had a sleepless night spent praying I'd make the right decision. It wasn't about who I loved more; it was about my family's survival. Then the contractions started. I was barely seven months pregnant, way too soon.

"Mama, I need you to take me to the hospital. Something is wrong."

Mama quickly got dressed, and we made the short trip to Pomona Valley Hospital. The staff promptly checked me into a room, and the doctor came in to check on me.

As I lay in the hospital bed hooked up to machines and monitors, I couldn't help but feel a wave of despair. How had I ended up here, in this situation? Was it all my fault? Should I have made different choices? These questions swirled in my mind as the doctors tried to stop my contractions.

"Mrs. Cameron, we will do everything to stop this labor. I think we can, but I want you to remain calm," the doctor said, explaining the next step. Mama was there, holding my hand.

"I need to call James. He should be here with you." Mama started making her way to the door.

"No, Mama, I want you to call Ellis. He's going to be this baby's daddy." Although I had a passionate love for James, now that I was in the hospital with a medical emergency, I suddenly realized that Ellis was the one I wanted to comfort me—it was always Ellis. My husband, the man I'd counted on for years, and despite his relapse, he was the father to my children and still my husband. I believed he had seen the error in his ways. If he'd agree to stop drinking for good, we could reunite our family. At 25 years old, James could go on to meet and fall in love with another woman, I told myself, trying to rationalize my decision.

"Are you sure, Dawn?" Mama asked.

"Yes, Mama. He's staying with Chuck and Talie. Here's the number. We will call James when we have more info, I can't have them both here fighting with each other." Mama left the room to call Ellis. I had made my decision, I was determined to stick with it. For better or worse.

It Had to Be You

POMONA, CALIFORNIA

WINTER 1959

Dawn Cameron

31 Years Old

Ellis rushed down the hospital hallway; the echoes of his hurried footsteps filled the air. Bursting through the doorway, his face etched with worry, his eyes met mine, revealing the depth of his emotions.

"You won't regret this," he said, determination lacing his words. "I'll make it up to you and be the best father any child ever had. I'll never leave your side again. I'm sorry."

His sincerity overwhelmed me, and tears welled up in my eyes. He placed something gently on the nightstand. "It might seem silly," he continued, "but I saw these at the store and thought of the night we met." My heart swelled with love as he revealed a tin of Almond Rocha, the very prize we had won at the dance contest long ago.

"I love it, and I love you. I believe, together we can fix our family, but only if you stop drinking for good. Can you do that?"

"I've been on the wagon for three months. I'll never touch another drop of alcohol for as long as I live. It's cost me too much. I'll go to those meetings, whatever it takes." Ellis held my hand as he gazed into my eyes.

As we soaked in the precious moment, the doctor entered the room, concern evident as he glanced between us. "Your contractions are slowing down," he said with a hint of relief. "We've been successful in stopping your labor. The baby's heartbeat sounds steady, but we need to keep you in the hospital for observation. You'll need to be on bed rest for the remainder of this pregnancy. It won't be easy, but it can be done."

"We'll do whatever it takes," Ellis answered as he looked deep into my eyes.

When I was finally released from the hospital, my family welcomed me home with open arms. The children surrounded me, their joyous smiles and hugs warming my heart. As sunlight filtered through the curtains, casting a warm glow in the room, I reclined on the couch. My heavy belly a constant reminder of the life growing within me.

"Can I get you a drink, Mama?" Susan had become

such a young lady over the last few months. Everything we had been through had made her mature beyond her years.

"That would be lovely. Thank you," I responded.

Ellis was in the kitchen attempting to tackle breakfast, though the clatter of pans and the occasional muttered curse betrayed his lack of expertise. I couldn't help but chuckle softly, realizing that some things never changed.

"Need a hand, chef?" I called out, pushing myself up off the couch with a sigh.

"No, you stay seated. You can't be up walking around. Doctor's orders." Ellis replied.

"Susan, can you help your Daddy with the food please? He's about ready to burn the house down."

Ellis chuckled, and his eyes softened as they met mine. "Trying to make up for lost time, you know?"

"There's something we need to talk about."

Leaning against the counter, Ellis responded. "Yeah, I figured."

Taking a deep breath, I attempted to find the right words. "I appreciate everything you're doing, but I can't ignore the fact that you've been hovering over me like I'm about to vanish."

"I can't help it. I worry, especially with everything that's happened." He sighed.

"That's the thing, Ellis," I replied gently but firmly. "I understand your concern, but we can't keep living like this. You're going to have to learn to trust me again. Mama took it upon herself to inform James of our situation, urging him not to cause any stress. He won't be coming around."

"I can't shake the feeling that I need to protect you, protect our family. I don't want that man around you. I saw the way he looks at you. He still loves you," Ellis firmly reiterated his thoughts about James.

"I chose you, Ellis, and we both need to find a way to move forward. James has moved on with his, and we need to as well." I had been hearing rumors that upon my rejection, James had run into the arms of his former love, Alice Kramer.

"You heard about that, too?" Ellis averted his gaze, his voice tinged with vulnerability. "Listen, I do trust you, and I'm sorry I've messed up badly. I don't trust James Lockhart. He was my friend, look what he did."

"We've all made mistakes, but we have to believe that we can overcome them. Quit worrying about him, and let's work on building our life."

Ellis met my eyes, his emotions laid bare. "I don't want to lose you, Dawn. I'll do whatever it takes. I know you're right."

"We're in this together and Mama will stay to help until this baby comes." I gave him a reassuring smile.

"Everything is going to work out now, I know it." His nodded with a mixture of determination and a hint of surrender.

Over the following weeks, I noticed a gradual shift in Ellis's behavior. He began to relinquish his need to hover, and we started to regain the trust that had been lost. The guilt I felt about James's pain still lingered, but I hoped time would eventually heal those wounds.

ON JANUARY 10, 1960, TWILIGHT DESTINY CAMERON MADE her grand entrance. She was tiny and delicate, with large eyes and fair hair reminiscent of James Lockhart, which filled me with worry. Our whole family had various shades of red hair. How would Ellis react to this blonde haired baby?

However, my worries were unfounded. Ellis kept his promise to be the best father ever, doting on little Twyla. He found a reasonably priced house to purchase and began fulfilling his dream of buying distressed properties, renovating them with his construction skills, and selling them at a substantial gain. Ellis turned a good profit with his real estate ventures and started saving to launch his own construction business with aspirations of building affordable housing all over Southern California.

James and his wife moved several towns away but kept his barber shop in Pomona. When Ellis was gone working all day, I made arrangements for him to stop by on his lunch break and meet his daughter. It was the first time I'd seen James in a while. He looked thinner and older than he had in the summer. My heart sometimes still ached for him, but I tried to lock up those feelings as I reminded myself of my choice to go with my husband.

"Ellis and I want to raise the baby the same as the other children. You can see her, but we don't want her to know she's different from her siblings. She won't know you're her real father," I explained to James with a lump in my throat.

"Why are you doing this?" James ran his fingers through his hair.

"It's for the best. People can be mean. I don't want her getting teased or called a bastard."

"I don't like it, but if that's what will truly make you happy, I'll try to respect your wishes." It seemed like James was giving in much easier than I anticipated. I'd almost been hoping that he would put up more of a fight for Twyla and me.

"Dawn, there's something I have to tell you. I'm with Alice Kramer. I ran into her, and she helped me get through this. She's carrying my child now." James gave me this news with a serious look in his eyes.

"The rumors are true. It seems like it didn't take you long to move on." Here I was trying to let James down easily, and he was already entangled with another woman. Part of me was devastated to hear of this pregnancy, but I also felt slightly relieved. If he had a wife and another baby to worry about, then maybe it would be easier for him to step aside as Twyla's father.

We made plans for me to take little Twyla to the barbershop to see him once a week. We'd worry about what to tell her when she got a little older and started asking questions.

"Does Alice know about Twyla and me? When is her child due?" I had many questions running through my mind.

"She's not happy about it, but she knows about you and the baby. She doesn't want me seeing either of you. I think with time, things will change. She's due next spring. We're going to get married." James looked at me with regret in his green eyes.

"Spring? These two babies will be little more than a year apart!" I responded. Little Twyla would have another sibling, one that wasn't from Ellis and me. It was extremely complicated, I didn't know how we'd all survive this situation. One jealous spouse was enough to deal with, now there would be two.

"I hope you know what you're doing, James," I responded, my voice tinged with worry.

"I don't have a choice, do I? What's done is done. I'm treading water now," James said as he headed toward the door.

Several months went by, and unfortunately, Alice never changed her mind about James seeing Twyla, and neither did Ellis. Both of our spouses were threatened by the love James and I had shared that long, hot summer of 1959. Every time I tried to make arrangements for Twyla to see her birth father, fights erupted all around.

Ellis and I were getting along well, but any mention of

James's name brought tension to the air. I didn't want anything to threaten our newfound peace and I hoped, with all of my heart, that we could find a way to make this blended family work.

My yearning for harmony remained strong. As the tangled web of complexities and unspoken emotions unfolded, hope burned within me. Amid this uncertain future and the fractured pieces of our lives, I held onto the belief that love could bridge the gap, binding us together into a family that would stand the test of time.

Someone You Loved

POMONA, CALIFORNIA
JUNE 5TH, 1960

Dawn Cameron
32nd Birthday

"Talie, can you drive me to the barber shop? There's something I must do, and I can't face it alone." I woke up on my 32nd birthday with a new mindset.

I'd spent the last six months trying to ignore James' desire to see his daughter and Ellis's never ending jealousy. These two men just couldn't find a way to get along and now I was going to do something drastic. I vowed to end this chaos. It was the one thing threatening my family, and I was going to do whatever it took to survive.

"I'll be right there," Talie replied without hesitation, her unwavering support evident in her voice.

"I'm going to take control of this situation, and I'm not going to be at the mercy of these men anymore. Ellis has been great, the perfect husband and father. But if he hears I've been taking Twyla to see James it might be more than he can bare, he won't have another man trying to take his place. I'm afraid he'll resort to drinking again. His sobriety is the most important thing to me now. If he loses it, I'll lose my family."

"You're different than the Dawn who was worrying about everything a few months ago. What's changed?" Talie responded.

"I woke up today on my birthday with such a weight on my chest. These men are driving me crazy, and I realized I can't live this way anymore. My family deserves peace, and it will never happen with the threat of Ellis and James breaking into violence every time they see each other."

"If this is your path, I'm right beside you," Talie responded as she drove to the barber shop. My heart pounded with determination. I had developed a plan, and it wasn't going to be easy. I couldn't continue to let the tension and chaos continue any longer.

As I stepped inside the barber shop, the familiar scent of aftershave and the sound of scissors cutting hair surrounded me, I was filled with an array of memories. This was the place where James and I had been reunited, and now it would be the place of our final goodbye.

James looked up from his work, his eyes meeting mine with a mixture of sadness and understanding. Without a word, he walked over to the cash register and pulled out a small box, placing it gently in my hands. My heart skipped a beat as I opened it, revealing a delicate ruby and gold ring inside.

Inscribed inside of the ring was a single word— "Always."

Tears welled up in my eyes as I looked at him speechless. It was as if that one word held all the love, all the memories, and all the longing we had for each other. But we both knew that it was time to let go, move on from the past, and embrace the paths we had chosen.

"You know things can't continue like this, and I can't keep this ring," I whispered, my voice barely audible. "It's too much."

James shook his head gently, his eyes never leaving mine. "I want you to give it to Twyla when she's older," he said softly. "To know that her parents, her real parents, loved each other at one time. I'm guessing I won't be seeing much of you anymore."

A lump formed in my throat as I closed the box and held it close to my heart. "It has to be this way," I managed to say, my voice trembling. "But I'll put this ring somewhere safe. I promise to give it to her when she's older and can understand."

As I looked into his green, soulful eyes, I knew that this was our final farewell. We both needed to let go, to find happiness in the lives we were building with our spouses. It wasn't easy, but it was the only solution that would stop all the fighting. If we didn't put a stop to it, I feared someone would end up dead.

"Dawn, it's time to go," Talie's gentle voice broke through the somber atmosphere, her presence a reminder of the bond of womanhood that tied us together.

I turned to Talie, her eyes filled with understanding and support. She had been there for me through thick and thin, and I knew she would be there to help me pick up the pieces now that I had said goodbye to James for good.

With a heavy heart, I turned to James, feeling the weight of the ring in my pocket, the symbol of our love and the memories we had shared. Taking a deep breath, I mustered the strength to speak, my voice quivering slightly, "Take care, James."

He nodded, trying to keep his emotions in check. "You too, Dawn. Take care of yourself and Twyla. Thanks for seeing me."

As I walked away, Talie placed a firm hand on my shoulder, giving me the strength to keep moving forward. Her unconditional love and support were what I needed now more than ever.

As we stepped out into the sunlight, I took another deep breath, hoping that saying goodbye to James was the best decision for everyone involved. The pain in my heart was still raw, but I felt a flicker of hope, knowing that I was

Dawn, like the sun rising through the morning mist, and I could withstand any storm.

Talie gave me a supportive smile, her presence like a lifeboat during this tumultuous time. Grateful for her encouraging presence, I nodded, knowing that our bond surpassed mere friendship—we were sisters, and she would help me carry on.

As we walked away from the barber shop, a mix of emotions enveloped me—sadness for the end of an era and hope for a new beginning. Regardless of the choice I made, I knew there wasn't an easy path to follow. Each option carried its own struggles. My ultimate quest was to find inner peace, a resolution that would bring tranquility to both families.

However, I knew deep down that wrong or right, this was my path toward peace.

Talie's voice broke through my thoughts.

"You're doing the right thing. It may be tough now, but in time, it will get easier. You'll see."

Epilogue

Dawn Cameron

90 Years Old

"Mama, are you ready to go?" Twyla, and her family have arrived, pulling me from the depths of my memories. These memories of the past that reside deep within me, like a second heartbeat.

I reflect on how much of myself I see in my daughter and granddaughter; we are like links in a chain—Dawn, Twyla, and Celeste, three remarkable women, illuminating the canvas of life with the strongest and most enduring light, each generation passing on the flame of resilience and love to the next.

These beautiful women have arrived to finally take me to my 90th birthday party in Redlands, California. A place where Ellis and I experienced countless joyous years together.

Ellis, at last, acquired his cherished horse property, and I had the privilege of hosting numerous gatherings, birthdays, and celebrations with flair. Our home was often filled with over 50 guests, including our children, grandchildren, employees, and friends. The Fishers, Talie and Chuck, and their children and grandchildren, our dear friends whom I'll never forget. Those years were magnificent, and I believe I found my happily ever after until Ellis' passing at 59 years old.

Can it truly be over 30 years since I last beheld his freckled face?

As Twyla descends the stairs, still as stunning as ever, I cannot help but notice the traces of James Lockhart in her looks and demeanor. There were moments in my life when I struggled to be as close to Twyla as I was with the other children. Her resemblance to her birth father reminded me of a path not taken, the secret I chose to keep about her paternity.

At the beginning of Twyla's life, when Ellis and I decided to raise her as his own, we never thought of the future and how this secret would eat at our family. We didn't look too far ahead, taking life one day at a time.

My childhood was focused on survival, and such circumstances often require living in the present and not dwelling on the challenges of the future. While I eventually had to learn to accept stability in my life, it felt like I was chasing the adventure of my youth, growing up within a nomadic life, never quite knowing where I'd end up.

Eventually, I had to learn to settle down, accept that families grow and change. Most importantly, I had to learn to have faith in myself and trust my own discernment.

Women today envision themselves as masters of their own destinies, a perspective I hadn't fully grasped when Twyla was born. I was always reacting to the events around me and it took a long time for me to get into the driver's seat.

My gaze shifts to my granddaughter, Celeste, with her huge green eyes, quiet intelligence, and understated sense of humor, reminiscent of James Lockhart, I see a woman who embraces her power and self-worth from within.

My love for Celeste and my entire family knows no bounds. I've endeavored to impart the wisdom my mother once shared with me to my grandchildren, emphasizing the importance of learning from our mistakes. "If you aren't making mistakes, you aren't living!" Mama used to say.

While I deeply regret the secrets we kept from Twyla, I did attempt to tell her the truth about her paternity many times, but the words never seemed to come out.

One thing I've come to realize is that avoiding problems won't make them vanish. Eventually, all those little boxes of unpleasant memories came crashing down in an instant. I've learned it's better to deal with things head on. It's less complicated that way.

I now seek strength in my faith in the Lord to overcome life's challenges, and I hope that my legacy will be one of love, resilience, and unwavering determination. Growing up during the Great Depression, we clung to hope even in the darkest of times, and that enduring spirit continues to shape my outlook on life.

Today is the day I give Celeste my journals, photographs, and scrapbooks—a treasure trove of memories. My dream of putting my life on paper can now be fulfilled by Celeste, who possesses a love for books and a gift for words. Through her, my legacy will continue to thrive.

"Celeste, go grab that box in the corner. I have a gift for you."

"A gift for me? But it's your birthday, Grandma." Celeste responds as she opens the box.

"Everything is there, everything you need to write the story of my life." I explain.

"Oh Grandma, are you sure?" I can see the tears welling up in her eyes.

"I'm sure, now come over here and help an old lady up the stairs." I ask for her help, not because I need it, but because I want to feel her close to me.

"Since it's your birthday, I'll humor you." She teases as she makes her way over to me and offers me her arm.

Together we head out towards the party, and the celebration unfolds, filled with love, joy, and the beauty of life. As we come together as a tight-knit clan, I realize that no matter the challenges we face or the secrets we hold, what truly matters is the love that binds us. With every laugh, every hug, and every shared memory, we strengthen our connection and build a foundation that will carry us through life's ups and downs.

My heart is full knowing that the legacy of love and resilience I have woven, will endure long after I'm gone. The laughter of my great-great-grandchildren echoes in my ears, and I realize that the impact I've had on their lives is immeasurable.

As I bask in the warmth of their love and celebrate the life I've lived, I know that the best is yet to come for my family, and my legacy will continue to thrive through the generations to come.

THANK YOU FOR PICKING UP A COPY OF **_EVERY NIGHT HAS A DAWN_** and giving it a read. I would love your feedback so please feel free to leave me a review here:

amzn.com/review/create-review? &asin=B0CK69L4M8

To Be Continued . . .

In the Spring of 2024 with *Twilight's Hidden Truth*, the second installment of the *Winds of Change* trilogy.

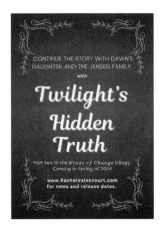

Authors Note

THE STORY BEHIND THE STORY

In 2017, my life was forever marked by two significant events that would shape the course of my journey toward writing this novel. The first of these pivotal moments occurred in June when my feisty 90-year-old grandmother, Nellie June, experienced a heart attack.

Grandma was a force of nature, possessing boundless energy and a spirited personality. Grandma June was there to give advice (most of it good) and despite enduring a heart attack and pneumonia, she fought tenaciously, refusing to let her body succumb. It almost seemed as if a higher power had granted Grandma June a little more time on this earth, to take care of some unfinished business.

My oldest aunt took on the role of caregiver to Grandma June with my parents and other family members taking turns staying with Grandma, who didn't want to be alone in her last days.

Even though I lived several hours away, I visited my Grandma several times per week, not only to help, but also because I knew that my time with Grandma was limited. I wanted to seize every precious moment with her. As the sole daughter in my maternal line, we shared an extraordinary bond. How I cherish the memories of her infectious laughter, her deep and husky chuckles that resonated in my soul. Her face would break open with a huge smile, and she'd throw her head back with laughter at the witty comments I shared with her about my life living in wine country.

My beloved Grandma June had an unwavering passion for reading and sharing her remarkable tales of growing up as a poor farm worker in the state of Washington. We would often engage in heartfelt conversations about her past, delving into the profound impact the Great Depression and World War II had on her life. It was during these moments that Grandma June revealed her cherished dream—to pen a novel capturing the essence of Washington State during those tumultuous times. She diligently took notes and conducted extensive research, but her writing had not progressed very far.

One day, Grandma greeted me at her front door, clutching a box overflowing with scraps of paper and envelopes—a tangible record of her 90 years on earth. Assuring me that these treasures would serve as my guiding light, she entrusted me with the task of bringing her story to life.

As I returned home, eager to embark on this literary journey, I opened up Grandma's box of memories and found a trove of lovingly preserved, old black-and-white photographs, letters and other reflections that spanned years of her family's life during the Great Depression.

Filled with inspiration and encouragement, Grandma urged me to reignite my passion for writing. Recognizing my affinity for books and writing she believed that I possessed the ability to weave her meticulously gathered research into a captivating tribute—a heartfelt love letter dedicated to Washington State, the place where she had grown up poor yet happy.

In the presence of her unwavering belief, I managed to complete the first two chapters of this novel. I had the opportunity to read them to my grandmother before she peacefully slipped away into the great eternal.

After her passing, when I couldn't sleep, I continued writing with tears streaming down my face, the words did not flow as they had when Grandma was alive. My confidence faltered, and I wondered if I would ever finish this novel without my muse by my side.

That night I had a vivid dream, of my grandmother as a little girl, running through fields of happiness. The next morning I awoke invigorated. Suddenly, I started to envision Washington at the time of my grandmother's youth, the place of her many escapades. The words began to flow, and I wrote for months, followed by many breaks to recharge my creativity.

I was determined to honor my grandmother's memory and her dream of sharing her story with the world. As the years passed, I found my way to the words and the keyboard, capturing her spirit and the lessons she imparted to me. It was a slow process.

It is my hope that, through the character of Millie Dawn, some of Grandma's spirited essence will carry on in this novel. Her story living forever within the ink-stained lines of these pages, etched in the very fabric of my heart and destined to endure the tests of time.

The second event that occurred happened on my birthday in September. Something was put in motion that would forever shape my life's journey. My husband gifted me with an Ancestry DNA kit, fulfilling a long-held desire to explore my heritage. Fascinated by genetics and DNA, I embarked on a quest for ancestral knowledge. While I knew of my German, English, and French heritage on my father's side, and Western European lineage from my grandmother side, my maternal grandfather's ancestry remained a mystery. His parents had passed away when he was young, and my mother had never met them.

I mailed it off that very same day and started the six-week waiting period for the results, but little did I know I would be opening a Pandora's Box for myself and my mother. An extremely shocking secret that threatened to break apart our family and change everything we thought we knew about our heritage.

The day after Thanksgiving we discovered a close match on my Ancestry DNA account. This close relative was someone I didn't recognize and turned out to my mother's biological father. Grandpa Al, although greatly loved and greatly missed, was not genetically related to me or my mother. My biological grandfather turned out to be the town barber and he was still alive!

In 1959, during a brief separation between my grandparents, my mother was the result of a year-long affair. It was astonishing to learn that her biological father was still alive, and we had the opportunity to meet him. Witnessing Grandpa Jack hugging my mother, their matching green eyes locked in a loving gaze, felt like something out of a dream.

Sadly, our happiness was short-lived because Grandpa Jack passed away six weeks later, followed shortly thereafter by my Grandma June. Upon receiving this shocking news and experiencing such a rapid succession of losses, I found myself reeling, and the need to write once again embraced me like an old friend.

While this book draws inspiration from the unfolding events in my life, it's important to note that it is a work of fiction. Writing became my outlet to express my feelings, my tool to navigate the labyrinth of emotions I was facing.

Once I started pouring words onto paper, I found it impossible to stop. For months, I immersed myself in this story, trying to process this information and figure out how my beloved grandmother could keep such a secret from my mother.

But as every writer knows, the dreaded writer's block eventually set in, and it became a painful struggle to put pen to paper. Motivation seemed to elude me, and I finally stopped writing it. Two long years passed and I rarely gave it a second thought. I was happy to let it go as nothing more than a cathartic exercise to process the tumultuous events surrounding my mother's paternity revelation. I lost faith in the possibility of this book ever seeing the light of day.

But then, as fate would have it, early in 2023, I contracted Covid. While my case wasn't severe enough for hospitalization, it wasn't mild either. During my quarantine, I tried my best to maintain my sanity, binging on *Emily in Paris* and *House Hunters International*.

Then, into the third morning of my quarantine the universe whispered in my ear, urging me forward. I began to have powerful urge to finish this book, and I couldn't ignore it any longer.

Secluded from my husband and daughters, I embraced the opportunity to write. I thought I might as well make the most of that week of quarantine, so I wrote and wrote, and then I wrote some more.

To my surprise, the words flowed effortlessly, free from the pain that had plagued me before. It had taken me five years to reach this point, but when I wrote during that time of seclusion, I felt alive, renewed, and inspired. The words shot out of my fingertips like lightning bolts as I typed away. My emotions left me and entered the manuscript.

Once I started, I couldn't stop. I became obsessed, waking up in the middle of the night to write for hours before returning to a restful sleep. When I finally emerged from my self-imposed seclusion seven days later, I had completed the book you are about to read. In fact, half of it was written during that remarkable week of passion flowing from my heart and directly onto these pages.

Now I am certain it's time to share our story, hoping to offer solace to others facing similar situations.

This book marks the first installment in the Winds of Change Trilogy, a series where stories intertwine with multiple layers. The inaugural novel, 'Every Night Has a Dawn,' delves into my grandmother's experiences growing up in poverty during the Great Depression. The second installment explores my mother's life, her coming of age in the chaotic 1970s, and her struggles as a teenage mother determined to raise me to the best of her abilities. Currently, I'm writing the third novel, which delves into my personal journey as a world traveler, recounting how I met and fell in love with my husband. It narrates our around-the-world journey, including our time living in Australia, and our eventual settlement in California. This final installment also explores the connections between mothers and daughters and how we are all intertwined.

With each book, I hope to peel the layers of our lives, allowing readers to glimpse the resilience and strength that carried us through the toughest of times. In sharing our stories, I aspire to offer a glimmer of hope and the reassurance that no matter how dark life may seem, there's always a chance for survival and revival.

Recipe

MAMA'S FAMOUS PIG N' WHISTLE CAKE

- 4 Eggs, beat Hard
- 2 Cups Granulated Sugar
- 1 Teaspoon Vanilla
- 2 Cups Flour
- 2 Teaspoons Baking Powder
- 1 Pinch of Salt 1 Cup Scalded Condensed Milk

Mix all ingredients and bake at 350 degrees for 30 minutes.

Topping

- 1 Cup Brown Sugar
- 6 Tablespoons of Milk or Condensed Milk
- 1 Cup of Butter
- 1 ½ Cup of Coconut
- ½ Cup of Mixed Nuts

Mix together and spread over hot cake.
Cool and Serve.

Acknowledgments

I extend my deepest gratitude to my husband, best friend, and soulmate, who continues to inspire me and remains the love of my life.

To my beautiful daughters, I am incredibly proud to be your mother. As you grow and face the world, my wish for you is to stay true to yourselves, standing firm in your beliefs, no matter what the world may think. Your unwavering determination and individuality make me cherish not only having you in my family but also having you as my best friends and ultimate Hype Squad in life.

Thank you to my loving parents, for reading my chapters, offering suggestions, and providing unwavering support throughout this journey. Mom, thank you for teaching me to be a strong person, and Dad, thank you for showing me to be a good person.

My heartfelt appreciation goes to my exceptional editor, Dori Harrell. Your unwavering support, keen insights, and expert guidance helped to shape this book and bring it to life. Your dedication and commitment were invaluable during the rewrite, profoundly impacting my growth as a writer.

I am deeply thankful to the Makah nation for allowing my grandmother's family to stay on their reservation in the mid-1930s.

Much gratitude to my cousin and fellow author, April Yarber, for encouraging me to finish my book and providing unwavering support during challenging times. I love you cousin!

To my dear friend, Laura Bianchi, your friendship and daily conversations mean the world to me and I will forever cherish our friendship. True friends are hard to come by and I know I have a true friend in you.

To my Grandma June, we did it! Your story has been published. Thank you for entrusting me with your life's notes and always being there for me. This book owes its existence to you, and so do I.

To my entire family, thank you for contributing to the development of this book and for being important and loved.

Lastly, I thank my Heavenly Father for creating, providing, and loving me despite my imperfections.

Thank You,

Rachel Valencourt

Editors

Dori Harrell, Jenna O'Malley, John Bowers

Format Designer

Dawn Baca

Images

Section and Scene Breaks—Golden Border Ornament (*Edited*) by Yodafunkyo from Pixabay
Pixabay.com/users/yodafunkyo-9881052/
Pixabay.com/illustrations/golden-border-ornament-design-4203142/

Chapters— Daffodil Watercolor by Tohamina from Freepik
Freepik.com/author/tohamina
Freepik.com/free-vector/set-watercolor-daffodil-flowers-clipart-white-background_64217327.htm

About the Author

Rachel Valencourt is a wife, mother, and an unapologetic lover of books. As a native Californian, she honed her writing skills at Cal State University San Bernardino, before embarking on an exciting career in travel.

From the cobbled streets of London to the vibrant markets of Bangkok, Rachel's passion for travel has led her on journeys that have left a unique imprint on her story-telling.

Following years of international living, she and her

husband now joyfully reside in their coastal abode in sunny San Diego County.

When Rachel is not writing, you'll find her at the nearest concert venue, rocking out with her British hubby and teenage daughters, proving that her love for adventure extends far beyond the pages of her books.

Join my mailing list to stay updated on the latest news and discover upcoming release dates.

http://eepurl.com/im5WFQ

I'd be thrilled if you'd drop by my website to check out my newest blog post. I genuinely enjoy hearing from my readers, so feel free to connect with me through the website. I'm always eager to engage with you!

https://rachelvalencourt.com

 facebook.com/RachelValencourt

x.com/rachelvalencourt

instagram.com/rachelvalencourt

Printed in Great Britain
by Amazon

30125723R00182